LONDONERS

Maureen Duffy is a British poet, playwright and novelist. After a tough childhood, Duffy took her degree in English from King's College London. She turned to writing full-time as a poet and playwright after being commissioned to produce a screenplay by Granada Television. Her first novel, *That's How It Was* (1962), was published to great acclaim. Her first openly lesbian novel was *The Microcosm* (1966), set in the famous Gateways club in London. Her *Collected Poems, 1949-84* appeared in 1985. Maureen's most recent poetry collection is *Environmental Studies*.

ALSO BY MAUREEN DUFFY

Fiction

The Orpheus Trail
That's How it Was
The Single Eye
The Microcosm
The Paradox Players
Wounds
Love Child
I Want To Go To Moscow
Capital
Housespy
Gor Saga
Change
Illuminations
Occam's Razor
Restitution
Alchemy

Non – fiction

The Erotic World of Faery
The Passionate Shepherdess:
Aphra Behn
Men and Beasts: Animal Rights
Handbook

Inherit the Earth
A Thousand Capricious
Chances: History of the
Methuen List
Henry Purcell
England: the Making of the
Myth from Stone Henge to
Albert

Drama

Rites
Solo
Olde Tyme
A Nightingale in Bloomsbury
Square

Poetry

Lyrics for the Dog Hour
Venus Touch
Evesong
Memorials of the Quick and the
Dead
Collected Poems 1949-84
Family Values
Environmental Studies

MAUREEN DUFFY

Londoners

An Elegy

VINTAGE BOOKS
London

Published by Vintage 2013

2 4 6 8 10 9 7 5 3 1

Copyright © Maureen Duffy 1983

Maureen Duffy has asserted her right under the Copyright, Designs
and Patents Act 1988 to be identified as the author of this work

The quotation from 'A Prayer for Old Age' by W. B. Yeats: Reprinted
by permission of United Agents on behalf of: The Executors of the
Estate of Grainne Yeats

Quotation from 'You Can't Hurry Love': Words and Music by
Brian Holland, James Edward Holland Jr., Lamont Herbert Dozier
© 1965, Reproduced by Permission of Jobete Music/ EMI Music,
London W1F 9LD

First published in Great Britain in 1983 by Methuen London Ltd

Vintage
Random House, 20 Vauxhall Bridge Road,
London SW1V 2SA

www.vintage-books.co.uk

Addresses for companies within The Random House Group Limited
can be found at: www.randomhouse.co.uk/offices.htm

The Random House Group Limited Reg. No. 954009

A CIP catalogue record for this book
is available from the British Library

ISBN 9780099587361

Printed and bound in Great Britain by Clays Ltd, St Ives plc

O voi, che avete gl' intelletti sani,
mirate la dottrina, che s'asconde
sotto il velame degli versi strani!

Inferno IX

I

Afterwards when you get indoors, for that's what it is, home being, as they say, where the heart, that old clapped-out, clapped in a barrel organ is, after the din of time being called, the last goodnights, see yous and the snorts of homing cars caught at the lights, afterwards you stand inside your own door a moment and listen to the house decked above. All the floorboards creak. The houses were well built in 1883 except that the joists have grown weary with so many feet over them and protest.

It's Léonie going lightly to and fro wakeful. How many of us pace and then twitch in the dark unless we've had enough to rock us to sleep? Tonight she left early after another evening watching each time the door swung, letting in a slab of night air and a new face to swim a moment, a pale questing John Dory in the layered smoke, unsure alone until it finds its own shoal and the drifting bladder splits in a grin.

The bar is a reef where we each have our own school with its territory to browse and snap on morsels of comfort. Ours is up against the bar flap by the door where passers to pee have to shove us aside as they go and come back and the pickers-up of glasses must fight us away from that little postern with hands full of fragile weapons.

I turn on the transistor and let music out into the room. At this very moment, I'm prepared to bet, half a dozen plastic boxes with their small silver nipples are squirting their liquid droppings into the air above me. If the giant came with his spade and sheared away one wall he would see us all; like opening the front of a doll's house. We each have a bed, a table, a chair, a radio and somewhere to put our clothes, a cupboard or a curtained rail.

I remember once at Tintagel or Iona, some sometime community of those who had left the world, seeing the cells side by side with their identical stone furniture, table, stool, bed, cupboard. They lived horizontally side by side; we live vertically foot to head. Each had a slab shelf that might have served as a personal shrine or altar, the guide book said. We have that too in the boxes that give us pictures and sounds from elsewhere.

In those places of rock and spray and wind-pared turf – as if the grass itself were keeping its head down – I can hear the singing. People have always made music in fields and chantries, dancing grounds and beer halls. Sometimes I wonder if it's all gathering somewhere across the universe, being analysed perhaps, the sounds trapped and nodded over by star-distant eggheads, or whether it's turned the corner of space and is on its way back to break into our receivers some time to come, all the music we have ever let loose on the air waves: song and drum, bones and horn and the plush sweep of strings. When I was a kid it was live from lips and throats, whistled and sung. Now I swing the needle and my shrine makes its own melody. It is time for a nightcap.

I shall draw the cork on this week's special offer: Côtes de Ventoux, thirty-seven and six a bottle, old style. Future scholars will have the decimal divide to contend with as we have the calendar. Perhaps I should set a little academic booby-trap by always writing in old money. *Footnote: We have been unable to discover the significance in what, as we have seen, is a consistent anomaly in this writer's work.* I shall be known as the master of the old minting, except that we don't get titles like *maestro* for word-spinning.

So then pour out a glass from the windy coasts. It tastes acid after beer, with an organic twang of piss or bile. Tonight coming back, for a moment I saw the still unleafed plane trees, my old friends, as Snow White's Disney wood of terror, a mesh keeping out the sky, a web above the streets that we scurry under believing ourselves free, the kind of vision that comes to the middle-raged. Remember you're still too young to be Prime Minister and be cheered.

As we live longer we shift the key points, imaginary watersheds and climacterics, forward, nimbling on into the eighties. Even so, I know I'm the eldest in this stack of lives. Right then that I should be the old mole in the cellerage with them all standing on my shoulders, and the only native, elder statesman, oldest resident of this little slice of Empire.

Léonie thought just for a moment when Raffael's face came round the door that it was Jemal's burnt-umber skin and conker eyes but there the resemblance stops and I felt her sink back on the narrow plinth of bar stool, all her trembling flesh settling again, becoming monumental, a Rubens madonna in waiting.

'Angel what are you doing here away from the Knackers on a Thursday? What are you drinking?'

He orders his usual white wine. 'Today I am too sad and tired to do business. I come here to relax. Today I have wept for hours thinking of my family and how ashamed they would be.'

Should I believe him, believe in this family in Gordon's Khartoum, home of dervishes and sandstorms, and in the tears they generate? His skin is paler than Jemal's, stretched smooth as a girl's. In profile his face is any carved pharaoh's. One gold ring hangs against the bronze neck which is girdled with fake lapis lazuli. The spotless white ducks cling to his bird-fine bones. He is a fawn desert leopard lazily waiting to pounce and when the smooth spatulate fingers pluck at a victim it sighs under the *coup de grâce*. This evening his light-coffee sweater was threaded with silver. He smiled charmingly at Léonie without the black pupils engaging.

'She is very unhappy,' he said when she left.

'She is in love.'

'Ah love. I am always in. But I am happy.'

'Yet today, you said, you were crying.'

'Just a little tears because of my family.' His eyes roamed the men's faces from force of habit in spite of avowedly not being out for business. Like all of them, boys and girls, he lives in the moment. Only sometimes past and future trouble them with ghosts of dead promise. 'Perhaps I will go along the road after all. I feel a little better.' The wine in his hand is almost green as if the glass were a lachrymatory for the afternoon's tears he sips at. 'Besides I see the Boche is coming in. I do not like them. They are not gentle.'

I turned to look over my own shoulder where his eyes had gone. Wolfgang smiled across. 'That one is quite mild.'

11

'They will never be friend with someone like me. They are happy to do business but then they are ashamed. They would like to beat me.'

'Anyway he's married.'

Raffael flings his hand in the air derisively and blows out of his soft-ridged damson lips. 'They are the worst for shame, the married ones. Take care darling.' He swallows the last of the tears and insinuates the tight white bum flauntingly through the crowded bar.

'Good evening.' Wolf is always correct. He bowed his head. He should be too young for the *Gauleiter* click of heels yet it hung in the air. 'You will have a drink with me please? A pint of bitter, *ja*?'

I held up the dregs of my glass in acknowledgement. He brought back two glass tankards with their heads frothed fit for a telly commercial with yeasty suds. 'It is good tonight.'

At first when he came to London he drank lager but now he's proud of his anglicisation to bitter and connoisseurs its clarity and head, holding up the brown agate jug for the light to fall through.

'How is the great world of finance?'

'It is very good, I think.' Strange how he still after eighteen months pronounces it 'sink' and it's too late at thirty-five for his tongue to learn to get round 'th' or my throat to make his gutturals. I wonder if such habits are rooted in the brain itself or just the muscles.

'Soon we are opening a new branch in Pakistan. We follow the flag.' He smiled, enjoying his own joke. 'Where you have been we go. Perhaps I will be the new manager.'

I wondered to myself how he would manage the brown skins and whether Raffael is right.

'Would you take your family?'

'I think so.'

'And business is booming even though England is still the sick man of Europe?'

'We are none of us in very good health now. But here is the financial capital of the world. And why?' He leant forward. 'I tell you. When I first come, came, here I heard my boss on the phone making a deal. When he put it down I said, "What are you doing making a deal on the telephone? First you must write, then..." And he said, "Listen, you have heard an Englishman's word is his bond. Here it is true. That is why

12

business is so easy. If it is agreed it is agreed. You can rely on it, absolutely."'

As usual I was caught between whether to smile and bow deprecatingly, acknowledging the compliment to perfidious Albion or to cry, 'No, we aren't like that. Don't let us kid you. Or if we are it's for the wrong reason.' Because of course it isn't as simple as he sees it and my own ambiguity is an echo of our two sides to every question that make truth a coat of many colours rather than a seamless robe, especially here in the Great When as it still is for so many who set down on its golden pavements.

> Now Mary this London's a wonderful sight
> With the people all working by day and by night
> Sure they don't plant potatoes or barley or wheat
> But there's lots of them digging for gold in the street.
> At least when I asked them that's what I was told
> So I just took a hand in that digging for gold . . .

What can I say to this child of an old enemy who wasn't even born until we weren't at war any more? He is kind, loves his wife and small son and daughter who live in a semi the firm has bought them in Putney. He works hard and looks for promotion, more money, responsibility. We seem shiftless and shifty by comparison. Sometimes I think Europe will never forgive us in its secret heart for not going down before Hitler. And even we sometimes feel guilty because we enjoyed it: the deprivation, the blitz jokes, screwing and scraping on the rations, our finest hour. All this lies between us every time we raise our pints and Wolf speaks praises he thinks I want to hear, and he sincerely believes, but it's my head it oozes out of like ectoplasm, that dubious substance mediums used to induce in the eyes of the beholder, to lie on the mahogany bar between our elbows.

His straightforward neo-liberalism is distressed by our class system, that he can't eat in the canteen with their lower orders. Our divisions, our infinite gradations, are a hindrance to getting and spending in this great metropolis of lucre, Mammonchester. He's too polite to say we should sweep them all away but every so often he grows red and stutters over his new-found fluency for the things he can't say. Only I see that the word that binds us, that makes his wheels and deals possible has a certain accent and is learned in a precise school,

13

that his sorters and packers from the mail room wouldn't want him earwigging on their dinner-time exchange of birds, bets and gobbets of gossip like balls of phlegm spat into hissing coals.

The music has run on, a whole concerto come and gone unnoticed and one of the minor gods has minutely changed the course of our lives. And there went forth a decree from Broadcasting House that all the nation should be taxed... But no *madame*, *je n'aime pas* Brahms. His linear malingerings are too like this endless monologue that goes on inside my own head and for which I need an antiphon not a counterpart. Perhaps it comes from a too early addiction to Hamlet's soliloquies; to pee or not to pee: that is the question. Who could have foreseen that as one of the side effects of a grammar school education?

There is a second shrine to this private temple we can all build for ourselves in our own homes, courtesy of Marconi and Edison, devils or angels in beavers and top hats. I can put a record on the phonograph, gramophone, radiogram, record player, stereo, hi-fi: its name updates with its technical guts.

I can bring you chattering in, my master. It's grown a little cold and you will huddle the rags of your robes about you as you cough and whine and pull at my glass of Côtes de Ventoux and drop your scraps of verse on my table. I have only to set a Dufay mass spinning and just by thinking of it already you're here.

'Why are you writing a book about a mediaeval French poet?' Léonie asked. 'Who will read it? The English are only interested in themselves, in English literature and Bloomsbury gossip.'

'Because he interests me.' I could have said: 'is me' but with even her near-perfect English she might not have understood the words and her Gallic nationalism might have resisted their meaning. I can no longer hear her soft pad overhead. Perhaps she has wept herself to sleep.

> *Se la face ay pale*
> *La cause est amer...*

That old spelling of *amour* makes an untranslatable pun of bitter love.

'Anyway,' I said, 'Villon is a folk figure, part of European culture. Now we are in the Common Market...'

'Pff!' she snorted elegantly in a comic-strip plosive. 'And you would be out tomorrow if you could. What have you brought us? The doubtful benefits of your imperialism.'

We both laughed, she at herself, and me with her, knowing she meant Jemal whom she loves, I suppose, literally to distraction in that he distracts her thoughts continually from everything else so that she is almost at times distraught, and yet she can laugh. But tonight she was angry with me, holding me personally responsible like an ambassador carrying his country's guilt or the runner with news of defeat. 'You are always complaining that you don't make enough money and yet you go on writing books no one wants to read. What do the English care for European culture or consciousness?'

'"And to hell with Burgundy!"'

'What is that?'

'An operetta of our parents' generation, about Villon, and then there are Weill and Brecht.'

'Bloody foreigners. We don't think much of him even in France. He isn't read.'

'That's your mistake. But then in some ways he is very English, perhaps because he grew up when Paris was British.' I am provoking her quite deliberately. She snorts again and smiles, seeing the trick.

'The wolves roamed the streets of Paris in winter, eating women and children. We all learned that in school.'

But she's right of course. It's perverse to be at heart a mediaevalist in the computer age, to have an imagination with a five-hundred-year time warp, to see the Paris of Joan of Arc and the London of Marie Lloyd as one eternal city so that the snows of yesteryear slop over the tops of my track shoes and soak the legs of my jeans ink blue when I step over my threshold into Oliver Gardens and trudge through to the Fulham Road.

Where does it lead me except esoterically astray into whining complaints to my purse or cap in hand from patron to patron?

> *Go my letters take a leap*
> *though you've neither tongue nor feet*
> *and make quite clear in your harangue*
> *that it's lack of money makes me weep.*

You, master, my guide are, for that's one thing about poets

15

they're ever present, a thief and a manslaughterer.

> *I am Francois, more's the pity*
> *born near Pontoise in Paris city.*
> *On a six-foot rope stretched one of these days*
> *me neck'll find out how much me arse weighs.*

I understand all the twists and shifts of that conflict, that fight to go on writing without conforming. You could have given in, trimmed the tonsure you kept like a bald spot in the middle of your thinning hair, half hidden but ready for use when the watch picked you up. You could have folded your hands in front of you and taken a job with the establishment, written sermons instead of ballades in thieves' cant, set yourself to walk the beat of the cloister instead of scurrying like a sewer rat through the alleys of Paris.

How to survive: that's what we all want to know. But you didn't, did you? We don't use exile as a punishment in Mother England nowadays, not physical exile anyway, presumably because there's nowhere to go on our right little, tight little island, no unhandy Siberia for poets to be sent to like your exile from Paris. Once there was the teacher training college in Porthcawl for writers to obscure out their lives in, being big fish in a little pond, flaunting a bow tie for the first year girls and dozing ostentatiously during department meetings. Now this brave new world of holy austerity has driven us back on the city where we're overcrowded scribbling, scrabbling rodents trying to gnaw ourselves a piece in the big cheese squeaking and pulling tails for a few reviews, or a chance to read for a publisher, to sit in judgement on young hopeful's manuscript for a tenner.

My view is jaundiced of course, blanched rather, bled white as yours was, my master, when you wrote *The Legacy* without enough even to buy a drink and warming your mittens at the candle flame you wrote by in your upstairs room alone while the Sorbonne rang its nine o'clock curfew knell on the day. Sometimes I'm more there with you than here; others you're here in this room with me. The record ends. Dufay's mass of love offers peace and the Côtes de Ventoux washes me towards sleep.

16

II

I wake in the dark, some dead hour that down here in my basement I can't tell. You are sitting hobgoblin on the end of the bed like Marley's ghost twittering for attention. What is it you want to tell me now? If you keep me awake gossiping I shan't be able to write in the morning. Your life won't advance and neither will mine.

My head is thick with too much beer and then wine plonked on top of it. In theory there's no reason why I should get up every morning at my customary eight. Who would know, let alone care, if I lay here like Oblomov supinely dreaming my life away? But I try to live an ordered life in accordance with the Puritan work ethic. I rise and bath and eat breakfast like any pillar of Watford society with a commuter train to catch, an office to go to, a second life to pursue.

Have you ever thought that some of our problems come from only having one whole, rounded, integrated life? Except of course for love: that brings another, children, houses, the butcher, the baker, the candlestick maker. Perhaps that's why so many artists, poets especially, do their best work when they're young and pouring all their attention into the one stream that's themselves. It's not that the brain begins to die: it's the sheer loneliness as the years pass that makes us want to get up and throw down the pen or brush, go out into the street and catch Ancient Mariner at passers-by (all the rest of the world is on its way to a wedding) and never let them go.

In the middle of this dogwatch I could despair, looking back. Where and when did I get into this strait, this sunken cleft? I cast around for other things I might have done or been

17

and see there was never any way out. You got what you wanted, the world says, don't bellyache now. Scribblers become unemployable at anything else, except in wartime when we're roped in for propaganda to make B awful movies about wearing a gas mask or saving silver paper. I remember the stinking jam jars of half-washed milk bottle tops sour as sick until the tin caps were replaced with cardboard discs. We took it to school, every scrap of glittery foil that could be salvaged and smoothed out, but I can't remember now who was responsible for collecting it. No wait: on Monday morning a monitor came round all the school, a boy from top class so it must have been Mr Powell.

The door opens as we sit there at our wooden desks with the bench seats bound to them by an iron frame, two to a desk with two inkwells, little hollow porcelain stoppers in the brown wood stained with blots of blackish green from generations of shook nibs and slopped flasks when they were filled on Monday morning.

Everything happened on Monday mornings: savings, dinner money, silver paper, notices while we kept our heads down doing the sums from the blackboard or copying out a hymn. I can hear now the dip and knock of the wooden pens against the rim of the china inkwells, the scratch of the nibs that were crossed from darting into the floor and then bent carefully forward and back to align the two prongs again. That was another Monday morning ritual: new nibs but only for those who really needed them.

When you sucked the nib to make it write smoother, holding its coldness like a pebble in the warm moist mouth with that faint fear that it might go down the wrong way and choke you, the little bronze scoop tasted of battery acid like the ink. Everything was rankly metallic to the tongue and the nose: dinner money held next to sweaty skin, the desk frames, the iron banisters and playground railings, blakeys on our heels. We grew up in the last of the iron age and our coin was the big round penny weight of the copper, Victorian bun. Now it's clean plastic and alloy pence.

Our learning to read and write and sum wasn't very different from your schooling though yours was early done in Latin, dead language that was a prize we were given for passing the scholarship. But the cheap pen and ink and heavy bench desk were conditions you would have understood and the cloister sound of a hand bell rung in the hall by a monitor on Monday morning to call assembly, the bang of seats, shuffle and clatter of children's feet on the barewood floors, silence and then the fluting into a hymn:

> *Morning has broken like the first morning*
> *Blackbird has spoken like the first bird ...*

The sparrows gorballed among the chimney pots. You could see the nit eggs sprinkled like fairy fernseed through the hair of the child in front and my own hair would stand on end, not in sympathy but in fear. Now every prep school in England reckons on lice once a year. Like fleas, or humans, it turns out that they love not the dirt we are ashamed of but the silken shampood curls of princelings, wall-to-wall carpeting and central heating.

Should I call you 'Prince' like you do in your own *envois*:

> *Prince, gentle as a falcon*
> *Know what he did before he went?*
> *He took a good pull on a flagon*
> *When he was ready to leave this world ...*

Or 'Frank'? What about that as a device for bringing you up to date? The use of the first name alone always makes the biographer greasily familiar with the subject. It gives that patronizing tone, nudge, nudge, with the reader. Look, this great personage, this repository of one of the world's myths of beauty, wit or talent is human like us, farts, belches, is no good in bed, spendthrift, neurotic. We aren't so bad when they can be brought down with a maidenly dismissive Jane or a clodpole William.

What about *The Life of Frank Villain, with the poems newly rendered into English metres.* You had to wait four hundred years to be done into English and then they only printed a hundred and fifty-seven copies. All right, so since then a lot of people have had a crack at you. You appeal to our letterdays as the unconforming romantic yet you took your cap in hand to your possible patrons, threw them off some verses for food and drink whether it was cant ballades for Coquillards to bang their pots on the pub table to or prize verses for the ducal hall or boudoir, in return for a pension, board and lodging.

Why do I go on talking to you, like your own dialogue of heart and body? I suppose it's because I don't believe in the ghost in the machine, in that classical dichotomy, antipathy. I

19

am my body. Yet I can understand the need, know it to my marrow for the running dialogue which is really a disguised, thinly, very thinly papered-over monotone, a shared-out solo.

Now you want to talk about love, or I do. Love and money, getting and spending, were your twin muses and the themes I muse on. It must be four o'clock if that's what my thoughts are running after. Soon the birds will start their break of day burble over the Spring city where the prunus is pelted, furred thick with pink and white blossom, Japanese printed or wedding caked with tissue-paper petals.

So your lady of the twisted nose had you flogged naked like washing on the stones at the stream's edge. You knew it all, didn't you: the lust of Fat Margot as she crushed your meagreness under her and the cold flirtation of Katherine who turned you inside out with her refusals, *felonne et dure*?

Why did your day always show the dance of death on the chapel walls when it's love that leads us a real dance? Léonie loves Jemal who loves himself or hates himself; everybody loves Raffaela and Wolfgang loves the nameless 'my wife' in Putney. And who do I love? No one. For the first time in my life my heart is whole, wholly flat as a wet paper bag.

Perhaps Léonie and I should comfort each other. But then we'd lose our comforting friendship and we'd both know it was only second best. You said you were the laughing stock of the city, known everywhere as the rejected lover, so what advice can you offer? You liked the city twang in a girl's voice but I've never found it a draw. Is that another offshoot of a grammar grub's upbringing: that you can't any longer hear love in your mother tongue, the accent that crooned over your cot and lullabied you? *Amour* comes to us lilting in standard English with received pronunciation not costermongering her wares in the gab of Wapping, Watford and Walthamstow.

Love kicked your arse for you out of Paris wearing your broken heart on your sleeve. You told the country girls on your way how hard you'd been treated, I bet, to move their milky breasts to give you suck while you were still hankering after Kate the canon's niece like an Abelard whose love lyrics had once been on every tongue in that city too. Do we, do I rather, leaving aside that biographer's cop-out, believe in that love of yours?

Do I believe in love at all any more or have I grown heretic in middle age or that middle-way agnosticism we're all supposed to fall into after our midlife crisis? In the old days it was conversion to faith now it's conversion to a convenient cloud of unknowing, where all things are possible because nothing's sure.

Oh yes, lying here in this dark night of the flesh it would be easy to recant, to say love has no power after all to put down death, except for such a little since Old Mort wins anyway that it's all St Elmo's fire, will o' the wisp, and wiser then to lie down with the Raffaelas who promise nothing more than a few minutes' forgetting, a scratch for the itch. But I can't let go.

> Venus you say you are old now
> you want to say goodbye to love
> and sit with your glass by the fire
> skirt spread to warm your thighs.

Is that what you meant by your ballade of the old whore lamenting for her youth with her gather-ye-gold-for-your-rosebuds-while-ye-may advice to the young tarts?

> But you brought me up in your worship
> though I'm old and ridiculous too
> to be panting after your favours.
> Yet what else am I to do
>
> imprinted with love of you through
> down to mind's marrow and heart's
> if it has any hand in this business
> and isn't just a muscle of sorts?

What would you have done in old age, you who cried you were old in your thirties with falling hair and teeth and gobbing tennis balls of phlegm? You too might have been like old Horace with thin tears wetting his cheeks for an unattainable boy or Yeats struck still by a memory of Maude Gonne's straight back on Howth station.

> Better to be old and a fool
> than pretend it wasn't worth the game
> of lighting a votary candle
> when you know you're still scorched by her flame.
>
> Better to be daft and obscene
> than be ashamed of what once has been
>
> Venus though the night strikes chill
> I burn still.

How will it look in the morning, in the cold light of day? It's best not to think of that. I go back to you warming your mittened fingers (is that the right translation?) and falling unwined or dined onto a straw bed. Perhaps your poverty was all a pose to catch the patron's eye and you're no guide to me there either, just a figure of speech to raise the wind, like filling in a form for an Arts Council grant.

It's a gallows dance with your feet in the air, a running life where if your sole touches the ground you're down and out. That's what you teach me, how to keep jogging on up the down escalator. The trick is to try at least to stay in the same place and not be carried down and down.

A lot of us don't of course and there's a piece of research for a charitable grant, Gulbenkian or Rowntree. Is the percentage of self murder higher among artists than the rest of the population, or which among the trades of painter, composer, scribbler is the most prone? We must be; gas, razor, water, booze and pills: the examples march through the mind like a ghastly parade for the Macbeths' At Home.

Love failed them and they failed love. I still believe in that divinity; I must. I dream of a girl like a glass of water, cool and clear as the adverts have taught me. If I'm to go on I have to believe still, because they are always there, haunting, flaunting at the edge of the mind those who didn't, who said enough: now you will notice me and daubed their message on the wall in their blood or became a bottle bobbing on the water with the words corked up inside.

You weren't tempted by that. Your need was to escape notice when you were out with a picklock after bread, but to scream like a Battersea mongrel, take me, take me, when you were caged in a dungeon and waiting to see whether the royal progress might touch your town and open the bars. Léonie would say: 'You English are hard, inhuman. You never give clemency. Your Queen goes to a city but no one is pardoned. No one gets mercy, like a free drink at the back door, only your British justice.'

We learnt that early on. We kept the rules and did our homework because, just down the road the secondary modern with horrid warning gaped wide ready to embrace us in its greasy arms if we fell from grace after love or money. Then it was the works or the factory and the end of promise. Whip and carrot were so enmeshed the donkeys had to go round and round with the wheel drawing up the water of a good life, the lure of a permanent job for us children of dole fathers, a house and a car and coming home in a clean shirt from work.

I bite the hand that fed me I know. We should be grateful but we aren't because we were taught subtly that it was our due, our dessert of tinned peaches and evaporated milk, for being cleverer, harder working, respectable ten-year-old pillars of society in our satchels and uniforms. We all show the same bench marks on our literary bums: arrogance, didacticism and a language that's a mouthful of gristle and old bones to be chawed and champed on for every dribble of juice, our own first tongue warped onto a web of Latin, like you again with your Parisian *bon bec* crowing Donatus. And it doesn't matter whether we first glottal stopped in the playground in scouse or cockney, by the time we'd been drilled by Caesar and led on by Virgil we had to speak our own language like a sharp foreigner, a tourist in a chip shop or at a family reunion.

I've become as much a stranger as Jemal or Wolfgang, more because they don't expect to be at home in my native city. They are the true Londoners, denizens of cosmopolis. My hometown was danced away round a VJ bonfire while yesterday's snows turned to slush and piddled off down the drain. If we had known while we feasted on our chocolate-spread sandwiches and wedges of fruitless dried-egg cake, would we have laughed and cheered for the end of that world?

For it's gone. As I lie here with the house like an archeological site staged above me I know my dad, sharp as he was, would barely have understood this grave new world. Does it matter that we make dreams that only half come true, that are sea-changed in the dreaming and making, so looking back we hardly recognize that country we plotted, and would hate to arrive there, since we're no longer the same people who set out and our dreamland changes as we walk?

You didn't make dreams beyond the next day, except for your lady of the crooked nose to stop twisting you around her slim finger. Is that then the message for these small hours, the night-scented stock to sweeten my dark and close my own eyes on, that scullery wisdom picked out with chicken-neck fingers, a nugget from the soda jar: tomorrow never comes?

I see them now: dad's tobacco plants opening their soft cream trumpets to the evening and letting fall their scent, a muted fanfare outside the back door when you went out for a pee, and mingled with the hot distemper smell of the lavatory walls and mown city grass with its bouquet of dry white wine, *blanc de blancs* to the country's moselle, drifting from a neighbour's back garden while the voices rose and fell on the twilight from fences and fences away.

III

It's right the words should be up in Latin over the lifts, immemorable portentous dog-tag to match the art décor, then the only fit tongue to write the things that couldn't be said, for war memorials or about art and knowledge. *Dulce et decorum est pro arte mori.* And those bronze sunbursts were brave and right too, affirmations like the labouring figures in bas-relief round Poplar Civic Hall. Even that was an aspiration to be not just any town or borough but somewhere new and prideful for the citizens of no mean city, along with the baths and the theatre, the Athens of E14.

The entrance hall used to be all roundly open like a cinema foyer, now it's rope-railed off into sections for security. Show your pass, prove your right to be in here, that you're not a bomber who no longer believes the legend of imperial truth we learned in the shelter or behind the invisible bars of occupation on our forbidden sets. Even then it wasn't true. That carefully calm delivery so unlike Movietone or Gaumont British news was lying, bending to conformity with its received pronunciation, passing code messages to guerrillas, propagoosing friend and enemy, our end justifying its means.

Those who really belong sail through with a wave of their club card, members reinforcing with this new security system that old feeling of exclusivity, the playground gang that wouldn't let you join. The rest of us are sent back by the immaculate girls with their flash teeth and smiles. 'If you will wait over there someone will fetch you.' We sit on the curving bench with our backs to the wall.

What was your equivalent for this my Frank master? The

contest at Blois, I suppose; a pension poem when you turned up as an exile bringing your mud and tatters into the noble hall, your chattering teeth to the Duke's fireside. He would have let you stay a day or so to get your breath and then the test. 'You've come at just the right time. I'm having a little literary tourney. I and my guests are trying our hands at a ballade, the first line of which is . . .'

You must have been numb with fright; so soon and the taste of dust still in your mouth. Could you do it, would the words come? Perhaps you went away into the garden to think or sat in a quiet corner of the fortress looking down at the fields beyond the moat through a gash in the cold thickness of stone and beating your brains for a rhyme to outdo the others, a motto to endstop each verse in this begging bowl ballad.

I die of thirst beside the fountain . . .

I am called by one of the paint smart girls. She whistles up a messenger. For years there was a man with a limp who always seemed to fall to my lot to lead me through these eternal corridors. Sometimes I wondered if he was part of the softening-up process, a deliberate attempt to induce shame and guilt as you followed him on and on, trying not to outpace him, to think of things to say, not to flaunt your two good legs. It seemed impossible that this was all our society could offer to someone who could barely walk: there had to be some other reason.

The passages were low and narrow with all-purpose, everlasting coffee paint. It's very quiet. We go through sets of swing doors that are marked with fire warnings. Sometimes a blue or red light shines a cyclopean eye down from above a closed door labelled studio. My mouth is parched with fear. I even long for a paper cup of ambiguous fluid from the vending machine. 'I die of thirst beside the fountain . . . laughing I weep . . .'

Perhaps I should take that for my device and for blazon a pen rouge above a pint pot argent. My messenger is liveried in old London Transport style. He has the same neat low-profiled Tommy Trinder features as dad, that say out of one corner of the mouth, 'Don't let them get you down,' and out of the other: 'I suppose you're doing all right but I wish you had a proper job.'

And here is the door with the name of power on it,

unpretentiously, chastely typed on white card. My guide leaves me. I must knock, turn the handle and go in with courage I don't have. There's another bright girl, two years out of Oxbridge, the handmaiden of this lord whose word is her law and whom she is so lucky to work for. Of course he has his little foibles but he's really rather sweet and so considerate when you've got a cold or the curse. She buzzes my arrival. The partition door is flung open. Jeremy comes at me with a brisk manly stride, his hand thrust forward.

'Al, marvellous that you could come in. Julie, could we have some coffee, sweetheart, from the foul machine... Milk and sugar Al? Makes it more palatable.' He winks; I nod. With a drinks dispenser you get economy and equality. No more differentials of executive coffee in cups on a tray, clerical in mugs and manual urned tea. No more tea ladies or tea boys. It's an image of the future they threaten us with when equality means uniformity not of prison garb but of consumable garbage. I am frightened and therefore I run quickly to verbal excess.

'Have a pew. I've asked Hilary to join us so that we can get this little problem straightened out.'

It is my script, my integrity, my child he is talking about. The chair seats are at shin level, presumably to save expense on the legs. You sink like glistening Phaeton never to rise again. The door opens letting in an upper echelon head above collar and tie with wings of neat brown, grey-darned hair brushed back. Suited shoulders incline round the plane of the door holding the head at an angle Marx, Groucho, perfected.

'Hilary! So glad you could pop in. You know Al?'

We lever ourselves up and I thrust out my hand. 'I don't think we've met.'

'No ... a great admirer of your work of course.'

'Would you like some coffee? Julie's just ...'

'I waylaid her as I came in and placed my order. What are you working on now?'

Julie makes her entry and a diversion, with three white plastic cups on a plastic tray that matches the walls, before I can answer. We cry out with gratitude and pleasure and pass them round amongst us. The thin white skin becomes pliable and too hot to hold. We pass them from hand to hand and then perch them on the floor or on the edge of a desk where they're in constant danger of being knocked over which is, I decide,

27

why the walls are painted that same colour.

'Hilary, I know you're busy and we mustn't keep you so perhaps if I tell Al about our problem . . .'

Their problem is cunt. Even as I wrote it I knew it would be yet I couldn't see any way out. I tried over the alternatives and nothing else would do. Vulva and pudenda are impenetrable for the common tongue and anyway not the language a retired madam would use to describe her private parts. Hole is coarse, hard and empty with no sea image of cockle and mussel flesh, soft-lipped and salty. Vagina is clinical and unidiomatic. 'My sex' would be coy.

'You realize,' I say when Jeremy has outlined their problem with a faint clearing of the throat in order not to stumble over the obdurate word, 'that were it a retired male prostitute lamenting his lost youth we could have described his shrivelled prick with hardly a backward look.'

'Oh, I don't think it's quite as simple as that.' Hilary picks up his collapsible cup respectfully. The chairs make any action dangerous and the bending of the head to bring the lips to a delicate brim is almost impossible. He puts it back on the desk leaving his mouth pursed for what he has to say next. 'I wouldn't want us to get hung up on a single word. It's the tone of the whole script, as I understand it from Jeremy, that's giving pause for thought. We do want to get it right.'

'Oh absolutely! You see Al, what we're increasingly unsure about is the fitness of this aspect of mediaeval culture for a family medium. I mean the, ah, Rabelaisian side. All this about the Devil's fart for instance.'

'If it were more balanced perhaps.' It's Tweedledee's turn now. 'If there was something you could bring out to emphasize the man's stature while toning down the other element it would get it in better proportion.'

'After all,' Tweedledum puts in, 'all that sixties permissiveness does sound rather old hat now.'

'You mean 1460s,' I say, innocently misunderstanding.

'In the mediaeval mind piety was always a counterweight to the sheer gusto of their physical lives and I don't feel you've given us enough of that.'

I'm ready for this. 'That may have been true of other people of that period, and it has been said of Villon, but I don't see much evidence for it. Of over two thousand lines in *The Testament* less than twenty can be read as more than

28

conventional piety in the "Thank God" class.'

'There's that moving ballade for his mother to The Virgin,' Tweedledum pounces.

'Yes, supposedly spoken by a woman who from her own words is poor and old, who knows nothing and has never learnt to read to the "empress of the infernal marshes", Mary as a kind of barely Christianized Persephone. Against that you have two poems to be spoken by a retired whore, one by the poet "in this brothel where we two keep house" just among the ballades...'

Hilary looks at his watch and gets up, abandoning the hardly tasted fluid in his bendable mug. 'I'm sorry to rush away but I've got another meeting. I'm sure you can sort something out.' To Tweedledum: 'You'll let me know, won't you, what you and Al decide.' He puts out a hand to me which I take. 'We have to think about our postbag. The complaints lobby is always more articulate than our satisfied customers, better organized too. As a public body we have to take account... Very glad to meet you.' He has ducked out smiling.

'That's good then,' Jeremy almost rubs his hands. 'You'll take the script home and have another look at it.'

I want to lie on the floor and howl. How have they got me to this position? I was fighting back; I even thought I was winning. He is holding out my typescript towards me: a little thumbed and rubbed, hangdog-eared, *usée* like La Belle Healmière herself in lamenting old age. Nothing has been said exactly but we can all read the shadow writing they have traced on the coffee-coloured wall, Revise, trim or no production.

I want to shout: 'But it's true, it's true. I haven't made it up out of prurience. The words are there in the poems.' And I see them both smile as at an impassioned idiot, the writer as child in the ways of the world, and hear them murmur: 'Truth is a relative thing, that lies in the eyes of the beholder, like beauty.'

What stops my mouth is that half of me acquiesces. I know my truth isn't theirs. I don't say mine is the only one but it's mine, given into my custody to defend by the peculiar historical accident, genetic, social that made me.

Did you have this trouble? Did church and state rail at you for your verses in thieves' cant, your cries of compassion for the blackened sinews of the hanged and the withered tits of the whores? Why did you write them? Did they pay you in pots of wine, free food and fucks? I tear at your double life for

29

understanding and the two halves come apart in my hands, a walnut I can't fit together again. I am going down in the lift, dazed, with the script in my hands, defeated, I'm not sure how, and my own face looks back haggard at me from the long lift mirror so many have patted their hair and arranged their features in going up.

The sunlight smacks me in the eyes as I step out of the charmed circle of the foyer, and the midday traffic, pedestrian and wheeled, batters at my ears. The world is out to lunch, to gossip in pubs and sandwich bar queues. They have last night to offer each other for novelty and this morning to exclaim over for companionship. Where can I hide in these streets in which everyone has a job to go back to except me, a desk to fit the knees under, a demand to be met?

I should go home to you to write but the morning has drained all the lively juice out through the soles of my feet and left me empty. I am blundering down Pickpocket Avenue where the cutpurses fleece the tourist and the tourist loots the shops, where the princesses of Araby, unused to carrying little tin counters or cheque books about with them, lightfinger the goodies, believing that husbands, fathers, brothers can always settle such things, and find themselves up before the beak like any overnight drunk.

The street is strangely tawdry, even the famous names: D. H. Evans and Selfridges, are staled by recession and touting cheek by heavy jowl with gimcrack and gewgaw, trumpery and vanity, gaud and trifle, unionjacked and bearskinned plastic made in Hong Kong. We took beads and looking glasses to colonize the natives in our Empire days and now they are sending them back coloured red, white and blue.

The metal spars of the bus shelter are chill and rough with scabby patches of rust. I have stood here in all weathers but mostly I remember it in rain driving under the tin roof and drenching the doomed who only stand and wait. Across the river of Park Lane Hyde Park beckons greenly. I could sit there in a deck chair if summer was further on. Instead I stand here with the rest, not looking at each other, bored and listless. Sometimes a bus pulls in from the endless surf of traffic to take one or two of us away. Today I can't even wonder where they're going or invent lives for them.

I've been waiting here so long I turn my mind again to the great dilemma of urban man: whether to go by bus or tube.

Tube is more certain but there are changes, underground passages to walk, a station to find. The bus will take me to my road's end, if it ever comes. Lassitude and sloth make me go on wilting against the metal frame like a feeble creeper that can only grow up some support however unfriendly, rather than striking out bravely for the nearest hole in the ground that will gulp me down to the tube. By now I know I was wrong, made the wrong choice but I go on standing because surely if I move away and am in the noman's land between bus and tube the '30' will round the corner and its two red decks will roar dieselly past as though it came, as the timetable lies, punctually every thirteen minutes.

When at last it comes I see that my conductor is an unsmiling Sikh, black-bearded and turbanned, the upswept wisps of dark hair at the back of his neck when he has given me my change and passed on up the bus as mysterious as the stray strands at the temples of a nun. Don't they ever cut their hair? Perhaps they unbind it from a topknot in bed and they and their wives clasp each other wrapped in a fine black silk shawl of their own weaving. Why don't they smile and are they Muslim or Hindu, or neither?

I think of the Hindus as more cheerful, inventive, sculptors of temple erotica, hard porn of twined stone limbs that are as fluid and rounded as Cranach's Eve, every manjack of them aspiring to be Krishna frolicking among the cowgirls. But the Muslims are of sterner stuff, no longer the magnanimous pleasure-loving potentates like Saladin the magnificent, but Islam militant. There was Daz who managed the Taj Mahal for a time, who giggled a lot but whose eyes would fill when he spoke of his mother and who went home to marry the fourteen-year-old she had chosen for him in what we called Bengal with its image of tigers and lancers, and there is Jemal who hardly ever smiles and breaks Léonie's heart.

They come and take our jobs and our women or rather our women take them and we give them the jobs the English won't do and the shops that can only pay if a whole extended family, grannies and wetback cousins, arranged spouses and multitudinous winning, willing small boys work them from ten to ten every day, an eighty-hour week. And they have colonised our imagination and our literature. Perhaps I should write a study: *The Impact of the Indian Sub-Continent on English Literature. Part One: The Conquerors. Part Two: Two-*

31

way Traffic in Contemporary Writing.

Why have they become our looking glass? An elegant elderly dame, her shrunk shanks brave in sheer tights and summer shoes, her bent shoulders clothed in thin navy silk and her head become small as a rabbit's skull with a soft chamois of aged cared-for skin tooled over it, bearing up a wide navy straw hat heavy with white daisies, offers the conductor a *bon-bon* question.

'Where do you come from? My father was in India. I was born there.'

'I am from Uganda.'

'Oh. I've never bin to Africa.'

Approaching Knightsbridge station she gets up from her seat beside the entrance, hanging on with two heavily veined hands to the metal pole as if she was going down with the ship while a ghostly band plays *Rule Britannia*. Does he see the game old bird she is? He is impenetrable behind his beard, turban and neat uniform so unlike our own dear boys with their mangled jeans, buttonless jackets flung wide for us to read the legend on their chests that tell of their coca-colanisation or mythical enrolment in the international Varsity club. The bus judders and jumps swaying her on her pole, marionette. She smiles when it stops, unclenches her hands, pulls down the rucked sleeve where her handbag has swung and banged like a shutter in the wind, and descends vice-regally knowing the world is watching. I give her my *grande dame* for gallantry.

We trundle on past Harrods, *QE II* of commerce, a twenties liner dressed over all with fairy lights at Christmas and now sailing through late Spring towards where mosque and oratory confront each other, clashing rocks in a Protestant sea, diagonally across the strait where the Brompton Road grows old and Knightsbridge dips down to South Ken.

What would Newman have thought of having a heathen temple new-built opposite and will they set out from their corner to convert the infidel or join hands with him in the ecumenical belief that any faith is better than none in this most agnostic outpost of Western Europe? It isn't the swart boat to hell we most of us fear but the inner circle underground of oblivion. Terror would be something; instead of which we have shifted it from the psychic reality of belief to the fantasy titillation of the horror movie. And there's no going back. We can't believe what we don't believe, what has no resonance for us and no ground in our reason to root in.

Hell has become Hades again, the shadow kingdom of the heart, not of punishment but of non being, of sighs not howls, a haunting ground at the back of the mind where the dead live in our forever, surfacing in dreams and guilts, laying chill hands on our lives to bend them towards their state. I get up and ding the bell for my request stop. Once off, my feet turn towards the Nevern. There I can get a sandwich and a pint. There I shall be known, welcomed. I step out of the sunshine into the subdued light and hum of the lunchtime bar.

IV

I fell asleep, of course, after a couple of pints, heavily, and woke with my head full of foam rubber that insulates me from the world, to be set upon at once by guilt as actual as any figure in a mediaeval morality play, except that it dwells tapeworm in the gut where its suckers are firmly dug into the soft flesh and all the nourishment of confidence that's sent down, praise, pride in craftsmanship, are leeched away to squit out through the psychic arsehole drained of goodness.

You take me by the hand and lead me up into the street again. No, not the bus this time. I will be brave and step out up the Earl's Court Road to the station. The juggernauts tank past making the air and ground tremble with their shock waves. It's four o'clock, the pause between closing and opening time when the city draws breath before the grand rush home. Once this road was full of old commonwealth Aussies and Kiwis, now it's new oil that greases its turning wheels. Three black-masked and chotied girls, with tempting glimpses of eyes and vizard frames of ivory skin, chatter on the corner by Smith's. A young man, spare as if fined down by desert sand and wind, in a long gown of white silk and a white lawn headcloth, delicately embroidered as my mother's best tea tablecloth only brought out for visitors, leads a curly haired child by the hand, beautiful as the soap-bubble blower in a Victorian painting but with the suds of ringlets dark round the smooth pale cheeks above the grey gown that doesn't hide one good and one twisted foot. Clinging to his father's hand he rocks from side to side round the corner into Earl's Court Square. They have come looking for a modern miracle from Western doctors, the

34

inheritors of Averroes and Avenzoar. The shops are calligraphed with the arabic script that is like sandwaves firm and flowing, from the brush of the wind.

I ride the five stops to Green Park, aware that I am wasting money, that if I had been calmer and able to shrug off this morning's meeting I should have dropped in at the library on my way home and saved myself this journey and the double fares. We are all feckless, spendthrift in some things and miserly in others. That's the true lesson of Scrooge, that he looks out of a cartoon of Dickens' own face, a linear echo of part of his own nature. We screw and scrape to save fivepence and blow it.

Tout aux tavernes et aux filles

just to keep the ink flowing in our veins. Shakespeare was Shylock taking the knife to his own white breast to carve a slice for supper. We are every one of us gnawing on ourselves for sustenance.

I climb up into Piccadilly and turn to pass the Ritz in whose ice-cream parlour I once breakfasted with an American editor on his way to the Frankfurt Book Fair where authors are bought and sold. Cue for a song-and-dance routine on the wide pavement backed by the park railings that become a gallery for art tat (or should it be tat art?) on Sundays to catch the strolling sightseers. I too have lived high and I didn't catch a single flea while I was there. It was a chance to choose Arbroath smokies, devilled kidneys, mushrooms on toast and scrambled egg, yellow as a pile of guineas, but the editor was a Jewish puritan and I had to copycat his rolls and coffee.

The traffic-light ford at the top of St James's has to be crossed and then it's turn down by Fortnums, a threshold I have never darkened in a quarter of a century of shopping, its interior more unknown to me than that of a Turkish mosque. I jog down Duke of York Street taking pleasure in dodging between cars, in my brisk citizen's know-all trot going places and veer left into the square.

The library has its back in the corner and a modest Edwardian entrance. It gives an impression of brownness and therefore of a place of learning. I don't know why knowledge is brown in my book: it just is. Perhaps it has something to do with that strange expression 'in a brown study' or is umbrous with the deep summer shade of the tree our first parents scrumped a sour apple from. Then again it may just be the brown desks and walls of Mostyn Road Infants and Junior Mixed.

The notice on the door about members makes it the only club I belong to, and each time I push through the swing doors I get this faint frisson of exclusivity. I hang up my plastic bag on the hat rack because bags must be deposited: even paid-up scholars pilfer. I take my pile of returns to the brown high counter that is like an old-fashioned bar before the sixties orgy of renovation padded them all in red leatherette with brass cross-hatching, and say my name softly hoping desperately and futilely that it will mean something to the superior youth who scribbles it in pencil on a scrap of paper he pops under the flap of the first book before he carries the pile away.

Sometimes I chat with the deputy librarian and that makes me feel known and truly a member but he isn't on today. Go over then to the shelves of the old catalogue bound in maroon, each as heavy as twenty of the volumes they list. The card index is more economical of space and the microfiche is better still but neither of them has the feel of scholarship that opening these heavyweights does and reading down their broad thick pages. New generations will be used to it, think nothing of slipping the plastic sheet into the magic lantern and running their eye over the green-lit column on the screen. They will make their own mythology of that in time I know, but some of us will go on hankering after the sheer physicalness of those iron and leather age operations. Now everything is done at a finger touch and we must learn not to need the thud of a heavy cover falling open, the weight of a square foot of sugar paper between our fingers to focus the mind. I finish my jottings on the scrap paper so thoughtfully provided, the secret code signs that only the initiate can decipher and that will lead you to where the treasure is shelved and turn towards the lift. I shall begin at Biog. on the top floor and work my way down to Topog. in the basement.

The whore goddess fashion reigns over these dusty fields. The lift door clangs open letting me out into Biography and Biographical Collections. It's very dim and quiet up here. There's only room to crouch between the stacks to look at the bottom shelves. Sometimes I sit on the floor like an eccentric of the rope soles and folkweave era and am embarrassed to be caught out there as if I were being deliberately ostentatious.

Today I don't chance it but bend and peer like a short-sighted professor in a vintage children's comic.

Touching a shelf to look through a book I hear the crack and feel the tingle of earthing static from the metal racks and the meccano grill of the floor. It's a new biography of Charles D'Orleans, interesting to us because he spent twenty years in captivity among the English. The whore goddess dictates who shall be written about and which among those already lifed shall be taken down and read. Before the Second World War, 'the War' as those of us who don't remember the Great War call it, I could have written a dialogue for the voices of these glorious dead but fashion says that's out. Not even *Punch* would publish it.

She's the modern face of that mutability the Elizabethans feared and deified. No that's not quite true, for they knew her and Shakespeare railed at her too under different names. It was Spenser saw through to her counterpart: the eternal principle of change, our constant inconstant we strive and kick against until it carries us into the grave where it's all change.

> *Woman's body that's so tender*
> *smooth and soft and fine*
> *must these evils too attend her?*
> *Unless she goes to heaven alive.*

Perhaps biography should be shelved by occupation instead of alphabetically. No doubt the computers will do it with their ease of double cross-reference. Someone will get a PhD for devising the Doughy biographical classification. Will the cataloguers settle on one job for everybody? Donne, John, theologian; Burns, Robert, customs official; Eliot, Thomas Stearns, bank clerk; Spenser, Edmund, courtier; Keats, John, medic; Clare, John, agricultural labourer.

I walk towards the stairs, aware of their lives clamorous around me and go down through Literature, French & Hist., French, to the deepest basement for topography so that I can follow your dead steps on their travels up and down the land, fleeing the flics or scavenging for a living in that yesteryear I can't find the perfect word for.

> *Where are yesterday's snows?*

And that *'mais'* at the beginning of the line: 'but', 'yet', 'still'; how do I translate that? Or do I leave it out? Like all perfect lines, it's untransferable without some loss. Virgil's *'lacrimae rerum'*, Horace's *'non sum qualis'*, Dante's *'Amor che a nullo amato amor perdona'*, are all heartbreakers. And yet they claim Shakespeare sounds better in Russian or Italian than in English. Tell me, my devilish hard master, was *'d'antan'* already archaic in your day? There's a winnowing exam question: compare and contrast Rossetti's 'But where are the snows of yester-year?' with Lowell's 'Oh where is last year's snow?' showing how each version exemplifies the period when it was made. And what shall I make of you in my turn, my maker, my mucker, and does it matter? *'Mais ou sont les neiges d'antan?'*

I hear the women scraping snow from the Moscow pavements with their iron shovels, their fingers and hands wrapped anonymous in black against the cold and their faces kneaded by it into one peasant wholemeal countenance that has bent over a handle or a furrow for centuries. You didn't wonder where they'd gone, only the lost beauties; Thais, Flora, Heloise whose names are like bells ringing triples of desire.

Topography is the lowest and dimmest circle of this limbo. Telly has killed the old travel book with its colour slide, shy fauna and glimpses down the throats of flowers more intimate even than the humming bird's tongue can know. Sinbad would have to take the camera crew and the videotape editor along with him now, not his notebook and pencil. I browse among Victorian and Edwardian fields with sketchpad and butterfly net to know what Angers, Blois and Orleans might have looked like before our century trampled over them as you exiled your way from Paris, chatting up the country girls like Keats Krishnaing among the milkmaids until he was clapped out in spite of their sweet butter and cream flesh.

I take my hoard upstairs to the counter. Rain is falling now beyond the long windows. When I've signed them out, I jacket the half-dozen volumes in my Bottoms Up plastic bag, patterned with ghostly outlines of wine bottles and push through the half-glazed swing doors into the darkening Spring evening that smells of laid dust.

V

After the last few days that brought that foam of blossom out in the parks and squares a cold wind has got up with the rain, hurrying me and my plastic bag down the road whose pavements are muddied already. So early in the year the sun hasn't really warmed the air and it chills at the first touch of rain, catching us out in our light jackets. We scuttle past, hands in the pockets of our jeans out of reach of the little barbs of drops that pock the skin with ice, and our narrow jacket collars turned up, dodging along, as city dwellers learn to slip by each other without touching, carrying an invisible envelope of space that may be only skin thick. The traffic at this time crawls towards the embankment and the bridges leading south, the wheels inching through the flash flood that gushes along the gutters. A smart arse in a small silver Mercedes nips into the inside lane and roars along it spraying the pedestrians with liquid filth. A boy tries to scramble away his carefully whitened loafers and pale blue cruise trousers.

The air is aromatic with fish and chips, roast meat from the great turning drums of Kebabed flesh, curry in battered samosa triangles, glossy with grease, and from the stainless steel vats of hot chick peas, mutton, ladies' fingers, saffron rice. I join the queue for a tinfoil dish of vegetable curry and a paper bag of onion bagia corms that look as if you could plant them in Earl's Court Square garden and there would spring up a takeaway tree.

Hannalore opens the front door as I reach it with my hands full of curry and books. A sports car standing at the kerb throbs and coughs as her evening out nervously flexes his accelerator foot and adjusts his silk cravat, old style sporty gent. She keeps one here in London for work days and one at home in Hamburg for holidays. Heartwhole Hannalore is cool with them both, considering their proposals of marriage and letting them lie on the table while she types away in a solicitor's office, tempting there too, uncommitted while Léonie is breaking her heart as she arranges tours, books holidays, fashions dreams for other people, knowing Jemal will never safari her off to Africa, that his parents have ordered him a more docile prey. For once I refuse to draw conclusions from them: cool German, passionate Gallic.

'Oh Al. You will help me please one evening. I have my examination for Cambridge Proficiency in two weeks, a fortnight, yes?'

'Yes,' I say. 'Knock on my door.' The M.G. growls. She looks down the steps at it. She will get in calmly without apologising. I'm not even sure that she deigns to sleep with them.

The hall is dark. I press the time switch with my elbow and carry my curried books to my own front door. There is dust high above mantling the halved hard-boiled eggs of the Ionic cornice, and the unstirred air is moted with it for the wind can't get its fingers through the heavy front door, steel-backed against the burglars since the last time they made a clean sweep of the beloved stereo and radio Lares and Penates.

I switch on my own little tin god, take the cardboard lid from the foil dish and begin to spoon up the brown sauce with its flotsam of orange carrot discs, white potato cubes and green pea globules. Tonight the black ceiling and white walls seem chaste and precise. Sometimes they are my tomb with the black lid screwing down tighter and tighter. How shall I spend the next few hours till bedtime? Or rather where, for how is always the same, only the place alters. Do I feel a need for the Nevern, or the Knackers, Léonie or Raffael?

Sometimes it's known as the Knickers, the Henniker Arms. The wind is stronger now. I stand on the top step looking across at the mirror houses opposite with their identical porticos making the street a temple, a long double colonnade with the empty road at its heart through which leaves and papers bowl. No children chalk the pavement with hopscotch. It is a street of the unattached, unadopted.

Right to the Nevern, Left sinister to the Knackers; the rain at my back going out or coming home? I set my face to it and run head down, push open the mahogany door with its bevelled glass etched frostily with a jovial Toby jug and shove through into the juke box niagara that pours through the bar in solid sound.

The voices murmur a ground bass to the electronic love singers. Across the road in the Fusiliers they will be standing elbow to elbow, the eyes moving from face to face seeking another pair of eyes to lock onto. The leather lads parade there in black-shirt skin blousons and pants, topped by a peaked eagle cap in servile parody of those who would put them down, jackboot lickers. Imitation is the sincerest form of flattery. Every night is *Adlertag*.

But the Knicker-Knackers is gentler, perhaps because there's more space between the bodies or because it's Queenstown. Though they drift or flash across the road between the two it's here they come to rest and gossip, starlings on a highwire of pot and poppers. I think all this as I shoulder through to a foot of bar, just vacated by a tall figure in a long overcoat that was once costly. The head on it is large, handsome, lined. Without hearing the voice I can tell public school, the Guards, Whitehall. We all wear our origins on our sleeves.

Hazel waves a plump white much-ringed hand at me and lowers mascara blackleaded lids. Her black lowcut dress is tight over the full bosom. She holds her short glass delicately, woman to the manner made, who might own a dress shop in Stockport without looking out of place. Only the jawline is a little heavy with my knowledge. I take my drink to the upturned ship's wheel in the middle of the bar where you can lean between the spokes if there's room, each in a small cubicle under the fan that turns as lazily as in an old lure-of-the-mysterious-East movie, the sort they don't make any more with sweat and the swish of bead curtains. You always knew the villain because his panama was limper than anyone else's.

Old bibulous slogans hang mispelt over the bar. *'Don't give in till the wine gives out.' Epicurus.* But not: *He that loveth not wine and boys is a fool. Ben Jonson.* The brewers' design department doesn't dare that. I look down at my feet and see them detached among the litter of dogends and wrappers, the lino worn and stained, blackened in small cicatrices with stubbings out.

Two teenage black boys, one plump with puppy fat, the other skinny as a bootlace, chatter beside me in their speakeasy jargon. They have come in for a breather, breaking out of the trade ring for a few minutes to consider, take stock for the best night's takings. They are so young their skin is glazed like a chocolate Easter bunny yet soft to the touch. They wear cheap T-shirts, blue and white, that show off their childish arms and necks, and faded jeans moulding their boys' buttocks and thighs.

A lean black comes between them, putting a hand on the shoulder of each, making their trio a frieze or a strung paper cutout. Only a slight roundness of the pectorals under the black skirt is giveaway. Here you catch at the minutest details, not to know who's who but who's what.

And here comes Raffael, princing, prinking, princessing, progressing through the bar from the other street door, pausing to chat, toss the head, flick the fingers, informal tonight in cream silk shirt and trousers, the throat bare so that the world can see the careless blue beads flung against the amber skin matching the one earring, 'rich jewel in an Ethiope's ear'. Who will be allowed to buy the first drink? He crosses to me. I bow and offer.

'I can't stay. I must do business.' The long-lashed eyes rove; a smile, another wave. 'That one he wants but I don't think so. It is a good atmosphere tonight. I am happy.'

'That's a pretty necklace.'

A slim hand goes up to finger it gently. 'A friend brought it back for me from Greece. And the ring in the left ear. Sometimes I put it in the right to confuse them all. Some they find it exciting. I don't like to be beaten but I like to make them guess a little. You see those two?' Raffael nods towards a little group where two stand together, one short and stocky with his arm round the other's neck. The other looks across the bar, his skin flinching from the touch of a dead love.

'He is out today after three months in prison for his husband.'

The short one is knotted with shoulder and arm muscles. His voice drifts across thickly laced with Scotch. 'I think the world of him. I'd do it again tomorrow.' What will he say when he wakes and realizes there's no longer any light behind the eyes that look beyond him? Those hands could take and break.

'He not guilty, Brian guilty,' Raffael marvels. 'When the

42

other one say to me "My wife coming out", I think he mean female wife. Here comes your friend. Once I think he is your husband or wife.' He smiles and rolls his eyes. 'He is very strong I think.'

'He is married.' I say it firmly.

'Ah yes to the little one with the moustache. That will not last. When he is free again I will talk to him perhaps. I don't make trouble.' He waves and slips into the crowd as Paul reaches us.

'No Frank this evening?'

'He's away to the movies with Barbara. David's coming over. I rang him when I couldn't get you.'

'I had to go to the library.'

We stand in the spokes of the wheel under the fan and watch the world go by. Everywhere the eye makes vignettes, picks out a detail here and there to hold up for inspection. The canvas is asprawl with figures, each dressed with care for a role as if the painter had hired them to come and stand just so. And the title of this work? Only a Renaissance artist could manage the scale of it, the crowd scenes for battle or judgement, the garden of earthly delights or the four corners of the world paying homage to prince, pope or Peace.

The wind comes in when the doors open and swirls the smoke in veils. Groups break and reform in human kaleidoscope. David presses his way towards us. I buy us all another round of pints. At the bar a young man in regulation T-shirt, jeans and moustache offers me a drink. Sometimes we talk when we're both alone, his words making no logical sequence but as pebbles flung into water, the splash confirming the existence of the throwing hand. I wonder if he is permanently high or has some disability that makes his words tangential, disconnected. I smile and explain that I'm buying a round. I offer him one but he has a full glass and only wanted to talk.

'Why has everyone grown a moustache to look like Proust?' I hand David his glass. His own walrus is new and fashionably Edwardian.

'It's our search for a lost time,' he suggests. 'Cheers! Or as the fashionable cant has it: for a cultural identity.'

'Why that one? Why now?'

'All very masculine; our father's fathers. The old guard or guardsman.'

'But why not a cultural identity with the great lovers of the past, the Greeks say? Alexander, curly haired and clean shaven.'

'A question: were David and Jonathan bearded?'

'And Achilles and Patroclus. Have you ever thought that the loss of one love, Helen, began the Trojan war, and the loss of another, Patroclus, ended it?'

While we talk Paul's eyes watch the door although he knows Frank is at the cinema and can't appear there. The heart always hopes against reason and sometimes it's rewarded.

'When is Frank going back?'

'He's got his ticket. His family rang him from Melbourne last night to make sure it had arrived. He was so uptight after he'd spoken to them we had a blazing row. Almost I'll be glad now when he goes.'

'How did you meet Frank?' David asks.

'Not here or at a club. At the Nevern. He was in there with Barbara and John Scarsdale and his mob. We kept eyeing each other all evening across the pub. I was in the saloon and he was in the long bar and I kept thinking: "Why does he keep looking at us like that if he's with them?" Then I went down the Fedora after and there he was. Came up and asked me to dance. Said he'd been watching us for weeks wanting to say something. I'd never even seen him. When I found out he was an Australian I didn't want to get in too deep, knowing he'd have to go back one day.'

'Why does he? Isn't it still Kangaroo valley here?'

'They won't give him another work permit. He's had three. And besides his family want him to go home. He's got to get himself sorted out. He told them on the phone from here. Three thousand miles.' I imagine the silence on the other end of the line as the news zings over land and water: your only son of a good catholic immigrant family will never give you a son of his own. Your name stops here. Then the recriminations: 'It must come from your side of the family'; 'You kept him in the pouch too long like an old lady Roo.'

Paul prickles beside me. Herman the German has passed close to us. He cultivates a cold eye and a crew cut. The eagle vicious-beaked is splayed across the front of his peaked leather cap.

'He makes my flesh creep. I can't stand him near.'

'Not a pretty sight.' David agrees with him. 'One wonders

44

sometimes why we fought the war.'

'To give her the freedom to play camp commandant.'

'Who'd pay for it,' Paul asks as he always does, 'when there's so much better going for nothing?'

'That's the socialist in you,' David teases gently. 'Some people only value what they pay for.'

'I don't know what I am any more. There's no socialists left. They're all out for themselves.' The beer is beginning to bite on our brains.

'Socialism is like other religions: it will come again when the times are ready for it.'

'I think the British are naturally conservative and traditionalist. That's why they invented a conservative and traditional form of socialism, Labour with its cloth cap and embroidered union banner that had its roots in the battle between landlord and tenant, guv'nor and worker, in rent and making ends meet.' It's time for me to add my groatsworth of boozer's wit. 'It looked to an ideal world where the state replaced the guv'nor and landlord but we went on being ourselves. But capitalism craftily changed all that by getting rid of rent and the landlord, except ironically for council housing. We've become yeomen freeholders again as we were before the industrial revolution with our houses and cars, neo-Elizabethans. There are only so many variations on the basic problem of ensuring you're fit enough to survive: two in fact, individual or collective, lone predator or worker in the colony.'

'So, as I said, socialism will have its turn again when conditions demand it. Are we having another pint?' It's David's round. We hand him our glasses. The evening is moving towards bell time, the British way of curfew with nothing political in its purpose, almost a form of coercion. Those of you who have to be at work early must get your drinking over and get to bed. We don't say you must be off the streets but we close the places where you might be, and the transport by which you might travel, having drunk more than we allow for safe driving, too quickly and unadulterated by food. Only the young unencumbered can dance the night away in clubland.

A last inward rush of wind brings in a gaggle of young trade, boys and girls chattering like a high wire of starlings before takeoff. Some drama always runs among them of pimp or client, of falling out and making up, of being picked up and

45

questioned or barred from this and that pub. Like migrating birds they vanish from one scene for a time, sometimes to come back but sometimes to drop into the ocean of the city as they cross and recross and never surface again. That one, I know from Raffael, is sixteen, pale, cream-skinned if she wasn't blushed with rouge, her dark hair clipped short up her child's neck to draw the lips down to it. Her eyes are black as a Spaniard's or Mexican's but when I asked, Raffael shrugged and said she was from Tooting. And with her is Sally, touched lightly with the tar brush to give her nose and mouth a snub soft telltale. She believes, or imagines, she would like me to take her away from it all and off the game forever.

'Here's Frank,' Paul says. I feel his body relax and then tauten again but with a different note. He smiles. Frank pushes through. The crowd has thinned at the door but is packed at the bar as the bell rings last orders. The juke box is in the middle of its evening swansong. It is a song about death but here it becomes the little deaths of youth and desire.

Bright eyes why do you fade so fast . . .

Where's yesterday's snow?

'Frank, what are you having? I'll just get you one in before the last bell.'

VI

The morning has broken on rain. It flecks the window and runs down the black iron railings of the area. On the path beyond them where earth has pushed aside the thin broken skin of tarmac the sparrows have a puddle bath of dust in dry and rainwater in wet weather. Only one can use it at a time and there seems to be some queueing system. Two are stacked up on the railing while one is whirring her wings in the bath. More males than females bathe. Those waiting sometimes cheep for the one in to get on with it and get out. Other birds may chirp, spadgers cheep. Have I discovered avian cockney?

We will do anything except write. Did you have that problem? Unless it's a fiction of your own for sympathy, you wrote at night while the candle lasted. Was that a late hour to be up: nine o'clock? Is that what you mean by putting that verse in? When there was no electric or gas people got up with the lark, at dawn, late in winter, early in summer, as animals do. You were cold, you said, so it was winter or a bitter late Spring. (Remember to try to look up the probable weather pattern in the fifteenth century.) There was at least one very bad year when the wolves came down and roamed the streets of Paris but was that common and was it as cold as say 1964 when the Thames froze, or was that, anyway, 1963? Dates slip unless history pins them down: 1666, the year of the Great Frost.

The Legacy you wrote near Christmas, that's what you say in 1456, but *The Testament* has no time of year to it, only an upstairs room in place of my basement. I don't even know if that was in Paris or in the suburbs as some commentators have said. How can I write your life from such scribbled hints, such

47

marginal glosses? There's nothing new I can say.

Yet I know a lot of this morning's doubt is because I have to lunch with Guzzle. It means that my mind isn't on my work, on you but veers about, and runs on towards my meeting with him and starts back. 'We look before and after and sigh for what is not.'

The truth is I can't hate properly. I'm angered by this and that but I can't hate cleanly. I always see the soft foot poking out from the shell where the thorn will go straight in deep with a mortal thrust. I can't hate Guzzle because he's a Jewish refugee and I can't shuffle off the collective Aryan guilt. I'm an inverted anti-Semite. Goetzle fled from Hitler and became a half millionaire with hard work and a row of diamonds stitched into his hatband so the legend goes. Probably it was nothing so romantic but a simple transfer of funds or an uncle in the rag trade. I see the young Guzzle, slim then, thin even with a waif's face saying goodbye to parents he will never see again as the train begins to draw away, huffing and shrilling as trains used to, a big black iron pot on wheels carrying Goetzle off in its belly.

Transplanted he thrives, Guzzle gets on though the story of his rise is obscure. Suddenly at the end of the war there he is with the beginnings of a belly and a publishing house, having bought out the old and respected Handyside Press. I meet him at a party where he's trolling for talent. In those days he has ideals and a poetry list. I become Guzzle's for life unless I can make a breakthrough and get off his hook.

We are lunching at La Bocca della Verità where the lies come thick and fast as Milton's autumnal leaves in Vallabrosa descending. It's time to leave you, master, and go out in the rain that will batter the blossom from the trees and smear it, each petal a brown glutinous fingerprint on the pavements. It's the first time I've seen Guzzle since his knighthood, on which I didn't congratulate him. It will be between us like a sword of course. So quickly our weather turns around, maybe it accounts for that perfidy the foreigner sees in us, a people conservative and yet changeable.

Today the tube smells of damp clothes. The earlybird tourists wear anoraks and cheerful smiles against the holiday rain. I emerge at Leicester Square and walk up through the edge of Chinatown, past the drab books and delicately painted eggshells of the People's Republic shop. They don't need to tart up literature to vie with soap powder for the people's pence. It sells on content not packaging. Or will that all change with their new dispensation and their jackets become glossy as tarts' mouths?

Shaftesbury Avenue that used to glitter as theatreland is now a stream of traffic between clothes shops, but I still catch a breath of Turkish smoke from a hubble-bubble long holder and hear the click of a bead fringe, background to a high birdcall laugh. I cross it and turn up into Soho proper, scene of my youth, Salad Days when there were still coffee bars and pavement pros instead of strip celluloid and weary turns in haze-filled joints. There was a year when the girls all carried parasols, then another when they had little dogs. They stood around as if posing for a Lautrec who would happen along any minute to make them immortal on his knees. They were perched along the pavements like a row of exotic birds as we passed to our rendezvous in the Spacca Napoli where the Gaggia machine hissed like a tamped down geyser and you could sit for hours slowly scooping every last bubble of capuccino froth from the bottom of the cup. If you got bored with talk there was The Freight Train where the music was loud and fast or The Alpine where you could play chess and buy a wooden bowl of soup.

I pass them now, the places where we spent so many evenings when we'd had enough of Queen's refectory and yet didn't want to go home. Here we could argue the hours away, feeling sophisticates with our intensity and Italian coffee after a childhood of the British Restaurant and cafés that closed at six and didn't open on Sunday even for meat and two veg with unidentifiable fruit pie and creamola.

We were the grammar grubs, first flush of free secondary education. We had nothing and knew no one. At night we went back to our parents' homes where we were sore thumbs and thorns in the flesh or to bedsits in cheap suburbs and student hostels smelling of over-boiled greens and distemper. We had no tradition, no knowledge of the city and no money. The city gave us what it could for free, the river and Senate House library and each other whom it had brought together.

You might say our education was all froth, from the coffee and from the converse of untutored minds rubbing against each other and against the pent-up hiss of a Gaggia machine. We had no one to tell us anything. Everything had to be invented or discovered. We even had to put together an image of studenthood out of fragments of continual café society glimpsed in films and *The Vagabond King* laced with *Carmina Burana*.

La Bocca was there even then, but we didn't know. (We knew only one Soho restaurant, that somebody's father, an Italian hairdresser, had once been to.) Was it a place with a bookish flavour in those days? Waugh and Auden might have been lunching there as we passed the door on our way to the Spacca. We did know that Dylan Thomas had got drunk frequently in the same street because one of our group was Welsh.

Perhaps I'm gentler with Guzzle because of Willy. We all loved him but none of us got beyond his too-correct English with the still guttural precise accent after twelve years. He had escaped, like Goetzle, but jumping from taxi to taxi as a nine-year-old fleeing through Berlin. As he talked too fast he jangled his change in the pocket of his English grey flannels. Guzzle's English is heavy and formal. He is waiting for me already at the table as the maîtresse d'hotel, smiling in recognition, ushers me into the upstairs back room. What will happen when she and the ginger cat finally retire? Will it ever be the same? She remembers even the least significant of us.

Guzzle is drinking a red Campari though his appetite never needs stimulating. His dark bulk in its good wet slate cloth makes the table in front of him look flimsy and precarious. He grunts at me and stretches out a huge hand. I wonder about the baby Goetzle with those great paws on the cot cover and why I never noticed them when we first met. They can't have grown; hands don't after adulthood. They are the hands of a peasant farmer but the Goetzles must have been city-dwellers, tailors or shopkeepers for generations. Perhaps the rest of his body has grown to match his hands. He is Johnsonian in his girth and by extension in his speech.

'You're looking well, Al.'

This enrages me. Guzzle cares nothing for my good or ill health. He is at the moment the most important person in my life and yet he knows nothing of how that life is ordered, runs smoothly or falls apart. He states that I am looking well; he doesn't ask if I am. Yet I know my anger is irrational and that he can't win. If he says that I look tired I think he is secretly writing me off, a has-been, done for. It's because of my dependence that I'm angry and unreasoning.

'Yes, I'm not dead yet,' I hear myself answer.

'Al,' Guzzle says, leaning forward a little gravely as if Buddha's great jade statue were inclining, 'it is surprising when you are so sharp that people are so fond of you.'

I am taken aback and ashamed together. Guzzle is claiming to be fond of me. How then can I hate him? He has become with a word my father more in sorrow than in anger. 'How is the book coming? Will you be ready for us to put it in the catalogue that goes to press in October?'

Again I feel the anger flare. These are such sensible questions and yet I feel attacked. 'It's up and down.' Even to myself I sound shifty. His eyes wander.

'That's Anthea Sedgebourne. Do you know her? She sells ten thousand in hardback.'

'Soft porn.'

'That's where the money is. And there is Carter Foster with Harris of the *Daily News*. Film rights sold pre-publication, a quarter of a million paperback of the last title. What was it?'

'You can't remember? Try *Armageddon* or *Apocalypse* or *Doomsday*. They're all interchangeable and no one will care in six months' time.'

'His publisher and his bank manager care. You could do it.'

'Your faith touches me.'

'You are a good writer.'

'About the poems.'

'Ah yes.'

'Shall we put the translations all together at the end in an appendix or shall I dot them through the text?'

'In the body of the text I think. An appendix looks so old-fashioned.'

'They would make a few more pages . . .'

'You must learn to write longer books.'

'A book dictates its own length.'

'Of course in an ideal world but today . . .' His shoulders shrug massively as if Everest quaked. 'What shall we eat?' His fist reaches for the white card menu. I feel a soft tension in him while he reads as if he had lowered himself into a warm scented bath. No ordinary tub would take him. It must be regal, Roman imperial, a prop from a Cecil B. de Mille extravaganza. Once I visited him in his apartment, it was too rich to be merely an English flat, when he had the flu and came from his bed to see

me in a vast wool dressing-gown the sort children wore thirty
years ago and that I thought you couldn't buy any more, and
certainly not in marquee size or the dimensions of those
Mongolian yurts we had to draw for geography, and pale blue
silk pyjamas with enough cloth in them to rig a sailing ship. His
skin was damp and his hair was ruffled from the pillow,
making him look vulnerable, almost childish, Guzzle who can
never have known a real childhood.

He ponders now. 'Is the fish good here? I can't remember. I
shall begin with a little fritto misto and go on to . . . rognogni
trifolati. And you?'

'I shall have melanzane parmigiana followed by penna alla
crema.'

'I drink very little these days but you have some wine.'

'Red, I think. Who was it said writers prefer red? It must
have to do with being bloodsuckers or is it the iron in our souls
we have to keep primed?'

I'm behaving badly again and Guzzle looks at me in more
sorrow over the top of his menu, his heavy lower lip pouting a
little. I stare into the rain runnels coursing down the window.
The light is reflected in them making each one liquid glass, a
little world already full of minute life, organisms and elements.
I feel the shiver in the people below under the chill Spring
rain. A small lake of muddy water with scum of dogends,
wrappers, matches and mashed petals blown from who knows
where has dammed itself round the corner of Dean Street. As I
stare a car dashes a wave of it over the pedestrians who shout
after the driver. One throws up his hand in a gesture from
south of Rome, inaccessible to the north and a complex
compound of the inexpressible.

'When are you publishing the next volume of party memoirs
and who is it to be?'

His sadness deepens. The upper lip pouts too. His hand
goes out to rearrange the salt cellar and pepper mill as
deliberately as if they were chessmen. 'I am in some difficulty
there.'

'Has the supply of distinguished widows of ex-ministers
dried up? Honestly you've been lucky. There've been all these
intelligent literate women working behind the scenes to some
great man, longing to tell their story, frustrated of their own
job all these years and now bursting to set the record straight.
No doubt they were happy with a small advance too.'

'That has not changed. But I am no longer a party member and in any case unless there is something exceptional in them, who is interested in revelations about a party in decline.'

I feel a little sick. Instinct not reason brought out this touchstone question I don't want the answer to. Goetzle is ratting: the ship will founder. 'When did you abandon the People's Party?'

'Has it not rather abandoned us? Come now, even you must have doubts.'

'Of course.'

'What do you really think of the men of the Left, and women too?'

'I think they have destroyed my party and disenfranchised me. I am very angry.'

'Have you considered the alternatives?'

Is Guzzle trying to subvert me? Suddenly my value goes up: I am worth wooing. But if I refuse? No surely not that: that would be corruption. This is England; we don't.

Because I haven't answered he continues: 'What do you think will happen at the next election?'

'Confusion and another right-wing government.'

'It could be different.'

'You can't ask it. You don't understand. Do you remember the quaint old term "class traitor"? I was brought up on that. And that's what I am, me and those like me. Even to be sitting in such a restaurant is a form of treachery some of us can never escape. Think of Williamson and those bitter poems about language and death. For us the class war is civil war inside our heads.' It's my turn to lean forward. 'Have you ever wondered why the supreme English novel invention since the war is the thriller? It's because it's all about class and betrayal. That's why we do it better than anyone else.'

'Don't you think all that is changing, that capitalism is moving us all, yes ironically capitalism, towards a uniform society of identical consumer goods and shopping precincts?'

'Of course.'

'Well then?' The big hands spread out showing the hairs on their backs like those on crabs' legs, black and stiff.

'No, it isn't "well". I probably feel as badly about it from my side of the coin as any old High Tory. Even so I don't want those bad old days of comradely poverty back. Don't you see there's no predictable solution. I know the English too well in

53

my marrow: they aren't socialist; they were Labour. They have no image of "the people" as other countries do. Their images are quite different.'

'The new middle class are changing it all. They will want a new party, a coalition. In the age of the computer the old two-party system won't do.'

I sigh. 'The English actually believed they invented it because they only study English history. They forget the Ghibillines and Guelfs and Dante's Blacks and Whites.'

'Exactly so: the two-party system belongs to the Middle Ages.'

'I can't,' I am saying again. 'I just can't even though I see the reasons.'

'You may change.' Goetzle leans back. He can wait. He is adaptable, a survivor; I am a dodo. My roots are too deep in my childish past, that backyard tap root that sucks up the nourishment I write on. Guzzle's are shallow, quick to take over a patch of waste and run in all directions because he has no childhood to betray. That's why the new party will be made from the free floaters who either want to forget or who have never known. I see it as a logical evolution as fewer and fewer have our lost times to remember, and still I can't.

Guzzle eats like a man who might starve. He eats for all those who didn't have enough, the walking skeletons of the camps. I understand it. I find it as touching as the child's dressing-gown but I don't watch. And I eat too for others: for the besieged at Stalingrad and the famished Indian, and to win the war. I can't waste. My plate has to be cleaned even though I bloat with the effort. These are the tattered bundles we hump about with us on our backs, sometimes, often, more ludicrous than burdensome.

'Will you go into politics for your new party?' I find myself asking, seemingly without premeditation.

'Perhaps. I am thinking about it.'

'You've been asked?' Suddenly it's all clear to me. Guzzle might become Prime Minister.

'Approaches have been made. Nobody knows yet.'

Goetzle's defection will cause no surprise. It won't be like that legendary going into the wilderness of Bevan. There will be those who say it proves their point that the party has been betrayed from within for years, soft-centred, and those who will feel more exposed as their outer wall is nibbled away and they become the first bastion. Every such leaving makes it harder ever to go back, for the party to be again the old consensus, heir to both Beatrice Webb and Keir Hardie. I look down into the street where the white snows of yesteryear slush muddily through the bars of the drain cover.

The menu comes again but Guzzle waves at the trolley with its standard medley of confections, a sophisticated sweetshop window where you know the choices: liquorice bootlace, gobstopper, sherbet dab, lemonade powder. He selects profiteroles and I feel the saliva start in my own mouth at the remembered rich simplicity of choux paste shells for chocolate and cream even though I don't want them and order just coffee. Guzzle digs in delicately and savours.

'Will the book be on time?' he asks again.

'I hope so. As long as I don't have to take too much away from it for earning a living.'

'You can't expect to live by writing, few people do.'

'But I do expect to. I shall go on expecting.'

'I can give you some reading.'

'You pay so badly it's hardly worth it.' Still it might be better than taking on another class. At least I can sit at home and read and have the satisfaction of turning other people down. 'I'll think about it if you'll pay me £15 a manuscript.'

'That's more than our top fee.'

'If I have to take on another class I'll be late delivering.'

'I'll speak to Jennifer.'

'How is she?'

'As difficult and indispensable as ever.'

'When are you going to put her on the board?'

'I'm considering it very seriously.'

The thought strikes me. 'Wouldn't it be good for your new image to have a woman director, give you appeal to the liberated middle-class woman voter?'

'As I said before Al: it's a pity you're so sharp.'

I get up. 'I have to go. When your new party takes over I hope it'll remember the arts. Literature has always produced interesting Prime Ministers: Disraeli, Macmillan . . .'

Guzzle doesn't answer but stabs with his fork at a cockle shell of profiterole sending it skidding across the plate.

VII

The rain has stopped but Spring has gone from the streets for now at least. I'm a little drunk but not very much as they teach students to say in the heat of the English summer schools for foreigners. How I stewed and sweated through that one last year; six weeks when everyone else had gone off to Gozo and Corfu as the back of the *Sunday Times* had advised them to do in bleak January and the city was given up to the invader coming in hoards to learn the English. For once it was hot. The busybody sun stared ardently through the plate-glass windows at waves of boys and girls on their three-week crash courses or slavered on the bars of the Venetian blinds to get at their firm, sweet young skin, run its tongue over bare arms and throats and mould them in a deeper bronze. They were gold-leafed already from their home summer while I was still the cellared bulb colour which is somehow natural to the British. The sweat left damp oasis depressions on the pages from the heel of their hands as they copied down phrasal verbs and idiomatic expressions which are the English substitute for grammar.

'Let's go, shall we? *Run*: run into, run over, run across, run up, run down, run through . . .'

To them it's all freedom so they don't see how the city drains of colour in summer. Our best time is Spring, and then autumn again, but not today. Almost the snow might come back it's grown so suddenly cold. 'Snow into magnolia won't go.' I remember carrying that line around with me this time one year and not being able to do anything with it, seeing the little mounds of cold flakes piled on the white petal flesh and it browning, corrupting under their weight of chill penetration, a

56

kind of inverse necrophilia where it's death that's the lover.

The grave's a fine and private place
But none I think do there embrace.

I shall be glad to be off these dark streets. I go up the steps and into the sad dim hall, pull back the scissor grill of the ancient lift and step inside to be carried to the second floor. *Never walk when you can ride.*

The building can hardly have changed in its century and a quarter. It's right that our gloomy deliberations should take place here in this chill murk. Nesta acknowledges my late arrival from the head of the table. She will have set herself up for the afternoon on decaffeinated coffee, not the red wine that's making me drowsy in spite of the cold.

'We're taking the second item, matters arising from the minutes, Al.'

'Sorry madam chair.' I slink in and slump onto a hard seat with wooden arms to pin you in place like an infant's high chair.

'Is there anything you wish to raise?'

'No, no thank you.'

'Then is it your wish that I sign these minutes as a true record?' She looks about birdily, expectantly, although no one ever answers this question. We sit in a glum rhetorical silence. What anyway is a true record since minutes are meant to be non-controversial, the agreed dilute? Are there then three truths to every happening: yours, mine and ours; each of them blurred at the edges and a little off-centre? I must concentrate.

'Item three, our main business today is to consider applications for the Sabine Baring-Gould.'

'Did you know that he wrote over a hundred books, all standing up?'

'The Victorians usually stood up to write,' Curwen says impatiently.

'Some did, some didn't. Edward Arber, you know: *Arber's Reprints*, lexicographer and anthologist was photographed sitting at his desk. I think Gould saw his writing desk as a kind of lectern or pulpit.'

'Why should he do that? Why can't a desk just be a desk?'

'He was a clergyman. He wrote *Onward Christian Soldiers* and had fourteen children. It was written for his parishioners to sing in procession.'

'I thought he was a folksong collector.'

57

'That too. Arber was run over by a bus while reading, like Matthew Arnold. Literature is a dangerous preoccupation.' I am getting drunker or more desperate by the minute.

'This isn't getting us through the applications. Can we take your short lists in turn please?'

'Can't we go through the whole list one by one and give our thumbs up or down?'

'It isn't a gladiatorial combat.'

'Isn't it in a way? Someone's got to come out the winner and we have to decide.'

'They're not in competition for their lives.'

'They may be. In a sense they are: for their literary lives.'

'Five hundred pounds is hardly going to make the difference between life and death.'

'It isn't just the money; it's a matter of recognition, of self-confidence.'

'I don't see why we have to top the money up as we do out of state funds.'

'The original one hundred pounds is barely worth applying for today.'

'"Two pints of beer and a packet of crisps."' Everyone laughs politely.

'If Al is right it should be the recognition that matters most. No one has to be a writer.'

'But someone must.'

'There will always be people wanting to write.'

'You might as well say there will always be people wanting to be nurses or vets.'

'Society needs nurses.'

'It needs writers too.'

'I don't see how in times like these you can justify the expense.'

'Then you shouldn't be sitting on a committee like this.'

I have gone too far. He bristles as retired colonels did in between-the-wars fiction. Curwen has moved further and further to the Right as he got older until now he's a caricature, almost fascist in his laissez-faire, sporting a self-conscious military toothbrush of black bristle under a white thick thatch. I'm fond of him though, as I am of Guzzle but I pray not yet lord, not that conventional middle-aged mellowing that runs down to an abandonment of all hope, a descent to the grave.

'You'll learn when you get older,' my mother used to say

over some piece of wilful, as she saw it, difference from the norm. 'I won't,' I would answer. 'If it's not true.' I say it still inside even though I know now truth is Joseph's multicoloured dreamcoat.

'If they're no damn good they shouldn't be encouraged by dollops of public money just because it's Buggins' turn. Anything that's any good will find its own way.'

'Sabine Baring-Gould was a best seller in his day. Did you know that? He knocked them cold with *Mehalah*, a story of the Essex salt marshes. On the other hand Henry James sold rather badly. I recommend *Mehalah* as a good read. Our tomboy heroine, a proto-feminist, is drowned by the man who has pursued her to the last chapter! They go down together in burning prose. That's what we are commemorating in this private charity topped up by the taxpayer.'

'Please, please can we consider the candidates. Now who wants to put in a word for Damaris Derry?'

No one it seems. Shall I, just out of cussedness? No, I've done enough for the moment. Next we put aside Sri Desai, a writer with a talent as gentle and refined as the illustrations to a book of ragas, who refuses to fit himself into the current image of statutory ethnic writer in green bile. Luckily for him he's our only 'ethnic' applicant or he would be considered too classical and middle class.

'Paine Humphrey, I think so, yes,' Nesta decides.

'Does he really need it?'

'How much do we take that into consideration? This is an award not a bursary.'

'I mean does he need any more recognition. Isn't he the most fashionable wordmonger on the circuit at the moment?'

'A fine poet,' Curwen nods.

'The darling of fortune,' I murmur acidly. 'Overpraised today and torn down tomorrow.'

'Envy, Al?' Nesta throws her head back so that two light bulbs hang suspended in her glasses blotting out the pupils.

'Yes, of course. In a way. We would all like to be fashion's child if only for an hour, if we're honest, or part of us would. Without that in our society your audience is the faithful few who've heard of your work and follow your fortunes. It's rather like being an obscure seventeenth-century sect or the preacher to one, jogging your tattered gelding from village to village seeking out the one or two who will understand your word.'

I've never thought of it this way before and the picture both surprises and comforts me.

'I find what you're saying another distasteful aspect of modern life.'

'Rubbish! There's nothing modern about it. It's called place-seeking. Shakespeare and John Donne suffered from it very badly. They were both dependent on arms of the state, the established church and the court, for livelihood and they both sought out fortune's smiles to get it while trying to keep their artistic integrity.'

'I'm glad you at least allow them that,' Curwen sneers. He has made himself so much in his own image that his very gestures conjure up terms from the *Boy's Own*. No contemporary laconic vocabulary will describe them.

'Anyway,' Nesta says firmly, 'Paine Humphrey goes in.'

'I think Al's right,' Henrietta Kingston, alias Lady Letchworth, speaks for the first time. She's been nerving herself for her opening remark since she woke this morning. Her three novels are skilled miniatures she sells eighteen hundred copies of in hardback. She has a large flat at the top of a tall house in St John's Wood out of her failed marriage, sparsely furnished with rush matting on the floors and a one-bar electric fire. Yet she feels a fraud, I know, sitting in literary judgement even though it's usually sensible, that is, corresponds with mine. I like her and would like to comfort her but I don't know how. The days pass and I don't ring her up and suggest we meet which makes me feel guilty every time we do.

The literary world is littered with sensitive fugitives from the upper classes trying to pass as ordinary citizens, not realising that their new roles although a release for them are just as extraordinary to ninety-five per cent of the population. Our latter-day Bohemia takes them to its crusty bosom and the fashion hunters still seek them out to trade on their titles for gossip. I must concentrate. How I do run on. Jim Banes. We have reached Jim Banes.

'Nothing but an organ grinder's monkey,' Curwen growls, resolving my own problem. Now I shall support Jim Banes.

'We ought to have a token performance artist to go with our other symbols.'

'We haven't got a statutory woman yet,' Henrietta points out bravely. Because she's nervous her contributions are either

60

hesitant or aggressive.

'Surely we don't choose people according to category but on literary merit. If no one's good enough we shouldn't award at all.'

'That's a very simplistic view. Everyone is themselves but also a symbol of something. We all fall into classes or categories in other people's eyes.'

We drear on. The committee has got into a sullen mood of rejection and the next half-dozen go down quickly.

'I can't see anyone of outstanding talent in this lot, apart from Paine that is.'

'Then you have no problem Curwen. You know where to put your vote.'

'You mean you don't know who to propose.'

'Can we please finish the short list? Now Celia Finnan?'

'There's your statutory woman.'

'Better than Damaris Derry anyway.'

'Can we be sure posterity will agree with us? Maybe it will find for Ms Derry and against us. That's the point of literary, indeed artistic judgements of any sort. They're a matter of taste.'

'But you must know which you think best.'

'I know what *I* like, as people who were unsure of their judgement used to say.'

'But if you're not sure of your judgement you shouldn't be on this panel,' Curwen says triumphantly now that the wheel has come round full circle to him.

'I'm sure of my judgement for me but I don't insist that it's the final or only one. We should have more than one award to give.'

'"Everyone has won and all must have a prize,"' says Henrietta.

She looks indeed a little like Alice I decide, with her touched-up hair still long and blonde and thick, and the rest of us are uncannily like the other wonderland inhabitants. I cast Nesta unkindly as the Red Queen. And me, what am I? Knave, White Rabbit or just supporting Dodo? Curwen, of course, is the Mad Hatter or perhaps the peppery cook.

'Where's Hugh to give his voice?'

'If you'd been on time Al you'd have heard me give his apologies.'

'Are we a quorum without him?' I am being wicked.

61

'We don't have to be. There isn't one. As a matter of fact he sent me his short list.'

Sent or handed to her across the pillow? No, the idea is absurd, or is it? Is the Red Queen blushing? That would make an interesting tie-up and only logical when you think of it, our tame radical academic with the chairperson.

'Now I think we have our short list. I suggest we number them one to four. I've got some scrap paper. Everyone write their selection on the paper, fold it and hand it to me.'

'Nothing but a bloody lottery.'

'Like life.'

'A waste of public money.'

'A measly five hundred.'

'I'd be grateful for even a hundred,' Henrietta sighs. She'll vote for Celia Finnan because it's a talent much like her own, precisely refined by craftsmanship, come too late like little mistakes of my childhood, the children of middle age. And perhaps I shall too because Desai has no other supporter but me and because Jim Banes isn't you my master, roaring boy, and when I set him against you as a populist, outcast, iconoclast I see him as a man not even of straw but of foam rubber.

'We seem to have a tie: two each for Paine Humphrey and Celia Finnan. Which leaves me with the chair's casting vote.' So Hugh has voted not for revolution but fashion and now she has a real conflict. Which shall she brave: the wrath of the feminists or of fashionable academe and her putative lover? The pot-bellied god of gold is laughing down at us, his puny priests who are enhancing his power with our haggling over a dole so small. I wonder if he is more prayed to for little sums than large.

'I think on balance Celia Finnan because at this stage she needs it more.'

Nesta has been courageous and if Hugh is her lover foolhardy. Sisterhood has triumphed over sex. But I may be wrong, their love affair a fantasy of mine and she has nothing to lose. We break up. Henrietta and I vow to ring one another. 'We must have lunch.'

'That would be lovely,' she ducks her head.

It's dark outside and the rain has come back. The rush hour flows down from St Paul's in a muddy Styx of struggling bodies and cars. Paul's is a gaunt sepulchre for Donne's bones

62

against a sky of smoking clouds. Clerks and typists and bookkeepers froth through the drizzle from Mammon's heart to Cannon Street and London Bridge as they've done for over a century, homewards to their suburban teas, through Eliotesquerie to Betjemania on the green Southern with its slamming doors, or deep underground for Central and District going east into the desolate fringes of Essex, Romford and Redbridge and on down to the sea at Southend.

I flow with them towards the Temple. The platform is packed. There can't have been a train for a long time. The indicator panel suddenly glows with a name like the announcement of the entry of a character in a Shakespeare play: Richmond. 'How now Richmond, what make you here among the law's quills and frets?'

'I come to pluck a new tune, my lord.'

We are stacked against each other now. There's hardly enough room to expand my chest to breathe. If anyone fell they would be trampled to death and those at the front must feel their calves ache and their toes tingle with apprehension. Before them is the dark bed of the track with its parallel dull silver lines of steel and the white china discs that mark off the live rail. I catch the flying rumours: there's been a terrorist bomb at the Bank; someone has fallen under a train, and there's a lightning strike of drivers. They flow to and fro among us like ripples running at a rock face and back again.

In the neon half-light the faces are gaunt, the shadows painted on them as children draw stiff-brushed in black the basic components of a face: eyes, nose, mouth. We are all a little afraid down here of the sudden blast or the fist of water punching out of a tunnel to roll us shrieking in a tangle of helplessly flailing limbs down the sewers of the city. The horror movies know what they do when they externalize such terrors. Suddenly I have more respect for them. They are the dooms on our chapel walls, demonic and punitive.

The lone signal shows its green eye in the far tunnel and the lit caterpillar mask of the train slides towards us out of the dark drawing its body alongside the platform. We can see the others, travellers who've got on before us jammed in its gut but for some reason the doors don't open to let some of them out and us in. The train hisses but the doors stay shut. For a few moments the awful patience of the British prevails and then something snaps though I can't see what.

Perhaps the first hammering comes from within but suddenly they are beating on the doors and windows from both sides, shouting though we can't hear those on the other face of the glass, only see their mouths opening in Munch soundless cries not of fear but rage. The fists and palms look as if they are pounding against each other as they beat the transparent glass and those in front turn their heads to shout at those pushing from behind.

All the frustrations of the day, and of the ordered lives of the city damped down, suddenly seethe and boil, at the getting up every morning to a task that seems dictated by society not nature until we grow sullen inside, carrying a scummed and festering pool that slops up in our throats, a heavy bile to be soothed with booze and pills.

The doors hiss open. Over the air comes the soft calming West Indian voice: 'Let them off first please. Let them off first.' We struggle on board, shaken. We have been near to riot or panic. Some faces are pale and sweaty with fear; others are flushed, the eyes shining from an access, excess, of adrenalin. One man clenches and unclenches his fists. The doors hiss shut and the train jerks forward. The mass of flesh hanging ape-like from rails and poles lurches and stumbles.

VIII

I fight my way out a stop later and am swirled along in search of the Bakerloo, most ancient of underground ways only just modernized out of its Brunellian high hat brick arches. I've always believed it's named after Sherlock Holmes or rather for him. I cherish such thoughts against the rush of humankind from work to home, a stream I don't have to swim with or against every day since I carry my work around in my head so that I can dip a foot from time to time in these waters. I'm amazed and appalled by it. The Martian looking down from his hovering space craft would marvel at our obedience to need and the clock. Are we the only primates to be able to behave like insects and laud ourselves for it, for our industry, precision, punctuality? It built the pyramids and the Great Wall of China but it's unnatural for the English who long always to get back to their cottage industries of gardening and Do-It-Yourself and for whom work is largely an interruption of life and the beautifying of their semi-detached castles.

Spewed out again at Piccadilly I lament as always Nash's Regent Street vandalized by commerce and cross over among the classical façades of Mayfair, remembering my first foreign film in the plush seats of the Curzon, treated to a lush taste of Italian poverty on a day's outing from my own. It's a further extension of the same irony that sites the *Peterloo Review* here among the silverware shops and chic galleries on the top floor of a tall narrow house bequeathed to it by William Silverstone, twice jailed for publicly burning his ballot-paper in protest for universal suffrage.

The bottom floor is a tourist agency, the first and second

peddle temporary jobs, the third is an import and export company which I've never seen open. I climb up the backbone of the thin house as I do every time with mingled pride and fear. Sometimes I think they should have kept the magazine's first name, bestowed by Silverstone with the building, the *Tower*, but an early committee decided that there might have been confusion with a well-known religious broadsheet.

The open-plan general office falls silent when I push open the door, and then the scattered group takes up its talk again.

'Is Phillip in?'

A girl with large glasses and a bowl-of-porridge face waves towards his room and goes on talking. I walk over to the door marked *Editor* and knock on the name underneath, knuckling the 'l' and 'd' of Golden.

'Come!' I turn the handle and open the door. Phillip is reclining in his swivel chair; his feet, in white moccasins and socks as this year's mode is below the bottoms of his carefully faded jeans, are propped on the desk. 'Al, how nice!'

'I did say I'd drop in.'

'Of course you did. How're things?'

'Busy. Just been to a committee meeting.'

'Ah committees . . . they're all the rage. This whole place is a committee now. I've made the company into a collective.'

'It seemed to be meeting as I came through.' I laugh and jerk my head back at the door.

'The boys and girls. Some of them are quite pretty. A little earnest perhaps. It makes my life very easy. I really have nothing to do any more except sign the cheques. All the decisions are taken by the collective.'

'Including layout and content?'

'Everything.'

'Is that why you did it?'

'Did what?'

'Made it a collective?'

'Oh, I don't think I had much choice. We can only afford to employ the young and fervent. No one with ties and responsibilities would work for what we pay. Naturally they bring their ideas with them.'

'You make it sound like luggage.'

'Rather, excess baggage. They're a bit cross at the moment because they want to sell this building and move into fashionable Wandsworth but they can't because of the terms of the original trust. Silverstone tied it up so that if the building is diverted from use for its main purpose of publishing a radical magazine in accordance with his principles it must be sold and the money given to certain specified charities.'

'As if he saw the shape of things to come. Where would he have stood now do you think?' I am staving off the moment when I have to ask the question I already know the answer to.

'It's very hard to say isn't it.'

'There must be a few bits of *Some Discourses* that would give us a clue.'

'You're always harking back Al. Who cares where Silverstone would have stood?'

'I do.' I'm remembering how I first met Phillip at a party given by that pair of lifetime lovers Tom and Harry, nearly twenty years ago. For a couple of years until I got to know him I had thought we were on the side of the same angels in most things.

'You've never learned to ride with the punches like I do, maybe because I'm a rootless antipodean who can never go back to the land of roast lamb and two veg on Sunday.'

'How's Terry?'

'As queenly as ever. You must come to dinner. We're veggie at the moment.'

'Silverstone would have approved.'

'Oh strictly dietary. Good for the heart if not for the fart. All those beans.' He's smiling at me as I squirm on my unasked question. Was there ever a time when I actually liked Phillip? I can't remember any more.

'What will you do about the move?'

'Fortunately there's nothing to be done. I just have to sit tight and spread my hands in impatience.' He does so. 'I shall still be here when they've tired of this small beer and gone off to play somewhere else.'

'The collective might sack you.'

'That's taken care of.'

I decide to taunt him a little. 'Don't you fancy Wandsworth? Isn't that really just the sort of place the *Peterloo* should be these days?'

'Can you see me going south of the river? It's virtually suburban. What was your committee about?'

'Choosing the Sabine Boring-Gould winner for this year.'

Phillip looks up eagerly. 'Who did you pick?'

'Read it in the *Bookseller*.'

'Always the puritan, Al. I suppose you want to know about your article? Let's ask the editor. Give them a taste of real responsibility.' He swings his feet down from the desk and stands up. I follow. It's my dismissal and now he's going to throw me to the cubs. I trail behind him into the outer office.

'Julie, Terry, everybody this is Al. Al wants to know if we're going to take the Villon piece; authors like to know that sort of thing from time to time.'

Julie is the bowl of porridge. She doesn't attract me and I'm frightened so I make these snap judgements I know I shouldn't. We share with our ape brothers an over-developed social sense and Julie and I can each feel the other's waves of hostility or so I believe. Suddenly she reminds me of Nesta and that doesn't help either.

'We discussed it at some length.' Her delivery is Cambridge rapid, the voice accentless verging towards middle professional, Girls' Public Day School Trust rather than boarding school. 'We couldn't see its relevance to the present phase of the conflict.'

'Shit to that,' I hear myself gearing automatically down into demotic, speaking in my mother tongue, though *she* would never have used a 'rude' word. The old man would have said: 'Arseholes!' I may yet do so. I feel a rage rising in me that isn't mine but theirs, that thirst for equality that runs through English history and breaks through the conservatism every so often ripping the fabric apart.

> *When Adam delved and Eve span*
> *Who was then the gentleman?*

'Show us how it's relevant then,' Terry wants to know. 'It's history and this country's got too much of that. People want their eyes opened to what's going on now.'

'We have a responsibility to develop the whole man – and woman,' I add hastily. 'Literature and history are part of our culture. That's the sort of principle the *Peterloo* was founded on.'

'Middle-class culture.'

'To a certain extent; that is middle-class in its distribution, not necessarily in its genesis or concerns. Anyway you can't say that about Villon. Not only was he a populist poet, he was a condemned criminal. I should have thought he was just the

68

subject for *Peterloo* readers.'

'It distracts from the struggle.'

'What does?'

'The historical approach.'

'What about Tawney and Thompson? Without our historians there wouldn't be a base for a popular movement.'

'Why now anyway?'

'It's the five hundred and fiftieth anniversary of his birth if you want a peg to hang on.'

'There's no sign of a proto-revolutionary consciousness in his work, at least as you've presented it. Indeed he seems almost sycophantic.' Julie's glasses flash like Nesta's.

'Artists usually are. They have to be, either to a single or a collective patron.' I am sycophantic myself now in arguing with them, trying to persuade them to take something they despise. 'What more do you want of him? He was imprisoned, tortured, sentenced to be hanged, exiled.'

'Perhaps that isn't sufficiently brought out in your piece.'

'Then publish the translation of *The Ballade of the Hanged*. Let him speak for himself.'

'Through your translation?'

'Yes. All right. Publish it in the original.'

'That's an elitist suggestion. How many of your readers can manage French let alone mediaeval?'

'That's why things have to be translated, so that they aren't lost, become inaccessible.'

'If they served their purpose in their time it may be best to let them go.'

'Human achievement is based on culture, on the remembrance of things past and building on it.'

'That's why we go on making the same mistakes. We have to scrap the whole system and start again.' Terry's short curls look almost damp under the light. He must be the one Phillip thinks is pretty. I grasp at irrelevancies to keep from despair.

'Poetry is a very suspect form. It can be made to serve any master.' In another age she would have said: 'serve the devil' and called it the great seducer.

'People don't need high art. They can make their own.'

'Yes I know. This country is full of writers. You've only got to announce a poetry competition and the entries come in in their thousands. It's the first thing the English turn to when they're bereaved or divorced or made redundant: writing poetry. But they need help. Just as they would if they took up painting or music and help lies in the knowledge of other writers as well as in practising your craft. Villon wrote for the people as well as princes, in thieves' cant, but he did it better than other people, that's why he's a great poet and worth writing or reading about.'

'That's your opinion.'

'That's what I'm arguing for: my opinion. I know that.'

'The editorial committee was unanimous.'

I don't look at Phillip although maybe I should. I grin and throw out my hands. 'Editors usually are.' Then I turn to Phillip. 'I'll see you.'

'Bye, Al.' He makes a little wave in the air. I nod at porridge bowl and the rest of them and turn for the door. Then I pause.

'"New presbyter is old priest writ large." More history.' I am shaking with anger and misery. I must be careful not to shut my fingers in the pincers of the lift door. I think I hear laughter from the room I have just left but that's probably simple paranoia. I have just enough reason alert still to tell myself that.

Out in the wet street again I cross over and look up the cliff face of the building to where the lit windows overhang the pavements dark now with spilt rain. I realise suddenly I should have suggested they print the dual text but it's too late and probably it always was. I have failed you, failed as your envoy. Either I have to believe that or to believe that your compassion is too great for these children of plenty, of Never-had-it-so-good time, your gallows print too ripe for them.

IX

I stand here still looking up like that sickly painting of *Love Locked Out*. If I had a brick I might throw it through one of the lit square panes but I haven't and anyway I could never shy it up there. I see it in my mind's eye wobbling underhand halfway up and toppling ignominiously back. I begin to trudge towards Green Park tube, uncheered this time by memories of breakfast at the Ritz as I pass its blazing picture-palace front where taxis are disgorging gorgers and the gorgeous. I get off at Gloucester Road, join a queue for chips and hurry the hot greasy paperful, smelling of childhood winter evenings, through the rain clutched against my coat to protect them from damp and cold, something I shall be sorry for when I put it on later and catch the reek of congealed fat.

My room itself seems bleak basement only tonight and nothing I could do would make it welcoming. It's a bolt hole, a cave for retreat where I can rub chipshop salt and vinegar into my wounds. Tonight the warm waxy fingers stick in my gullet and won't go down. There seems to be a lump in my chest that makes swallowing hard, a lump compounded of tears and cold boiled potatoes from a school dinner I'd refused to eat and was made to sit over in the emptying hall that served us as a dining room, pushing the mess about my plate and trying to choke down alternately a piece that crumbled to flour in the mouth, coating the tongue and throat with starch dust, and a knob like a candle end but tinged green on one side, a gobstopper to gag on.

I pull down the blind, shutting out the railings and dust bins it's too dark to see any more and the rain-pocked window.

Music, I need some music. '*Music for a while, shall all thy cares beguile.*' No, not that. I'm still angry. Something rougher. I shall come to the beguiling later. Dejaneira's aria from *Hercules*; Janet Baker at her baroque Handelian best: in full cry of madness, guilt and jealousy. '*Where shall I fly, where hide this guilty head?*' The adagio opening and then suddenly con brio:

> *Chain me ye Furies to your iron beds,*
> *and lash my guilty ghost*
> *with whips of scorpion.*
> *See! see, they come*
> *Alecto with her snakes,*
> *Megaera fell,*
> *and black Tisiphone.*

Why should they come to me, when I'm the one sinned against, to cry their murder. That's what rejection is: a little piece of murder, a strangling of the infant, a stab in the author's guts which are heart and pocket. And yet they come to prey on us with old guilts and self recriminations. You knew it too.

> *Hé! Dieu, se j'eusse estudié*
> *Ou temps de ma jeunesse folle . . .*

If only we'd worked harder, not wasted our time, got a better degree, loved more wisely and not too well, sucked up to the right people, not been so pig-headed, joined the dinner-party circuit, got into Oxbridge.

And then they hold up that Medusa head that turns to stone: failure of nerve. What if I can't do it any more? Maybe I shall never write again, or paint or compose though I think writers are more prone to tightrope wobble because they've no 'objective correlative', nothing outside themselves they can look at apart from a pile of MS that sickens you as your eye follows a sentence you've written like a regurgitated morsel, cat puke in the corner; no note that will answer them back from an instrument that isn't just the hollow bone of their own struck skull. Isn't it after all called '*writer's* block'?

Did you ever know this dread or did you die too young while the poems were still pouring out of you? What about the end of *The Legacy* where you couldn't finish it because your head was whirling and when it stopped your ink was frozen and the candle gone out so you wrapped yourself up and fell asleep: '*Et ne pens autrement finer*'? Was that really because of the cold or because you'd run out of words? And how long did that last? Was that viprous head held up before you, calcifying the imagination and freezing the ink? Questions, unanswerable questions, unless I can ravel out the truth from your own words. I know I impose on you and the porridge bowl was right. I twist you into the shape of my own concerns. But I don't believe I'm far out; I believe we have a community of experience, give or take half a millennium. You can't answer except with ambiguities.

The evening aches ahead to be got through. '*Which way shall I fly?*' The Knickers or the Nevern? But not yet either. It's too early yet. In my haste to be home and dry with the chips I forgot to buy an evening paper. I shall go and see how the world's wending. That will pass a bit till pubtime. I put on my jacket, open the door and climb up into the hall. On the top step I pause looking through the hatching of cold rain before I launch myself into it and run for the corner and the brightly blazing Asian newsagent's open till all hours. I pick up the evening paper, pay and go out into the fall that smarms down my hair with cold fingers and darkens my denim shoulders and trouser bottoms into deep navy.

A phone is ringing as I push into the hall. Is it mine? I gammy leg down the stairs and throw myself at the front door, fumbling with the key. Thank god I didn't Chubb lock it for the short trip to the corner and back. Don't stop! Whoever you are don't stop. I throw myself across the room and pick up the receiver afraid it will die in my hands.

'Al? Where've you been all day? We've rung you several times.'

It's one of the laws of life that a sat-by phone never rings. 'Sorry. I've been out. I had lunch with Goetzle. I thought I told you.'

'Some lunch.'

'Then I had a meeting and so on . . .'

'Anyway, I thought you'd want to know that's why I'm ringing this late from home because we've persuaded them to give you a half-hour Radio 3 programme to talk and read from your translations of the poems. They'll get someone in to read the originals, some native frog they've got up their sleeve or wherever.'

73

'Brilliant.'

'I thought you'd be pleased. We're still arguing over the fee but I'll speak to you later in the week about that.'

'Marvellous. Thanks for letting me know. It makes all the difference to tomorrow's stint.'

'Good. I'll talk to you soon.' He hangs up.

My guardian angel, agent, friend, rescuer. The whole evening changes. I can still do it. Everything will be all right. Tomorrow I'll be able to get on with the next chapter now, just get up and get on with it.

What do you think of that then my frank friend? I haven't failed you, not quite anyway. You're going to be on the radio after all; your voice will sound from the shrine, will oracle out through my lips and your own. You will speak and I shall be your priest to translate, just as it should be. I shall go to the Nevern. Perhaps I'll knock on Léonie's door. I can hear her now overhead, sounds of movement my misery blotted out before. First I'll look at the paper I bought in another country ten minutes ago.

A face I recognize looks out at the world from the front page through the blurred, furred and spreading rain drops darkening the newsprint. For a moment I can't place it. My eye begins to move along the headline and down into the columns of words. *Ex-diplomat Found Murdered in Chelsea Flat.*

I see the face now turning away from The Hennickers bar above the grey suit and overcoat and two held-out glasses while the voices and the clamour of the juke box fall back. I see the strand of greying hair that wilts over the broad forehead. In the picture the eyes are hooded, almost wary. They were blue or grey as I remember.

Past tense already. The Knackers will be alive with it, buzzing and fearful like any other animal colony a predator breaks into. I read on and try to tease out a story. There are hints at MI6 involvement. Cuthbert Wheeler, I learn his name too late, was a minor official in the Foreign Office until his retirement eighteen months ago, early retirement I note at fifty-seven. I know at once he was Bertie to his few close friends and to his family. He will have a sister in the shires, married with two children. And a mother; alive or dead there has to be a mother but not a father, not in any sense that mattered.

The report speaks of his 'elegant apartment'. Flats can't be elegant, the syllabic rhythm isn't right, and his dwelling was no doubt apart from the rough and tumble, riff-raff of the Knickers. Did they steal anything other than his life? Only the money in his wallet it seems though there were other things they might have taken. I picture him, or them, going down the stairs with a French carriage clock striking the golden hour under the sweaty jacket.

If they didn't come to steal it was a sex crime of lust or rage. The paper doesn't say but I read between the gaps that there was no sign of a break-in. Bertie had brought someone home to bed or perhaps just to talk. Was it a friend or a bit of trade, a trull, street troll? Did he even with his height and broad shoulders from a manly upbringing, at Harrow the paper says, Harrow and Cambridge, have a hankering for butch boys wielding Alecto's snaky whips and live on the edge of the abyss in his grey worsted and aggressively subdued tie? Was it an ex-lover who took the money to make it look like a queer being rolled? This paper won't tell me. Tomorrow the scandal sheets I scorn to buy will be full of innuendo and prurience.

This settles it: definitely the Nevern. My small peace, delicately negotiated ceasefire, isn't strong enough to take on the Knackers tonight. Suddenly I am against calling on Léonie too. I shall go untramelled by other people's ills and guilts, their emotional stocks and shares that rise and fall with every quotation. Do the other animals fall in love or is it, as in so many differences between us, one of degree rather than kind? Is their love like their language the embryo of ours?

My trousers and jacket are still damp. I raise the blind a bit and look out into the service road above the railings to try to see the slants of rain tacked against the darkness. If it's still pissing down there's no point in putting on dry clothes but when I try my jacket it strikes cold and heavy across my neck like a yoke. I find another behind the curtain that serves as wardrobe and let myself out into the hall again. The rain has stopped but the sky is still strung with sagging sheets of wet cloud. As I pass the gardens the prunus is a ghost of itself, the petals drenched and still.

The familiar pub noise gushes over me as I open the glass door, muffling the ears like water. I want to get a little drunk, just enough not to think, to laugh and unwind. I push towards our corner. Jemal is already there but it's too late to turn away. He watches me forcing between the stacked bodies.

75

'Hallo Al.'

'How's things? Have a drink.' He lifts an almost empty sleeve glass and drains it. I hand it to Felicity-behind-the-bar to refill and order my own pint to go with it. I turn while she's drawing the drinks to look out over the crowded bar, picking out vignettes, the small scenes people fall into as they talk. Other animals when not on the run are still life: humans make cartoons or genre painting. Rarely a face stands out in portrait. Or is it perhaps that since Lautrec the eye is trained to such sightings? Can one artist's view change the whole world's way of seeing the things he has seen, on and on for generations?

I don't want to turn back to Jemal, to the questions I must ask and he doesn't want to answer. But Felicity will be waiting for me to pay and I've no right to keep her standing there while others queue to be served. There's no real get-out from responsibility. Every small exchange involves it for those moments. Civilization runs on an acknowledgement that she will serve me what I ask for and I will pay what she says, with equally orderly procedures for when the first transaction breaks down. Only passion, frenzy release us from order for a while. The graffito on the sepulchre wall reads: Madness is divine.

I hand Jemal his full glass of pine-pale lager. When he first came here he drank bitter as a Briton for a time and then as disillusion grew in a symbol of protest took to lager. The protest was complex, and involved rejection of the cheaper drink, the workman's tipple as well as a preference for the foreign, unEnglish unRaj. Over the years the image has inverted. Now it's the blue boatrace boys in sporty blazers, this season's Jerome K. Jerome fashion, who call for bitter. Jemal rejects them too.

'Cheers Al.' We raise glasses and drink and I look out again into the pack, delaying speech. My eyes go from face to face and when they fall on a familiar one I grin and raise my pint a little to the wave or glass lifted in turn. Beyond the lattice partition a cheer goes up. Someone has won a darts game. I know all the regulars, their stories, their weaknesses. They are those whose home is really here, and here they play out their lives against the shifting backdrop of passing trade, tourists, droppers-in, those who come only for a pre-dinner drink. The regulars are in night after night and often lunchtimes as well. They have their set hours for coming and going. Some are lunchtimers only and never seen at night. Others are six to eighters and Sunday dinner timers. The pub is a wide estuary with different species taking up their territory to feed and squabble and mate but the tide-lines that mark out their boundaries, cliffs, high flotsam, shore or shallows are temporal as well as spatial. Again I see the dominance of order, of habit that dictates that John Scarsdale's crowd will be divided half each side of the palisade so that some can play darts and yet stay in touch with those who don't but want to lean their elbows on the bar as they perch on the high stools, or their backs against it if they stand, at the ready for the cry of: 'You're chalking Ian!'

Snatches of dialogue go past and are lost. Ellen, lifelong virgin, her grey hair still cut in a childish bob licks a Guinness moustache, same colour with the yellow froth that boils from a mudflat, from her upper lip. She leans away from a questing hand. Its owner bends over her.

'Don't be afraid of me Ellen.'

'It's your hands I'm afraid of, not you.'

'Is Léonie coming in?' I ask Jemal at last.

'I don't know Al.'

'If you don't who does?'

He shrugs. 'She knows where I am. If she wants to come in she can. The pub is open to everyone.'

'Are you still going home?'

'I will go when I am ready.'

'Now Zimbabwe is independent, it'll be harder for you to stay unless you register as a student.' I pause '... or marry an EEC citizen.'

'I could do that. Perhaps. But I won't register as a student.'

When he came first he came to study but threw up his course after a year. Now he hangs on from passport renewal to renewal, working in a small plastics factory, sent money by relatives who beg him to come home to the family business and the girl they'll find for him. Mother and sisters hanker for him, their littlest brother-son alone among loose women in London. Behind his eternal student's hornrimmed glasses his eyes are as wary in their dark depths as those that look off the front page of the evening paper someone has discarded on a nearby table. Jemal permits himself to be loved but not to love.

'Léonie would marry you.'

'I know that Al. She won't leave me alone. She smothers me.

77

I tell her I don't want to see her any more but she won't accept it. What can I do?'

'If you don't do something they will deport you. You know the routine: two policemen at the door at five o'clock in the morning when you're still half asleep, and before you know it you're on the plane.'

I am arguing against what I believe should happen for Léonie's sake. It would be better for her if he were gone but he lingers, postponing the day when he has to give up alcohol and his freedom. When he's middle-aged, plump and sleek what part will this time play in his remembrance, his London period? Perhaps he will warn his grandsons against the snares of foreign cities.

They all come to London, not England. That's what they call it; that's the allure. I remember an Australian returned for a sentimental trip reliving: 'I loved London but the poverty and the cold made me go back.' At once the city is Dickensian. I look around at us, The Nevern regulars, drunks' army, and try to see again how we appear to others. We're not poor, not as I grew up to it, but neither are we rich, nor even comfortable. Our homes are one room for the most part, two if we're lucky. Only John Scarsdale's contessa, as I call her, has a whole mansion flat. Margaretta over there is Monroe blonde, a Rhinemaiden Loren that Hitler would have set to breeding. Her Danubian blue eyes open wide to swallow yours up and lay you between the soft snowy Alps of her Viennese cream whirls.

'Why you not come to see me?' she asks whenever we meet, and once after a party: 'You dance with Léonie. Why you not dance with me?' And I couldn't say: 'It's because I don't want to be tantalized with fruit held out and then withheld.' Margaretta's riches are all warmly on display but once she told me: 'I am quite faithful while I am with someone. I am very loyal.' When she sits up on the high stool the whole bar lusts after her. Can she help that? Can she help spilling out promise from every moist pore?

Too hot and too cold are both heresies in love's creed. Jemal uses Léonie, lays his cold hands on her to warm them while Margaretta pours a steaming bowl and regretfully draws the rim from your lips. Can either of them help it? Can any of us?

X

Jemal leaves after the pint I've bought him. I loiter a bit but it's dull tonight: low Thursday. In the Knackers they'll be dole high and on the edge of hysteria. Being in work makes Friday the Neverner's night to wind down for the weekend. I go out into the street again where the rain's stopped; starless, unmooned, the sky is a cloudrace. I conjure pathetic fallacies all the time: the adult version of not treading on the black lines to hold off bad luck I suppose.

It's too early and I'm not drunk enough to go to bed. I don't want the wireless. Now that I know we're going to be on it, listening becomes work. Let's see what the magic box can give us, master. What would you have made of this? Would your talent have adapted to it or would you have been one of the lads on the poetry circuit with every reading the opportunity to pick up a night's lay? I remember those singing sixties when poets were still tin gods with boy and girl devotees clamouring to be noticed, and that time in the Greyhound when a couple of us, me and Harry Wilson I think, took bets on how soon it would be before Macshane was mopping and mowing in front of Roetke, that night's star reader, with offers of an interval drink in return for being allowed to send him some of his poems. Macshane, Macshane. We saw his ambition, felt the pent rage and alternately laughed at and were scythed by it until it turned on himself and he let his blood out all over the bedroom, the great sad sack of flesh deflating as the tap ran ketchup. For it wouldn't have been real, that daubed blood, not if you'd been the one to go up the stairs and find it. It's been more real to me all these years since I go over it again and

79

again, opening the door on his pain.

There it's become a chorus in my head: Macshane, pain, again and again. What was it our mutual tutor at Queen's, the Raven, once said: that even my essays were in blank verse? We were rivals then in a way although I'm not sure how conscious Mac was of it and now he's a decade dead, copped out while I shamble on and I still don't always know whose is the braver part. Switch on the box that lets the talking heads have their say.

I've never quite understood about Bacon's brass bonce, whether it ever really existed or whether it was just a myth put about by his enemies to prove he was a magician. How would he have worked it? A bellows perhaps like an organ pipe, *vox humana*, or ventriloquism. The learned doctor was maybe no more than a music-hall turn.

'Hallo, hallo, Friar Bacon what shall I tell you today? Would you like to know the date of the second coming or when man will fly to the moon?'

Perhaps what he foresaw through his lenses and engines, ingeniousnesses, was so strange that he needed lips of brass to utter it. Or perhaps the shapes in his mind's crystal ball drove him mad. He would have found our magic box completely comprehensible, more so than you, master, whose learning was only skin deep, something to be paddled in and peddle, not a rite for total immersion.

The box has gone into its mid-programme tumble of erotica designed to tease the pence from our pockets and I haven't even noticed yet what's on. I suppose these gaudy snippets will some day become a classic art form with a cult following like Victorian posters and trappings, a museum to house them and scholarly analyses of forms and developments. They are after all only the logical extension of bead and featherwork and cave paintings. Yet I do mind them, not the cartoons themselves, although sometimes those too, as weak or bad of their kind, but I mind their use as constant propaganda, their emphasis on the home beautiful, on consumption and throwaway living while the bits between toss us sops for our conscience about pollution and faraway famine with children clinging onto life like stick insects.

Ah, I know those faces now. Between them panders the interviewer to make this brief coupling of our minds and theirs, to lay out their dowry of dreamstuff for our inspection.

He's everyman to ask them the questions we should all want answers to but more boned up on his subject than we could ever be; incisive: that is with a schoolteacher's bitter tongue to winkle out confessions of rules broken and forbidden fruit gums fluffy in the pocket. He'll get to the bottom of them for us and terrier out the truth.

That one dipped his fingers in the till of local government though it can never be proved. The monuments to his high rise are cracked ceilings and broken lifts, flats abandoned as uninhabitable eight years after they were built under Teg Potter's chairmanship of the Housing Committee, walls distempered green with mildew. Teg prospered. He owns the party's club premises so how wouldn't he be elected; doesn't he hear what his constituents want as they down their pints?

That other grew up in comfort, was privately educated, Oxbridged, has never worked a day in his life except at being a politician, would remake the party in his own image and bend people to it. *'The swollen sheep look up and are not fed.'*

And what do they offer us except faction and division, a focus for envy for some and revulsion for others? Maybe you were right not to tax your mind with anything beyond survival, and it was politic enough for you to say again and again that poverty was sin and crime.

> A man needs money to make him whole
> Money is honey and balm for the soul.

They lean out of the box to lecture us. That one lilts, the other lisps. David knows the lilter; the whole valley knows him yet he was chosen against the lisper's candidate because she offered the improbable and the undesirable when all they want is jobs and houses and a share in the consumables with a holiday every year in the sun. She called them to struggle when they want to put their feet deep in the wall-to-wall carpeting and let the cocoon of central heating enwrap them keeping out mortal cold. Every Englishman's home is still his castle.

If I turn down the sound the mouths open and shut, dubbed with silence. Who can tell t'other from t'which except that one face has the stare of the fanatic while the other is fatly complacent. Between them they forbode political exile and the wilderness and I'm tired of being a Jeremiah on the shore with hair streaming in the wind calling down the lightning. I want some hope and comfort too: I dream of a girl by a stream in sunlight: Thais or sage Heloise. The interviewer is bowing them all out. Time for bed. I take my golden girl in my arms and carry her with me.

Was I asleep? What's that? The doorbell or the phone? Struggle up from that deep. It's the doorbell. The phone would still be ringing. I pull on my pants and shirt. The unexpected is best met dressed.

'Hallo?'

'It's David. Can I come in?'

He wouldn't be there unless it was some kind of emergency. 'Yes, come on in.' I push the button on my entry phone and fumble for my door key.

'Come in, come in. What's happened?'

'Have you got a whisky?'

'Yes. I'll get one. Sit down. What is it?'

He can't sit; he roams the room. I go into the kitchen slip for a glass and pour him a stiff one. If I sit down myself maybe he will too.

'What time is it?'

I look at my watch. 'It's two o'clock.'

'I've been there two hours. It was the only thing that kept me going: the thought that at any minute I could be knocking on your door.'

'Where have you been?' I'm trying to be calm.

'Can I have another one of these?' The glass is empty. I half fill it again. 'I've been in the copshop.'

He's trying to make a joke of it but I see his hand is shaking.

'What for?'

'I went to the Perseus tonight and picked somebody up, or rather we picked each other up. I'd had a few drinks and when we left we were holding hands and he wanted to stop and kiss once or twice. The second time a car drew up beside us and there were two plainclothes police. They said someone had rung them and complained about indecency in public.'

'Christ!'

'They took us both down to the station and took all our details. He's a carpenter, only just twenty-one.'

'But you weren't doing anything were you? You weren't having it off in the street?'

'I suppose it was a rather passionate kiss. You know what the young are: they don't have our middle-aged inhibitions.'

'So what's going to happen?'

'They'll prosecute. They said they had to because there'd been a complaint. One of them was very hostile. I wouldn't want to be left alone in a cell with him.'

'You'll have to get in touch with your solicitor first thing in the morning. Maybe they won't go on with it.'

'I think they will. They seemed determined.'

'Have another whisky. Do you want to stay the night?'

'No I think I'd better go home. Thanks; I feel better now.'

'If you have to go to court I'll come with you. You mustn't go alone. What about the boy?'

'His name's Henry Peters. At least I discovered that from it all. I'll have to ring him up and find out what's happening. He wanted me to go back with him when they let us out but I was too shaken. The young are more resilient.'

'Is he trade?'

'No, I don't think so. There wasn't any suggestion of that. Do you think it will be in the papers?'

I hesitate and then say with I hope complete conviction: 'It's so trivial I don't think anyone will bother. Frankly I don't think it's exciting enough.'

I see him out and sit cradling a whisky myself, knowing how he will swing between bravado and terror, a state you inhabited all your short life, master, up to the very last words you left: that plea to Parliament and a self-congratulatory pat on the back to the prison gatekeeper. 'What do you think of my appeal, Garnier? Was that the time to keep quiet?'

Toute beste garde sa pel would make a good motto to hang over the bed. S.O.S. Save our skins not our souls. They have to take care of themselves when the body is under siege. Whatever happens, David mustn't fall into despair.

Sleep's gone. It hardly seems worthwhile going back to bed but I've never been any good in the small hours, the black-dog hours. Better to try to lie still and stare into the dark until it draws down the lids. I think of all the sleepless now and forever. Like so much of the human paraphernalia we hump about with us our insomnia is an inflation of a primary piece of animal behaviour, of those feral catnaps with half an eye open for predator or victim. We don't know what images chase in their brains while they do it, whether we're really the only ones to make a movie out of watchfulness and turn it into wakefulness. Shakespeare and co were great tossers and turners: '*Sleep that knits up the ravelled sleeve of care; the*

certain knot of peace; carecharmer sleep, Brother to death . . .'
And I always think of the soldiers in the Great War as sleepless
in billet or dugout though realistically I suppose exhaustion
should have poleaxed them each night. Sometimes, like now, I
can see all those sleep-hungry thoughts spiralling up into the
night, the detritus of care, floating up, empty paper bags and
snapped fishing lines, feathers of fragmented dreams and old
bus tickets for journeys never finished, and the rainbow
confetti of hope staining the pavements after rain.

XI

I will make a grand assault on the day, go up into the hall and sort through the pile of post on the table. Some's been there for weeks because I haven't been doing my self-imposed job of taking it down to my room and writing *Not known at this address* or *Return to sender* on each one. Gone away, so many, or never even lived here. There's a plot for a radio play or even a theme for a poem. X, the solitary wanderer, gives somewhere as his residence. How does he get in to collect his post? He'd have to disguise himself as a series of traders, gasmen and plumbers. Would he get away with it? How would it end? You'd have to avoid making it too Kafkaesque. Or would you? Surely the great thing about Kafka is that life really is rather like that or perhaps only our lives are in the netherworld of a city. Perhaps all cities at all times have been, are surreal. *'Hell is a city much like London.'* Who said that? Or is it: *'London is a city much like hell'*? 'Dis hellhole of a city,' as the West Indian might say.

Even my post is surreal. There was nothing yesterday so today's a conglomeration. I think I must be on some common mailing list. Here's a man wants me to buy his platinum knick-knacks. At least he purports to be a real person, signs his name and has managing director under it. Could I afford even a pinhead in platinum? I doubt it. Some days these mailings make me angry, others I can read them with interest and even amusement. Out there must be people who're seduced by this kind of touch, rich people who'll be flattered by an ink signature into giving each other these space-age necklaces, bangles, anklets, all made with vulgar tastefulness.

This one wants a donation. Would I give; should I? Don't I believe such needs ought to be seen to by all of us and not just the subject of private whim? Yes but then you cut off the spontaneous impulse of giving, the imaginative act of impersonating another's pain and need, as well as the superstitious crossing of the fingers that charity masks, the propitiation of blind fortune.

Here's a request to take sides in some far-flung war when I can hardly grasp the one on my doorstep, and yet not to know, not to try to understand is chicken when every time I buy a shirt or a jar of instant coffee a ripple from that action fetches up on some remote shore, a child starves, a dog's beaten. What are otherwhere's snows? Knowing is everything. Villon didn't have to bother with floods in Bengal or oppression in the Horn. Paris purlieus were the bounds of your empire. Everything you ate was probably home grown in France, bread and wine the simple communion with the land, even ink and candles, your luxuries. A bit of me would like to live like that while another wants all the twentieth-century trappings.

Now this is better: an invitation to read in Newcastle on Tyne, land of saints and seals, miners and football. Overnight accommodation and expenses and what fee would I charge? And what's this? Bill's postmark. Maybe it's the BBC contract. No. It's just his 'With Compliments' slip paper-clipped onto the opaque coded message of a royalty statement. So I owe Guzzle nine hundred and forty-two pounds twenty-one pence. That much is clear at the end but how we get to it is a maze, a numerical labyrinth. Oh it's a kick in the gut every time to see how few copies are sold. Better perhaps to circulate in samizdat, 'sugared sonnets among friends' than be slapped across the face every twelvemonth with Guzzle's notional loss. Out of 1,750 copies sold at £7.95, say £8 for ease of summing, which comes to £14,000, I have earned at ten per cent £1,400, which means on an advance of £2,300 I owe Guzzle £900 plus £42.21 for copies of my own books which I have purchased at trade price, hence the ludicrous twenty-one pence. Do I get written down in Guzzle's debits column in his annual accounting? Or do I get into the credits because in theory I owe him that? If I were run over by a bus today, Matthew Arnold style, would I appear as a gain or a loss?

Since I'm early and in such good form I shall start the day with a bath, nip in quick before the rest are up. I take my towel, bundle the washing kit into my sponge bag and go up the stairs again, across the hall and on up to the first floor. Living alone makes you rehearse every action in your head as if, since there's no outside observer or commentator, it's the only way of confirming that you're real, a moving, acting being, locked into the web of the world. When I'm in love I can shift that, talking to the loved instead inside me. Feed the tenpenny pieces into the meter mouth and turn on the tap.

There's a bleakness about bedsit bathrooms because they don't belong to anybody. No one leaves a toothbrush in here. We hurry our things back to our cave so that no one else can use them and no one can pick them over, see the stains on the brush and the curling bristle, the tear in the face flannel, the hair like a cheese wire across the wash smoothed soap cake, stubble scum in the disposable plastic razor.

Here Léonie lies floating her white breasts like giant water lilies and Jemal his dark prune and fig. How many pub names are really euphemisms for cock and balls? Heidi fits in her long bones, the thin haunches poking into the enamel and the tits as small as daisies. Do they all lie toe to tap or do some cushion their heads between the chrome and let their legs float free? Then there are the bath wankers and the piddlers with their secret infant treat of letting warm pee flow into warm water and watching the yellow stain spread out in a fluid cloud. We soap and soothe ourselves and dream and turn over to lie like Hermaphrodite or the baby on the rug. I must get out of here before someone comes banging on the door. That spoils the therapy, the gentling of a bath. There ought to be an Old English poem somewhere called *Bathes blisse*.

> Bathes blisse
> as soote as a kusse
> y wisse

Perhaps I could get a scrap of parchment, scratch it on in my blood and sell it as a newly discovered fragment from a codex, set the scholarly world spinning with a literary Piltdown, do a Chatterton, strike an Anglo-Saxon attitude. How I wish I'd paid more attention to Professor Sibblethwayte when he was lecturing on Old Norse. I could have resurrected a whole Edda by now. That's where the future of forgery lies: in Gaelic and Norse, Orcadian and Frankish. Or Gothic; a fragment of Bishop Wulfstan's gospels. What a career I might have made as a faker! And if they let the living scribbler starve while they squabble over mediaeval laundry bills they deserve to be conned. I could leave a list of my inventions in my will so that the truth would out at last. Meanwhile it would be amusing to keep a catalogue of eminent collectors and libraries where my gobbets were being reverently preserved. Setting up the discovery would be an act of fiction in itself.

Enough; breakfast next, a good one to face the day; no going out on a couple of cups of tea sloshing around the empty belly. Dad never approved of that: an army marches on its stomach. Meditations on a boiled egg. Are all politics nothing more than Swift's big and little enders? I always break mine at the little end, but I can't remember whether that makes me Whig or Tory or even whether he identifies them. So many years since I read it at Queen's, each part getting progressively angrier and sadder until mankind was nothing but the stinking yahoos, the ultimate image of misanthropy, that the details have gone leaving only a, probably misremembered, outline. Present pushes past farther and farther back until maybe at last the press is too great and the dead begin to push back again, shoving present aside with all that weight of times forgotten. The answer to your question master may be that old snow is piled high in the mind's attics waiting to inch its way downstairs.

The letter says Committee Room 16b, at 10.30 a.m. The morning is bright again with sugary meringue clouds piled on a plate of pale blue sky. I join the tourists with their maps en route for the Mother of Parliaments, the Queen Ma'am and the mummies of the British Museum. It makes me suddenly wonder what sex London is. Other languages have to sex their capitals because of their own primitive genders but in any case there's no doubt. Paris is female, so's Vienna; Berlin is masculine, Rome feminine. London is androgynous: all things to all men, and women too. We make our choice, make her in the image we need to love or hate. In that sense as well Johnson was right and he that is tired of London is tired of life. This morning because I have a purpose, belong, am not shut down in my casket with pen and paper, she is bridal, promising. When I get out at Westminster and come up beside the bridge with the great liner of County Hall moored on the opposite bank 'earth hath not anything to show more fair' as I wait for the traffic waves to fall back at a red eye. Some head of state must be visiting: Parliament Square is dressed overall with union jacks and the quartering of an Arab moon.

I state my business to the usual copper on the door at St Stephen's entrance and am let in, bypassing the tail of general public queueing for the Strangers' Gallery. I am here on business, part of the organs of government. I have my briefcase searched and step through the security check. No bell rings or red light flares. I'm clean. If I'm to do a Guy Fawkes it will have to be by spontaneous combustion or the build-up of spouted hot air. Beside me the gloom of St Stephen's hall falls away; easy to see in its half-light the royal dais with favourites at each elbow, in front the suppliants humble or haughty, and the assassins behind the arras under the blackened beams. I push open the gothick swing doors in school library light oak, and go on through the fake cloister with pictures I half recall from my classroom walls that should have put us off English history for ever. As always I find the building ridiculous rather than impressive and yet I don't think I want to be governed from the spun glass and concrete of a Strasbourg.

Is it possible, though, to respect government if you can't admire its seat and the whole ambience that's half club, half public school? I shoulder through more swing doors into the diving bell of the central lobby. It was meant to be the secular equivalent of the crossing below the dome of St Paul's I suppose. The light's dim and religious enough. The fishes come and go through it, waiting to see or be seen, the suppliants nervous and shifty as if they had a bomb in the pocket, the elected members (just like a club) hearty or professionally attentive with slightly inclined head to give the impression of total concentration on your problem. I cross the stone flags as confidently as if I too belonged here.

You had to deal with princes of church and state, and the city bureaucracy, police and parlement court but poet was still a profession not the purveyor of goods in a free-for-all market. Now when I come here cap in hand I feel I have to begin by justifying our existence. Maybe I'm just having first night nerves. More swing doors and now I'm mounting the stone staircase on the right. Why do I find it so disturbing to think that this vaulting is a copy not an original fan flight of fancy? We all incorporate, make over, dally with the past. Is it because they didn't cannibalize; they tried to clone? Or is it the nature

89

of gothic that it can't be reworked by another age while classical can, endlessly into palladian and barococo and Victorian town halls. Only fascism made it blockish, misunderstanding its spirit, seeing only strength, mass not its sense of proportion.

'Committee Room 16b, the Select Committee on censorship?'

Through more doors into a school-dark-on-a-winter's-afternoon-before-the-lights-were-switched-on corridor. You will be summoned when it's your turn to give your evidence. The direct question is my equivalent of your choke pear and iron boot, master. No one will stick a funnel down my throat and flood my lungs and guts with cold water merely pour it steadily over my arguments and send me off shivering.

Sometimes I think this place really belongs to the porters and policemen. They're our guardians at the gates with their rule books and now their gadgetry, the devices of their hearts, that suss out evildoers with green unblinking electronic eyes. They're respectfully contemptuous of the happenings here. The place exists. They have to run and guard it but those for whom it exists are all children playing at games that must stop at bedtime. The porters laugh and chat among themselves, the grown-ups. They will know every wart and wrinkle: who drinks too much in the Strangers' bar, who's got an eye for a pretty constituent, who's a cow when crossed. Many-headed Cerberus has false teeth, thinning hair and dandruff sprinkling the grease line on the dark serge collars. One steps towards me to move me on, motioning with the head and a finger to the lips as he opens a library door.

After the gloom the light itself is almost interrogatory. I am being waved to a seat at the end of an oblong table. Far away opposite, I take it, is the chairman. Heads incline to look at me. Two are female; the rest male, too many to count in one go. Concentrate. The chairman is introducing himself and them. He is thanking me for my submission. We are making the gestures of democracy.

Yet we all know we're probably wasting our time. Very few of these reports that committees make ever get acted upon, translated into legislation that will change people's lives, make David less frightened. I've almost forgotten last night, this morning. Did it really happen or did I dream it?

Why did I spend precious writing time on a document we

shall seriously consider this morning but that will end up with the other pulped tonnes this place generates in monumental papery turds? The chairman finishes his resumé of what he thinks I've said. Professor Harris, young, incisive, ambitious academic he will offend only so far as is acceptable. He ends with the compliment delicate: 'I much enjoyed your book on secular and sacred love in mediaeval lyrics.' I bow my polite acceptance. My dissent there was scholarly or could be so read. This morning is different.

'Do I understand your paper correctly? Are you in fact suggesting that this country, and especially the media to use the fashionable term, is riddled with censorship?'

The name tag in front of him says Commander Purvis. Be careful. This one may bite as well as growl. '"Subliminal censorship", I think I call it.'

'Could you explain that more fully.'

'It takes two forms. First there's pressurized self-censorship which we all consciously or unconsciously bend to in search of publication. I don't think I say that it's good or bad; I merely point out its existence.' I am being cunning too. If I say it exists, bring it to attention I have already loaded the dice slightly, sleight of handily. I mustn't be overcome with admiration at my own subtlety. That way you get careless and make mistakes.

'Everyone practises some form of self-censorship. Is that it?'

'Yes, that's it exactly. Then there is external censorship of a subliminal kind which includes all the things we regard as editorial freedom and judgement.'

'Surely you're not suggesting that absolutely everything written, or at least submitted, should be published . . .?'

'Or performed. It applies as I think I point out to theatre and broadcasting too. No, I'm not really suggesting that.'

'Some people say too much is published already.' Miss Jaine Wheeler OBE now leans towards me.

'I know and I would probably agree. Where we would I think differ is on the selection. I would like to censor, heavily, dog, gardening and cookery books.' I laugh; they all laugh. Dare I take it further and say I seriously think another *Book of the Corgi* would undermine democracy? Better not. Time for a little more of my argument now we're all smiles. 'What I'm saying is that in our society we can muffle the impact of a work either by not presenting it so that the public, the consumer has

91

no freedom to choose it or by presenting it in so low a key that in competition with better promoted items the public's freedom of choice is curtailed. That's one aspect. Then there's the other of having editors, including script editors and directors, as middlemen, interpreters with the power to cut and alter and wielding the ultimate weapon of oblivion, non-publication if the artist doesn't conform. It's a very old problem of course: the Church demanding that Michelangelo drape his nude Christ is the classic example. Artists and society have always been in conflict in this way. It may even be part of the artist's function to be so. Graham Greene certainly thinks it is.'

'And so do you.'

I smile again.

'If it's universal and perennial there seems little point in this committee attempting to do anything about it.'

'We have to be aware of it all the time and not think that censorship is something that happens elsewhere but not in a democracy, in our free society. We have to be vigilant against our own subtleties. Neglect, and the economic deprivation that goes with it, is perhaps the commonest and most effective form of censorship and yet it's the most easily justified and the hardest to deal with. Sometimes artists in a democracy long to be jailed just to be convinced that someone out there takes them seriously or is even listening.'

'I think that's a very personal point of view.'

I bite back: 'All points of view are,' and smile benignly instead. The important thing in this particular argument is to give no hint of paranoia which offers the opponent the weapon to dismiss what you're putting forward. We are fencing or playing chess; I'm not sure which but I know it's a civilised and complex game, part charade yet capable of letting my blood. Not theirs. Only I can be wounded and limp away to nurse the gash.

'How then do you think this, as it were, in-built weakness in our system can be combatted?' Harris is doing his job.

'I should like to see a greater spread, more true choice offered to the public, not just the same handful of the currently fashionable.'

'You can't make people appreciate things.' The Commander horns in.

'No but you can find all sorts of ways of expanding the

range. For example: the Arts Council could have promotional schemes of various kinds for new artists in all fields. They woudn't be difficult to work out. Galleries for unknown painters, publicity for first novels, more performance schemes for drama and music. If the commercial entrepreneurs can't or won't do these things the state, that is society, must, to redress the balance for its own sake.'

'I'm afraid that kind of sixties liberalism isn't possible in the economic climate of the eighties.'

I want to say: 'And you're glad,' but I don't. I smile again.

'Don't you believe that talent will eventually be appreciated?'

'No I'm afraid I don't. Both Botticelli and John Donne disappeared for several hundred years. No one can know whether there aren't important works of art in all fields which are never published in the widest possible sense because of an editorial consensus based on fashion, dignified as the Zeitgeist.' I must stop. I am giving myself away.

'So you want still less censorship when most of the people who have written to us want more.'

'They're thinking about sexual freedoms. I'm thinking about intellectual and cultural ones which get obscured by arguments over whether you can simulate bestiality or necrophilia on stage or screen.'

'Well we've been most grateful to you for coming here to talk to us and for your submission.' They are all nodding politely except for Commander Purvis who is stabbing his blotter with a pencil. I get up and bow too.

'Thank you for seeing me.' I am ushered towards the door. A porter, the servant of Black Rod opens it and I am back in the corridor gloom. If I shouted and beat on the door, cried, 'No, no, let me in again. You must listen,' he would step out after me, others would run up and hustle me along to the legendary room in the tower for those who threaten the sanctity of our Mother. I shall go quietly officer, smiling all the way downstairs, across the aquarium lobby filled with watery shadows and out into the bright light of common day. Big Ben, straight off the sauce bottle, says it's only 11.30.

93

XII

Pausing on the kerb I fill eyes and lungs with bright, lead-laden air that shapes itself round my ribs to make a casket for my thudding heart. The flags in the square hang damp tea towels in an element not brisk enough to stiffen them. I cross over to St Margaret's under a sudden wheel of pigeons circuiting before touchdown in Trafalgar Square. I cross again and take Sanctuary in the park. How quickly the city dies back from water and trees and the green ground thatch of turf. Not having anywhere to go I'll walk a bit and be calmed by pelicans, pouched billy-cans, ducks and drakes skimming the water in take-off and set-down and the umbrella dip of swan necks goosing the Serpentine.

Away in the distance between trunk and branch move the brown Stubbs of horse buttocks above the slim crackable shanks and the polished black tapshoes on their way back from changing the guard where the tourists have been pointing lenses at them and pressing the tit. Strapped to each one is a blue and silver uniform manikin. Only the horses trotting with Houyhnhnm dignity are differentiated by colour and shape. They're the pageant we clothe war in, though they no longer say: 'Heigh, heigh' among the trumpets. We keep them for the holiday face of violence we can let children cheer.

Yet once they were the cruise missiles of their time, Tartar or Mussulman Arab or Norman cavalry, trampling the flower of Saxon foot, the professionals running down the English amateurs who came out for defence and went home for harvest. Oh in logic the bombers were right to spew the guts of pretty men and animals over the greensward because we've made soldiers our sewermen to do the dirty slaughter jobs our violence creates, policing the territories of language and culture we invent and knocking down the Aunt Sally enemies we rear up.

There go two more horsemen stalking through the trees, one male, one female in black and blue the colour of bruises, our reins and spurs to keep us in the tracks we lay down. One dappled grey from the merry-go-round hitches its tail to plop down steaming bran cakes without halting a step. Vegetarian browsers can do that; carnivores and carrion eaters crouch to crap, can be caught with their pants down.

We all tussle for place and mate though, as if Empedocles was right and the universe is held together by discord, each straining against the other and only the coming of love would bring the chaos of harmony, the falling apart that follows when one side of the tug-of-war gives in. Love is the big bang that brings the generating flux life springs from again. It's a tidy upside-down concept, worthy of a man who threw himself into a volcano to prove he was a god. In those days every town of any importance had its poet-philosopher-in-residence whose job was to consider life and come up with a few suggestions about its purpose and pursuit. Nowadays we have a kind of post-Christian scientific consensus: life is and is to be lived. Only the means, the politics of it is up for discussion. In that sense positivism has triumphed. Sartre and Co. were the last philosophers.

Where did the quest for the ideal die; in Auschwitz or the supermarket? Or are they both our dehumanizing plants? Maybe what we have now is the inescapable effect of sheer mass, of an animal population that's learned to control infant mortality and broken the built-in safeguard of evolution that only the fittest survive, replaced natural selection with artificial protection. Now, since everybody has to die, we've had to invent megadeath on the roads, in war and in the diseases of age most of us didn't live long enough to suffer before this century.

The weight of us all must make us numb. Once death was intimate, close, one of our own circle; now we can see the world's dying. Is it any wonder the mind staggers and then armours itself against shock, scales over the nerve ends, hoods the eyes and ears? Perhaps I should elect myself philosopher-in-residence for Earl's Court, colloquizing among the waterbirds about mortality, set myself up on a pillar in Nevern square. Which department of the Arts Council should I apply to for a grant for that? Or perhaps I could get commercial sponsorship. As long as I fixed a plaque to the bottom of my pillar or put a ribbon round it advertising Tweety-Pie budgie seed or De Mortuis Life Assurance they might send me up free telly dinners on a plastic tray. If I erected my column beside a parking meter they could buy me a season ticket for that as rent. Then I'd only need some firm to donate a Sleepwell duvet to wrap myself in against the cold and I'd be set up.

I could charge for people to come and consult me. That's what the saints and philosophers did, not in dirty money of course but in kind, in kindness, food and drink, and clothes unless you had an unfortunate reputation for nakedness. The trouble is no one would come. Most of the questions philosophers got asked or worried themselves with, science can provide an answer to if we wait long enough. Speculation now is out on a frontier beyond where the average person has thought to. Diogenes in his rainwater butt could gnaw himself to death before the prime minister would come knocking on the rim for guidance. No, as a profession poet-philosopher-in-residence is a non starter.

The last of the tourists are pressed up against the railings snapping the façade of the toy box with its lead soldier. I shall go left into Buckingham Palace Road and catch a tube from Victoria. Or should I go right to Knightsbridge? The choice is between the dosshouse and Harvey Nichols. Victoria is nearer.

What did they say when I'd gone, the lady and gentlemen of the select committee? Did they dismiss me as a nut, a raving impractical idealist? Did anything I'd said find root at all, does it ever? A tub or a column at least gave you some sort of status. You could speak with the tongues of men and angels now and unless you have a handle to your name, letters, a position, the words trickle through a sieve of politeness to the nearest gutter. I almost meant that about imprisonment although it was designed to shock too.

Victoria is always that first trip abroad, the flight of the Golden Arrow: queueing with a battered suitcase under the iron cathedral roof behind the magic sign that says *Dover-Calais-Paris*, the boat train, the first escape from England, home and duty. Perhaps it's so important just because we're an island, a womb set in the silver sea we have one day to cut ourselves free from or be strangled, smothered. That journey was a true magic first with the pain of the third-class slatted benches all part of the pleasure. Looking out of the window as we waited for the train to pull out at Calais after that scramble from the boat with a thudding suitcase you could see French porters in their royal blue blouses and black berets just like the pictures in your first French reader. And then at Paris you stepped out into the Gare du Nord and that palpable smell of coffee, gauloises, garlic that was as exotic as a houri to those who'd never eaten anything stronger than an onion boiled for two hours in a brown stew.

We took to it as if we'd been drinking a quarter carafe of wine with every meal, bar breakfast, all our lives except that everyone else got the trots. For the first time I smelt grape-instead of grain-based pee. The acid stink in the hotel lavatories was part of the adventure along with the cocoa-tin pavement pissoirs and the stripper adverts of Montmartre. It was bliss to wake in that dawn and realize at once that it was all there outside the window, and to feel knowing and a bit wicked by osmosis. Even the pillow smelt faintly of garlic.

That was when the bombs and guns had been quiet for a few years and we were deep in the new Ice Age of the Cold War. Perhaps that gave my first taste of foreign such relish. I don't know whether that Paris of the imagination ever really existed or was fabricked out of literature and myth: Abelard, Baudelaire, Les Impressionistes, Jean Gabin, Simone de Beauvoir and *Bless the Bride* and of course you, my master. I knew it was the place to play poet in or painter.

Outside the world had turned Orwellian upside-down, enemies and allies were reversed. Sometimes I think the Gary Powers spy trial ended my innocence. I knew instinctively that he and we were guilty and that Russia was therefore probably guilty too. The sky grew daily darker with the sun replaced by that implosion that would blow us all to bits. Were the winters really more bitter or was it just our doomwatch that made them seem so? Sunsets were bloodied with the desert testing. The sea boiled, the underground caverns quaked as the earth's bowels and the deeps were fouled with it. We became a river of chilled blood winding across the earth as every man looked at the next and saw the same impotent fear that, all unwilling, we would kill ourselves and each other.

In other times people went out to the hilltops to watch for the end of the world. We got up each morning, poured milk on our cornflakes and wondered if we would be sitting down to tea. It must have cracked something, that second frozen passion when the war itself was over. We had put all our strength into that, into surviving and ending it all and absorbing the vileness of the death camps. There was nothing left to meet this new betrayal and terror so soon when we were still raking over the ashes of the victory bonfire and picking up crumpled paper hats from the street party. We could never be the same again after the century's midlife crisis, that dark wood we had stumbled into. It became everyone for himself and no tomorrows, the day of the spiv and the racketeer; the double agent was the mirror of our new ambiguity. Now we've lived with damoclean violence so long we've grown numb to it until a little war wakes us and we go back to the fife and drum fusiliers, aproned bombardiers, Dunkirk and D-Day when the god of battles still had a human face.

The carriage sways between stops. In the window opposite, my own face looks back warped by time and the glass. It's a game I remember playing in adolescence: the who-am-I of the mirrored stare. Always you hoped to see something different, more suave, more elegant. Not many people can be content with what they see. Yeats thought he had 'pretty plumage' when he was young but that was an old man's hindsight to comfort himself. I look at my neighbours' faces and see them hollowed and shadowed too, the features in caricature and steal sly glances along the row of us to compare the originals. What the glass shows isn't them or is them seen with a jaundiced eye, Swift's for spotting the blackheads stippled about the hairy nostril. Lovers may still beautify them with their eyes. We are how we are seen. I know how that woman's face looks on the pillow on the high peak of love when women are most beautiful, how the damson lips will be brushed velvet and the temples silken where the black wings of hair come down.

The train and I are going west; going, going, gone west. All the rest of the world is at lunch. It's strange that other animals can get by on one meal a day while we need three, as if we were halfway between the continuous grazers and the hunters, with our human flexibility showing in this too that we can either munch or fast all day, but tempered by our desire for order that spaces out meal times and lays down hours for them.

So, pretending that I'm like all the other members of the working world, to a cheese and pickle sandwich in the Knickers and a pint. By day the Earl's Court Road is surrendered completely to the traffic. Great congers, hammerheads, bluefins of pantechnicons and artics full-bellied shudder and deafen the walkers going south in a shoal of minnow cars for the river crossings. The pub strikes quiet after it. The great dead fish in its glass case on the wall above the door wallows in a shaded backwater. A monster pike with Behemoth's pliers for a nose, it was caught by Jack Murphy in running Irish waters, is amber with age and varnish, shoaled relic of between the wars. In the front bar there's a handful of workmen in worn stained castoffs or overalls dusted with mortar and brick, drinking pints with crisps. From the back bar comes a love song oddly subdued in the half emptiness. I order my drink and round. Across the way lunchtime trade is brisk but in here it's the dreamtime, hair of the dog time, the slow awakening of those who don't sleep till the small hours, of dole lives that have nothing they must do.

The rent queens come here after a hard on night. They can't fake as the girls can. They have to spend, spill their milk till the last drop, no easy lie back and groan with feigned pleasure. The whole place has a beaten look this morning.

'We had a punch up here last night at closing time. Had to sort a few out.' The barman wipes a slow cloth through the sloppings of beer.

'What was it all about?'

He shrugs. 'Some of the young ones were a bit high. I could feel it early on. It's like that sometimes and when it is anything can set them off.'

Raffael pauses a moment in the nimbus of the open door looking round, then spots and comes towards me. 'Would you please buy me a drink. I'm all shaking.'

'What do you want?'

'A white wine.' His eyes flick about automatically. Today his dress is almost conventional: a white shirt and sweater, blue pressed jeans and black boots. He takes the glass and sips quickly, looking out over the rim.

'Isn't this early for you to be in?'

'I had to. I've been to police station. They come to my house and ask me to go. They want to show me something, ask me question.'

99

I picture his slim body between two heavyweights, plain clothes in macs or copper blue. 'What did they want?'

He nods towards the poster I hadn't noticed before above the juke box. From here I can only read the word *Murder* standing out blackly from the sheet and see the sadly closed and quizzical face under the falling shroud of dark hair. 'It was about him. They ask me if I know anything, have heard. I say no. Then they show me pictures.' He shudders and sips and rolls his eyes. It's an act but real terror peers through it. 'It is somebody hates us. His cock was cut off and stuck in his mouth. Why would anyone do that unless he is mad? It could happen to any of us. You think someone is nice and you go with him and he is a maniac who murders you and cuts off your cock. They say it is my duty to tell because of this. They ask me to suggest someone who might. I say I don't know anyone. This is the second time. You remember two years ago was that man, very quiet, distinguished like this one, a stockbroker perhaps. They show me picture of him too. All the same with his cock in his mouth. Perhaps it is some queen who has had the operation. My head goes round with all these thoughts. How can I tell them? I say I will let them know if I hear anything. No one is safe, yes but it would be terrible to point a finger at someone and be wrong. I look at everyone now and think, "Is it that one?" How can you do business like this?'

XIII

Closing time has rung us out; Raffael to his small corner, I to mine. I telephone David. He answers blearily from a deep recess of sleep but he does answer. I had been afraid of the double note sounding on silence and what I would have to do then.

'I didn't go in today; told them I had a stomach upset. True in a way.'

'I thought you might have the day off to recover.'

'I've slept all morning.'

'I should have a bath and eat something.'

'I don't feel hungry.'

'No but try. What about a drink tonight?'

'I think I'd better stay home and out of mischief.'

'All right. I'll ring you tomorrow.'

I put the receiver back wondering if I've done the right thing or should have said more, whether I should go round there now and make him eat. But a drowsiness is falling on me too, from the blizzard of pain and violence that makes me want to lie down and let sleep snow me under six feet deep.

Outside my lit room the Spring afternoon has draped itself in a soft grey teagown, a crêpe de Chine of unmoving cloud. A buddleia grows opposite the window from a cranny of dirt beside the cinder service road. Its twigs are scratched on the whitewashed wall of the far block dulled to cream with several winters' deposit since the last painting. In summer the buddleia grows with a spindly strength, a green persistence that ends in purple pokers for insects to browse on. The fireweed roots there too but I expect that, knowing how it

101

crept across bombed London, lacing over scars and fractures with its green lances of leaves and flowering pink starfish. But the buddleia belongs to childhood, to a humming beehive of a bush where red admirals boozed on the honeyed fists of mauve blossom in the vaccky's country air. In the city such persistence becomes a symbol like the prisoner's canary, caged along with him and still singing.

Suddenly I am stifled down here. I must get out or fall asleep to wake thick-tongued and alien from myself. I have to rove out as the folksingers have it, to walk out my early Spring afternoon (early Spring is like early Renaissance fresh and wondering), although it isn't May yet, for to view the fields and to take the air, even though my fields are Yeats's 'pavements grey' and my air mostly carbon monoxide. I lock my room behind me, go up into the hall and step through the front door onto the street.

Down the road is one of London's myriad oases, a little park I sometimes kip in in summer. I'll go there now and walk up and down the central path where children tricycle in sunshine, and look at the branches and the hardy sparse grass. Lorries and cars going south make a white water that has to be dammed by lights before I can cross. I walk along the far shore beside the tall cliff façades until I'm opposite the grey and grime church, High Anglican I believe, carrying on the faith of the Rev. Eliot, Stern Thomas in a cloud of self-conscious incense. I know it all though I've never been inside, just as I can sing the *Te Deum* right through, chant changes included, as part of my early twentieth-century heritage. Each moment of history is like the new stage in the life of an insect that we drew in our biology books: larva, pupa and then the winged flyaway that was the mature creature. Now I wonder if each stage should have been seen as valid and complete in itself, not just an immature form, a prelude to the last soaring and usually ephemeral maturity. 'May flies, the creatures of a day.' Who said that? Somebody must have done. 'Fair daffodils we weep to see you haste away so soon.' No that's not it.

Anyway where was I? I open the little iron gate that's for keeping children from running after a ball onto the waterfall road, and go in. The garden is like an oriental painting on some fragile substance, china or rice paper; partly because of the wing-petalled prunus, partly because of its miniature scale. There should be a bit of mirror pond under that willow with a lead swan on it from the gardens I made in bowls as a child. The hasting daffodils stand along the edges of the cruciform path and there are green, as yet unopened tulip soldiers and the purple prick heads of crocus. Of the trees only the long-haired willow shows green. I always thought this was Ophelia's drowning tree but when I looked it up that time the entry said it wasn't introduced until the eighteenth century, so she must have fallen from one of our natives; maybe the Crack Willow, the bitter withy, broke and let her down or the Grey Sallow that commonest old inmate of black twigs and buds. There's names to play with.

Did she fall or did she jump? The Queen, is it, tells Laertes she fell but she may be lying and if she fell why won't they bury her in consecrated ground with full obsequies? Because then we couldn't have Hamlet and Laertes fighting over the grave, which was a good sensational scene the Bard wanted in as part of the Revenge Tragedy trappings, like the car chase in the last thriller reel.

There's a tramp or a wino asleep on the damp bench at the end. The bristles start out of his reddened skin, mixed black pepper and salt grains. Funny how their skin is always sown with open pores full of dirt as if surface dust rubs off while, without washing, the little invisible craters and pockings fill over the years. There must be clean tramps but the ones I see are grainy, their hair greasy and uncombed. They all wear grey suits too, the same worn smooth elephant-hide cloth with all substance and nap gone from it; never navy or brown, just grey.

They frighten us. I know I shall keep down this end in case he wakes and becomes importunate. The reddened eyes and the long black nails fill us with fear and disgust because we're all asking: 'Could I?' Would one slip plunge me down like Ophelia from her cracking willow if, that is, she didn't jump? Some madness may be a form of slow suicide like the drunk and the junkie and the other naysayers.

The far end is a hedge of laurel sealing off the streets beyond, suburban shrubbery not Apollo's bay, that last image of all those women writers who cut their wrists, themselves their own muse while he ran them down: Anne and Sylvia whose limbs set into rigidity, and became the leafy branchings of a Daphne. These are the deathly dusty laurels that never die, of the plastic foliage, stitched on not budded out. Break a

103

twig and no white blood flows although their fingers are sinewy and resilient. They used to cover the way to the lavatories in the park, bitter dark curtainings for a private act that was still shameful and subject to pretence. You shouldn't be seen going in or out because then everyone would know you'd gone to pass water. Modesty didn't even let us pee. The very word was full of loudly splashing yellow fountains. Inside smelt of stale piss and cement mixed with mildew. The walls were scratched with graffiti brown-streaked with shit though I could never understand how anyone could linger long enough to decorate them in that dank dark.

Some of the dead become bitter fruit strung among the branches, others tumble Icarus into the sea. The etchings of them on the mind's retina don't go away or the questions their going left. Was Jo really fishing and flung himself accidentally after the line or did the moiré waters dazzle him down? People in glass houses shouldn't throw bones. When we first met as first novelists he was growing in a greenhouse for cheapness' sake while I rocked in an old tub on the river. Then he lent me his New York walk-up, empty except for the cockroaches who drove me out after one night. I see him sometimes in dreams with a thicket of green weeds filtering a Jack-a-lantern light and I can't tell if he's under glass or water.

You didn't live long enough for that, master. Sometimes you must have wanted to die to be out from under Thibault's torture but mostly you just wanted to live more. As far as anyone knows that is. That last curtain of silence, nothingness that muffles the date of your death could have come down on a hanging man but my bones don't feel it. Your mind wasn't cast that way. Murder's more likely or pneumonia in a bleak barn.

There must be some mediaeval saw about knowing a tree by its leaves. Certainly I'm no good at naming them without, except for the laurel and those big holly bushes. Why was the holly the male when the girls get its name? Or rather the other way round. Ivy I can see as the traditional clinging female. Perhaps it was because holly was used for knobbed staves, sticks, pricks. The green man's club must have been made of it but I can't remember for sure. Now it's civilized, de-glamoured by all the imitations on cakes and cards, and stands cosily in this park but inside is an angry god still who could bleed green gore if you tore his flesh.

Think back to the summer trees when you lay under them on

104

the grass. That's a plane I know by the patch-peeled bark, a Londoner. The spirit of Etherage could be locked in there to spread gracious palms over the passers by. And there are limes by the gate that hang their sweet pea scent in the air above the traffic on warm evenings: Cavalier poets carved by Gibbons fine-grained. Those high climbers must be acacias, the feathers of Prince Henry James. Maybe Ophelia was right and we should hang garlands in trees, make groves into poet's corners all over the city; little gardens of remembrance for those who were rooted here.

It's colder now. The tramp turns in his sleep on the bench. Time I went back. I wonder if I shall be here in summer when the young mothers bring their toddlers, the skinny septuagenarian comes to do his keep fit, the loose skin shaking on arms and thighs, and the language students sunbathe, covertly eyeing each other.

The homegoing rush slows the millrace traffic to a packed sardine crawl, each little fish in its tin nose to tail. I need tea and bread, a carton of doctored milk and another of orange juice, my subsistence diet. Ramon's face creams into a smile when I reach the till with my wire basket.

'I am very glad to see you. I have a big problem and I don't know who to ask. Now I see you.'

'What is it?'

'My sister's son; I have introduced him to you.'

I nod. I have indeed met this putative nephew.

'He needs a paper to stay here with photographs signed by someone of position.'

'You need a J.P. or a lawyer or someone like that.'

'We don't know such people. You will sign? I will show you.' He goes into the back of the shop and re-emerges with papers, postage-stamp pictures and his sister's son who stands smiling shyly. 'He is a student but sometimes he helps me a little in the shop or his cousin in the Tandoori.' He passes me the snapshots taken in a station booth of the boy looking seriously into the lens as though it was graduation day. 'You must sign on the back please.'

If I refuse he will be offended. He won't understand that writers in our England aren't pillars of society, their word law like doctors and teachers. I carefully inscribe my name and add my degree as an afterthought with the potent word 'lecturer', hoping this will be enough of a bona fide to see 'my sister's son' safe.

'Thank you, thank you. Please you will take this.' He reaches behind and puts a bottle of whisky into my basket, holding up a hand to still protest. I know too that I mustn't refuse or they will be perpetually in my debt, uneasy with me, expressing continuing gratitude and looking for ways to even things up. We murmur gently at each other bowing a little. I wonder what ways Ramon's children will absorb, especially the dusky Shirley Temple, plumply imperious, he carries about with such tenderness.

I take my white plastic bag of goodies he has packed and holds out to me, smile at the nephew and ask, 'What are you studying?' out of politeness, knowing the answer beforehand because it's always the same:

'Business studies.'

'You will be a great help to your family with that.'

I long for him to say English literature, history, classics or any of the old humane, liberal quadrivium, trivium before such empirical, useful subjects were thought up. I want him to be a poet when he must be an accountant and all his beauty will be in his looks. Did you ever see a brown face in your Paris, master? Was there a Moorish quarter for traders from over the border in Saracen Spain?

Suppers are being cooked throughout the house: noodles dropped into boiling water, beans ladled onto toast, instant drumsticks drawn from beds of limp chips. Each animal in its box sits down to eat alone. A godseye view with the lid off the dollshouse would show us like laboratory rats in solitary. Some munch reading; others gobble. I unwrap a tallowy slab of cheddar, slice a bright tomato, peel the dark green snake-skin from half of a half cucumber and segment the crisp inside, enjoying the fresh sweet smell and thinking of Oscar Wilde.

My room seems stale, full of unstirring air after the little park and its trees. I open the window at the bottom. Sometimes a blackbird sings high up and unseen, vesper or hesper from a cold chimney pot but not tonight. I finish my slicing with the long wedges of an orange carrot and the hard white flowers of a cauli. But I'm not allowed to begin.

There are catcalls outside, mewed questions. I open the window a bit wider. He is standing on the area wall with black head inquisitorially through the railings. 'What do you want? Some milk? Come on then.'

I turn away and go into the kitchen recess where the fridge talks quietly to itself like a rumbling belly. I get my cardboard jug of milk and a little dish and bring them back to hold up at the window. He jumps across onto the sill and insinuates his thin seal-sleek blackness through the gap, ducking his head nervously and peering about before dropping onto the floor and putting a muzzle down to the white milk. Now it comes out of the fridge but I remember it coming to the door in a can measured with another into a jug and sitting on the table under a little beaded cloth as if it were a covered chalice of wine on the altar, only the cloth was a boiled-out flour bag that hemmed up might have made handkerchiefs too.

Driblets of milk speck the brown carpet as he laps, lifting his head to listen at each sound, rangy alley cat, uneasy inside as a housed gypsy. When the dish is cleaned his tongue takes up each spilled drop. Then he uncoils upward onto the sill, looks each way, makes a little miaowing sound and goes out into the evening. The room seems very empty without him. I pick up the dish and take it to the sink and switch on the radio before turning to my cold supper.

I feel I've been neglecting you and that you're sulking. I ought to have another go at 'Brother men' or should it be 'Comrades'. English isn't very good at fraternity, the language for it is all jargon, latinate cant disguising Anglo-Saxon true feeling as distinct from Romance emotions. Maybe I should try 'mates' or 'pals'. *Freres humaine qui aprez nous vivez*: literally I suppose: human brothers, you who are living after us. Well done Al. Very nicely put. Where are your snows, yesterday?

Someone's shouting above the radio. Where's it coming from?

'Help me, someone help me.'

How long has it been going on? I haven't noticed it till now. Footsteps are running along outside, in the service road; no, in the area. The sky's a black sheet in the window I haven't closed or drawn the blind on. I must get up. There's a face: a young man. Hands come through the gap at the bottom and begin forcing the sash up.

'Let me in. Please let me in. They're after me. They'll kill me.' Blood drips from one of the forcing hands. I step forward.

'What do you want? What is it?'

'I won't do any harm. Just let me come in.' The blood smears

107

the white window frame and splodges thickly onto the sill.

'Come on then.' I haul him through the gap and shut the window behind.

'I'll never forget this.'

'What's the matter with your hand.'

'It's cut. I'm sorry for the mess.'

'I'll get a bandage for it. Let me look. Come to the sink.' I urge him into the kitchen and take the thin bloodied wrist. The cuts are deep and long. They need stitching.

'Stay there. I'll get a bandage. You'll have to take it down to St Stephen's, to casualty and get it stitched.'

I find a roll of bandage in the bottom drawer and bring it to him, washing off a little of the blood to see where to bind the gash. Great drops fall on the wet stainless steel and spread out like shock waves.

'Are you all right? How do you feel? What happened?'

'Someone's after me. The mafia.' He looks back over his shoulder towards the window.

'I'll pull the blind.' I go to the black oblong panes and try to peer out. The service road seems empty and quiet. I go back to him and bandage up the mouths of the wounds as tightly as I can. 'No one seems to be there.'

'I'd better get going in case they come in here after me. I don't want to cause you any trouble. I'll never forget this. I'll pay you back.'

'What for? Are you sure you're all right to get to St Stephen's? You can pick up a taxi outside the door.'

'I'm all right now. Thanks for the bandage. I'll just get down there.' I hold his elbow as we go towards the door.

'You sure you can make it?'

'Sure; thanks for the help. I'll put a thank-you postcard through your door.'

I follow him up the steps to the front door. 'Do you want me to go out and look.'

'No, I'll be fine.'

His good hand is on the door catch while he holds up, a dog, favouring its paw, the one with my bandage on. 'Get down to St Stephen's won't you.'

'I go there now.'

I turn away downstairs aware of the congealing blood I shall have to wash away. My room feels torn, wounded itself. I begin swabbing at the browning scabs and smears on draining

108

board and window frame. Then I see a trail, almost invisible, a snail track that only catches the light at a certain angle on the carpet and I fetch a bowl of water to wash it and a piece of nylon sponge. As I dip it in the water flows red. I feel almost lightheaded and a bit sick.

'Help me, someone help me!'

What now? There's a confused shouting and cries beyond the window but not close.

'Oh God! Help me, please, someone.'

I reach for the phone as the cries go on and dial 999. 'Police and perhaps an ambulance.'

I am through. The cries punctuating my voice as I answer the questions. 'You'd better hurry. There's a terrible row going on out there.'

I put down the receiver, switch off the light and let up the blind but I can't see anything. I sit by the black window and stare out listening to the distant shouts, a running babble of cries and pleas. Suddenly they stop. Everything is quite silent. I sit on until I see the bobbing light bubbles of torches that show up dark shapes of men and hear a mumble of voices. It must be the police. They are passing my window out on the service road. Now it's quiet again. Still I sit on.

I must draw the blind and switch on the light. Somehow I felt safer sitting in the dark, the watcher unseen. If it was the mafia or someone after him I don't want them coming through my window. Enough of visitors for one night. I shall open the door and go upstairs, see if anyone else is about. The house seems so silent. There's a policeman at the front door.

'Is it all over?'

'For the time being. We want everyone to stay in. You weren't going out were you?'

'No. What's happened?'

'Someone's dead.'

'Dead? How?'

'We don't know yet.'

'Someone came in through my window earlier. He was bleeding; said someone was after him. I bandaged him up. Then after, there was a lot of shouting and I telephoned for you.'

'Well, we'll want to talk to you later, tonight or tomorrow. Where are you? What's the name?'

Had he murdered somebody and I've helped him to escape?

I pour myself a scotch and sip. It's only nine o'clock but it seems like midnight. Did he really come through there and drip blood into my sink? What else could I have done?

XIV

I didn't think I'd ever unwind so I poured down the drink till I could fall into bed. Now I'm thick with sleep and languor. Did any of it happen? Should I really expect the police to call? I eat my breakfast as usual and when I'm dressed go up into the hall. The morning is grey and still: Saturday, I remember, and the inmates lying in. I look up the stairwell and then begin to climb though I'm not quite sure why. At the very top there's a window open. The sill is smeared with blood as mine was and my bandage dangles forlorn, grubby and bloody both, from a jutting overflow pipe to the left just below. To look down from here dizzies the mind. The desolate rag hangs quite still above the wall, a banner of defeat.

Why is it there? Should I retrieve it or leave it as some sort of clue? In the end I leave it because my fingers are too squeamish to reach out and touch it. I had thought he was the murderer but perhaps he was the victim. They had been waiting for him outside. He had turned back with them after him and run upstairs. And then?

I feel sick at either thought: that he's dead or has killed.

'I'll put a thank-you postcard through your door.' The white tiles of the wall are streaked with rust tears from the ancient plumbing and the ground below is puddled and littered sparsely with assorted rubbish. A dank, stale, fungoid smell drifts up. I turn away from the windows. I shouldn't close it to keep the smell from flowing in and down the stairs making the whole house rancid, in case I interfere with some bit of evidence.

I wonder if it's got into the papers yet. The house seems so

111

quiet as if nothing had happened. Yet my bandage dangles there, witness to me if to no one else. I wonder when the police will call. Why didn't they come last night? Shouldn't they have taken statements from everyone? If it was my intruder who has died I may have been the last person to see him alive. Guilt strikes at me. If I'd gone out with him and put him in a taxi, even gone with him as far as to St Stephen's he would still be alive. I was too concerned with clearing off his blood and now it's on my hands. But he may have been the killer. No, I can't believe that. I feel increasingly that he is dead and that I failed him. I trail downstairs again. No one can tell me what really happened. They are all at work or dead asleep behind their doors. I sense that I'm alone in the house.

When I reach the hall again I find the post has come: a rejection slip I recognize at once from my own writing on the envelope and a second: no, a copy of a *Guide to Literary Awards and Prizes* I sent away for and had almost forgotten about.

What prompted me to this I can't now remember but, with the returned poem and last night's happenings, work this morning just won't as somebody once said, so I sit down with the booklet and a mug of instant coffee.

At once I can see I've not been systematic in my approach to a literary life. I could have had all sorts of perks, from malt whisky to a paperweight through innumerable pens, quills to a brass carriage clock to show me how time hastes and is, like all life, relative yet inevitable as any writer could have told Einstein before he began. Most of them require a book you can tout around and the say-so of a publisher but there are others that if you drew up a chart for, a kind of Scribbler's Calendar, you could be sending something off to every month. The thing to do would be to buy a word processor and programme it with bright chippy phrases, meaningful fragments, and tell it to toss them out in a sonnet, ballad, villanelle, a kind of synthesizer for verse.

The real analogy is with cup-a-soup, just add water to the dried shrunken parings where the form is the fluid the images swim in, tadpoles or sperm. It's been tried in some university and the results weren't too good, but that's probably because they didn't have a poet writing the programme. Once you'd done that with your own machine it would have your tone of voice and poetic syntax. That's your true concrete verse: just

112

add water and see what shape it will set in.

Now again there are voices outside my window but daylight makes all the difference. I'm brave now. I go and raise the sash and peer out into the service road. Three men are poking about half-heartedly, peering over the railings and then standing back to stare up at something. They come down the steps. I shall call out. 'Did you want someone?'

They look up. 'Police. Someone was killed here last night.'

'I know. Someone came in through my window. I told the policeman on the door about it.'

'Could we talk to you?'

'Come round and I'll let you in.'

I'm glad they've come. Now I shall find out; now I shall be able to see or confirm, which will be a kind of easement, my own guilt. I go up into the hall and let them in. My room shrinks with their bulk. They introduce themselves but I don't hear their names, only their ranks. I'm telling my story as plainly as I can while the sergeant makes notes.

'Was this him?' The inspector offers me a photograph. There's a number underneath it and the face stares out blankly, passport or mugshot, his official face, younger, the hair longer, but unmistakably my last night's visitor.

'Who was he?'

'Eamon O'Halloran. A drug addict.'

'What happened?'

'He fell off the roof.'

'He's dead?'

'Killed instantly.'

'So he must have turned back when I left him, doubled up through the house and then. . . ?'

'He seems to have climbed out of an upstairs window onto the roof. We think part of the coping gave way.'

'He was up there a long time calling for help.' If they'd come sooner before the cries stopped, I think but don't say. 'I've been worrying about what I did wrong, didn't do. I should have taken him to St Stephen's.'

'It would have happened sooner or later. Don't blame yourself. It was only a matter of time. He had a lot of incidents of violence against himself. You did more than most would have.' The young inspector manages to convey that perhaps I have done too much, that I was foolish to let him in at all.

'Where was the cut from?'

'He put his fist through the chip shop window. There was some mention of shots by another resident. Did you hear anything like that or see anyone?'

'He said the mafia were after him but I didn't see anyone else. I thought when I heard the second lot of shouting and dialled 999 that it was someone else out there, lying injured somewhere. I didn't know it was him.'

'He said the mafia was after him?'

'Yes, he thought he was being chased. I suppose it was just a paranoid fantasy. He must have been stoned but he seemed quite rational when he was in here, otherwise I wouldn't have let him go.' Guilt strikes me again. 'If I'd kept him here . . .'

'It was only a matter of time.'

'How old was he?'

'Twenty-seven. It's probably best this way.' They get up, closing the notebook.

Eamon O'Halloran is dead and no one seems to care. I still can't take it in. Last night he was standing here with his live blood flowing into the sink and now he's quite dead, wasted. The police treat it with fatalism. It was inevitable, just a matter of time. He was not to be cured, changed. He and his life were no good and best done with quickly. I want to turn back the clock, run the film in reverse so that he gets up from where he's lying crumpled and flies up to the rooftop, runs down the stairs backwards and opens the front door. Freeze it there.

The noise of the street, the people and cars passing must have triggered his sense of persecution. Even so he might have fallen and just broken a few bones; instead he smashed himself to bits, a tree down in a gale of terror with the snapped limbs and roots sticking up into the air.

The police must have sighed with relief and rubbed their hands when you were finally banished from Paris, master. They must have said: 'Good riddance. It won't be long before that bad lot ends up in a ditch with his throat cut and then he won't ever be back to bother us any more.' I've come to the conclusion that you were probably an inefficient criminal. You got caught too often in your short time for you to have been any good at it. What must have narked the authorities was your singing and versifying about it. That was truly seditious, dissident. How they must have hated to be on everybody's lips, the butt of the boozers in every tavern. How they must have longed to see your feet dancing on air.

The police were here for half an hour and the morning's still young enough for me to get some work done before lunchtime, as I've learned to call it. If I go now I can put in an hour or two in the Reading Room before going up to the zoo to meet Hector. Gather your things together quickly. Where's the right notebook? Sharpen a couple of pencils. That's it. Am I decent enough, as the old man used to say, to lunch with a distinguished man of letters? Is my nose clean?

'Clip my ears for me, Al,' and I'd take the little scissors and trim the sprouts from the smooth top curve and the shell orifice of the fleshy mussel shapes that were almost too fine for a labouring man. Then he would snip at his nostrils and jerk the long whiskers that bushed out his eyebrows until he was Jack Buchanan again. Strange that the hairs on face and head were unruly while his body was whey white all his life with just the blue etchings of shrapnel like miner's marks here and there.

I seem to live half my life underground journeying. I travel about like a corpuscle in the veins of the city, red or white. Writers should be both, like oysters changing their sex every seven years. Sometimes we nourish the body, feed the imagination, and sometimes we fight off its enemies, the invaders that would destroy and pollute it. That's the theory anyway.

Still I feel such pride going in through these iron gates with a flock of tourists, knowing I have business here, opening my briefcase to be searched as I run up the steps, going through the revolving doors and across the main hall while others stand awed and look about them, flashing out my reader's ticket and funnelling through into the hush of the Reading Room. It won't be the same at Euston in a new building.

There's a place just where I like it, beside the state papers on the open shelves so that I can rummage in them until my orders come. Now round to 'V' in the catalogue, haul up the big red volume and turn the stiff pages. Fill in the order form and take it up to the little wooden tray by the requisitions section. 'How long is it taking today?'

'About forty-five minutes.' The slim black fingers reach out for my slip.

'Ah Al. Is it you? Long time no see. Hang on while I put this in.'

My heart is sinking or my stomach. Mathew Givens is someone I could have done without today. 'They're taking forever as usual. Come and have some coffee. We haven't had a gossip for ages.'

Gone my peaceful half hour looking for clues to Charles of Orleans' English imprisonment. I allow myself to be herded towards the restaurant.

'It's squalid as ever. Have a cardboard bun with your murky brew. Tea and coffee both taste the same. If there were any respect for scholarship in this god-forsaken city, country we'd have a readers' common room.'

Mathew Givens still hankers after plate-glass dondom, the groves of m'acadam, where the young and beautiful can saunter, more camp than campus, hanging on his every word. A too close reading of *The History Man* spoiled him early on for the uncloistered life and so he rails, shut out of his imagined Eden where he could have been a bright fruit on the tree of knowledge tempting a succession of ripening Evies.

'So what's new? Amuse me in this drab world.'

'You tell me. What are you doing with yourself now?' I know he doesn't really want to hear about my affairs nor do I much want to talk about them.

'Well I've found a way round their closed shop at last. I've set up my own university.'

'Oh?'

'The Walden College of the Humanities.'

'Oh.' I don't know what questions to ask. He is tense, with gleaming eyes, leaning across the plastic table, his hands squeezing the life out of his coffee cup.

'We do the international bachot. I advertise abroad and get more applications than we can handle. I've designed a gown for the students to wear on campus. We do English language classes as well. That brings in the money.'

'You should go in for business studies. That's what everybody wants. How did you get a building?'

'A great red Victorian hotel above the sea with a clifftop golf course. Just the thing and no one else wanted it. I don't approve of business studies. They're not a real subject. I do a lot of the teaching myself. There's nothing to it as I've always expected. Any time you want a job . . . They'll try to keep me down of course with their rules and regulations but there are always ways round if you have a good lawyer on tap. One day they'll have to recognize me. Take me into the U.E.A. as an extra-mural department. What are these tin-hut provincial universities anyway? Glorified grammar schools for nice head girls.'

As so often with Givens I'm driven into defending the indefensible. 'I thought everyone complained that there weren't any grammar schools any more, only nasty comprehensives.'

'It's still the conformists who get to the top. You're nit-picking Al. You know what I mean. You were one of the goodies too.'

'So were you. The pride of Redditch High School for Boys wasn't it?'

'It's independent now. The Jacob Morrison.'

'And who was he and why the Walden College?'

'Some nineteenth-century ironmaster who endowed it. Walden because it's a distinguished English name and we're not all that far from Saffron Walden as the land gull flies.'

I suspect Frinton or Clacton but am suddenly tired of the sport. Who am I to judge? Maybe I should be knocking on his door for a job.

'Everything's a con anyway. That's life Al: the nightmare death-in-life if you want a literary allusion.' He laughs. 'The best you can do is spoil their little games, show up the farce for what it is, play it for all you can get.' He is a coil of rage waiting to spring up and smack you in the face, blinding and lacerating in his anger. Did he kick and pummel in his mother's womb and thrust himself howling into the world, I wonder.

I look at my watch. 'I must get back and see if my book's come up.'

'Let's have lunch.'

'I can't. I'm having lunch with Hector Spalding.'

His face darkens as the muscles tense. 'I thought he was dead. Well he has been for the last ten years. Have fun.'

I get up and lift a hand. 'You're not coming back?'

'Not yet.' He will sit and brood on my defection.

The great bowl of books is soothingly quiet. I take mine from the reservation counter and go back to sit turning the pages until my abraded nerves stop jumping. Givens makes me feel like Job's advisers: 'Curse God and die.' The adrenalin must flow through his body like green bile. After a meeting with him I find myself contaminated by his wrath, all life sickened and muddied by it. Anger fuels him while me it enervates. I have to be sustained by hope, poor bitch shut

117

down in the corner of the box.

The words flowing into my head gradually comfort me. I am washed in the ocean of them that has gathered from all the fountain heads of every time and place until now we can all dip and drink as much as we like and the waters still rise added to year after year, flowing through culverts and conduits and along aqueducts, gushing up in fountains and lying still in pools and reflective in lakes; the waterways of words, knowledge, wisdom where sprat trivia dart and dazzle as they catch a moment's light. Sometimes, as now, for a moment I can take off my clothes and just float on them.

XV

It's odd to lunch at the zoo, rather like that strange eighteenth-century pastime of dining with the lunatics, supping in Strangeways. As I get closer I can hear strangely non-indigenous noises, that I wouldn't have thought would stand out so in the middle of the city. At night, I've read or heard somewhere, you can hear the lions sad svelte nocturnals, at vigil pacing insomniac the narrow concrete veldt of the cage floor. The moon calls up their hunting blood. We think we're so different of course. We reflect; they react. Yet the lines must be muddied between the two. I *think* I will go to the Asian supermarket and buy a packet of instant noodles; the lion or rather usually the lioness gets up on waking and slopes away to the water hole for a wildebeeste and I'm to believe the quality of intention behind those two entirely similar actions is quite different. *Cogito ego sum.*

Habit must be our extension of instinct, our ability to put ourselves on automatic pilot when conscious thought has mastered a process. Memory responds to a familiar trigger. Reading becomes instinctual or instinctive, I'm not sure which without a *Shorter Oxford*. I shall have become totally eccentric when I actually begin carrying one about with me and consulting it in public. I could probably get one on tape and carry it in my pocket with a set of headphones. Everyone would assume I was listening to music, not dictionary definitions.

Here's the gate for members and fellows, away from the gawping public entrance. As usual we have built in a hierarchy and can always find a justification of convenience for it. Give

Hector's name and I am checked off on a list. I go down an alley, as I remember, and come out at the members' bar and restaurant. You wouldn't know there were imprisoned creatures just beyond, their exotic lives urbanised to NW1.

The building has nothing to suggest the zoo's history either, no seventeenth-century touch of cupola like The Royal Observatory. It's more canteen than classical, a laboratory where the cloths could be whisked off the tables and the bunsen burners coupled up in an instant. But there's Hector waving at me and the place is humanized by his charm and his smile. I cross the room self-consciously, the reflex human reply to the possibility of being stared at.

'Al, lovely to see you. You're looking well.'

I look into his face and see the skin scorched by the years and his travels, the eyes the blue of a seafarer too under the white lion's mane, bleached by sun and time. Our soft pigskin becomes reptilian as we age: turtle, tortoise, frog, lizard. Hector is a smiling, leathery washerwoman since sex too leaves the head before the rest of the body, the outside of it that is. Inside it snuggles down against the onset of winter, hibernatory, waking to feed and observe how the snow fell whitening outside its burrow while it snoozed off its hoarded fat.

'How's life?'

'Oh that old thing!' He laughs. 'Will you have an aperitif?'

'I think I'll wait for the wine.'

'Red or white?'

'Which do you like?'

'I'm supposed to drink white at the moment. I was rather ill a couple of weeks ago and the doctor said white wine and whisky were fine but not red and brandy.'

'What about gin?'

He laughs. 'I didn't ask him but it's probably all right without the "it" don't you think?'

'Anyway how are you now?'

'Oh fine, much better. A little fever in India started it but that's all over now.'

'And how's Bill?'

'He's very well and the business is surprisingly flourishing. People still want to buy antiques as much as ever or as little. It was always steady and seasonal and still is. Americans in the summer; the round of the antique fairs and a steady dribble of

120

the discerning. Now what will you eat?' He indicates my menu.

I want to ask him how he can go on eating at a zoo but I don't, not wanting to draw attention to our differences, only to what we have in common. I fall upon the *oeufs florentines* with relief.

'I shall have the whitebait because they're so Dickensian. Writers seem to have gone in for fish. Think of Arnold Bennett and smoked haddock. Perhaps it was the myth that it made you brainy. And how is Messire Villon or is all that behind you?'

'He's still my alter ego.'

'You know I've never written a real biography but I've always thought that could happen to one. Bill would be jealous if I spent so much time with another man.'

'Even a dead one?'

'A kind of spiritual necrophilia.'

'What about another woman?'

'He would know that wasn't serious, merely an impersonation.'

'I think you do have either to fall in love with your subject for a bit or become them if it's to work.'

'I'm sure that's true. And then I suppose you don't want to let them go until, like an old lover, you're tired of them.'

'Isn't that heresy from you?' I tease him.

'Higamus, hogamus, Hector is known to be monogamous. But I can say with Enobarbus: "I have affections and often think what Venus did with Mars." I know how the world wends even if long ago I decided not to wend after it. I saw how destructive it was for too many. Wystan and Chester for instance. So I decided that what I would have with Bill was a marriage. The new lot, what I call radical camp, say we're role-playing and imitating the structures of straight capitalism or some such twaddle but I decided life outside, and inside with my work, was too absorbing and exciting, and that I really couldn't take constant emotional and domestic upheaval. Too distracting. You get nothing else done. As it is one has to spend far too much time being a token "*gay*" when one ought to be writing. Yet one feels one must do one's bit. Isn't this a divine pink, like mouthwash!' He sips at a campari. 'But you ought to be thinking of getting back to something of your own, I mean completely your own.'

'I don't seem to have the will. I'm going through a sort of

mid life crisis, a failure of nerve.' I'm into the sentence almost before I've thought and now it's too late. I take it I'm uttering some cry for help, a caged thing straining at bars I've made for myself. 'I know it's not very original. Did you ever have such a thing?'

'Oh my dear yes. After *Pearl* I didn't write anything for two years. It was the most ghastly time of my life and Bill's too. I gave him hell and he was marvellous. That's another reason why I'd never hurt him. I mean wouldn't have. Not now of course; I'm too decrepit. No one would want me.'

Yet I know they would. Some new boy would comb his white hair and sit on his knee, or rather go on his knees for his name and his money. Should I tell him this? We all long to be comforted against *annus terribilis* with the thought that we're still attractive. I wonder why I keep falling into Latin today, into a classical stance, a safety net of irony.

'But it goes you know: I mean the block thing. Suddenly. It's as if you've exhausted all the reserves and have to lie fallow for a year like some bit of mediaeval plough.'

'"Then Barleycorn sprang up again and so amazed them all."'

'That's it. The birth cycle is so vital a part of us all, don't you think?'

'But will it be? What will happen to our myths and symbols with genetic engineering, the re-making of the seasons and so on? Eventually we shall be able to programme daffodils to bloom all the year round. What will that do to our collective psyche, let alone an understanding of past literature, Hector? That worries me more than the actual effect: the loss of symbols, of the soft furnishings of the imagination. What stuff will the dreams be made of?'

'I know, I know; it is very distressing.' He joins the hands, fine still, though freckled and corded with veins, as if in prayer. 'But I can't believe we won't find replacements, new growth.'

'Plastic transplants, pacemakers for the heart.'

'They sustain life.'

'I am hoist by my own imagery.' I have to laugh at myself.

'I think that's why I like India so much: the problems are still quite different.'

'They have their own bomb.'

'Yes, because they are tremendously clever, but they are

essentially a peace-loving culture, at least the Hindus are.'

'And goddess worshippers.'

'Oh very much so: both the old witch mother-in-law figure Kali and Laksme, every heart's desire; two faces of the same principle. I find it so much more attractive than "cold Christ and tangled Trinity". No doubt the psychologists would say I was in love with my mother. But you now ... we were so upset when you and Celia split. You seemed such a perfect couple. Everyone took it as a personal loss. No one was prepared for it if you see what I mean. It's been a long time now. What you need is the love of a good woman.'

'A bad one would do to be going on with but I can't seem to find the energy to go hunting.' The little black prostitute from the Knickers crosses my mind momentarily but how could I make love without saying: 'I love you.' I've no practice at it. Maybe I should try to learn. 'What about the future of literature?'

'Talking books. Videos of flowing poetic landscapes with voice-over. Factions. The game, the play of words will go on, even if the rules change.'

Hector hasn't grown old and tired or bilious. He believes still. I am lifted by his sprightliness. 'No, I mustn't eat puddings my doctor says. Isn't that a pretty gateau. But I will be strong. Tell me the latest gossip to take my mind off it.'

But he is telling me because he hears it and I don't. Now I am out in the white sun again with the wine distancing the world, something that only happens when I drink at lunchtime. Afterwards everything runs as though in some very heavily expressionist film where the wrong significances are constantly being underlined and the colour is drained to sepia. Hector has reinvigorated me and I feel as if I could sit down now and toss off an epic. I know this sensation fades very quickly so enjoy it, Al, while you can. I am walking about nine feet tall, full of lust and invention.

The house is still in its daytime slumber. I shall make some coffee and try a line or two. I have a chant going round in my head. Is it the *Carmina Burana*? A pounding of 'Venus, Venus!' The Veneriana. There's that postcard David sent me from his holiday: Strozzi's *Venus and Mars*. 'Venus, Venus! Lovely Venus!' No that's not it.

Lucky bloke she's got you down there

          while the imp pulls off your boots.
          That's a something to remember
          when you're twined by daisy roots.

Two pairs of legs are going past the window, one in jeans, the other in grey cloth skirted by a dun raincoat. What now? Open the window and call out. 'Hallo! Did you want something?'

The legs turn and come back. They bend to let their owners look down. I crane up. The jeans come into a crouching position. The grey legs belong to an older man with haggard working-man's face that reminds me of my father, framed with thinning fine hair blown a little awry.

'There was a man killed here yesterday.'

'Yes, that's right. He came in through my window.'

'He was my son.' The voice is quietly controlled as if it might break.

'My father and me are trying to sort out what happened. No one seems to know.'

'Come round to the front door and I'll tell you what I can.'

What can I say to this father of a wasted son? I go through the happenings as I've done to the police. The brother too asks me:

'Was there anyone else? Someone said there were shots.'

Suddenly I understand that they want there to be someone else. It will ease the pain. It's better if he was killed; not tumbled ignominiously or jumped in despair. The father still has his Irish accent. They will be Catholics and suicide a terrible sin.

'I think the coping broke and he fell. I didn't hear or see anyone else.'

'The police won't tell us anything.'

'I don't know what we did wrong. I've always worked hard.' His bewilderment looks out dull-eyed from the drawn face.

'I should have gone with him to the hospital,' I say again stupidly.

'You did what you could.' They stand up. 'His mother will be grateful there was someone kind to him at the last. We owe you our thanks.'

I think that an English workman wouldn't have known how to put it, would have been locked into habitual non-saying. At the door we all shake hands gravely in memory of the dead man

124

whom we have failed and who has failed us, and in recognition of this moment when our lives touched and we were able to speak to each other. Four people at least mourn Eamon O'Halloran, us and his mother at home waiting for some news of her son's dying so that she can take it into her and be eased of the pain.

I go back to my scribbling: Venus, Venus! Against death there is only love, the fragile thing we neglect or rend. The chorus is swelling in my head again:

> Predatory Venus grips you
> shoves her tongue into your mouth.
> That's the stuff to get you going;
> That's true rainfall after drouth.
>
> Spiritual lovers tell us
> how the clouds their souls enmesh
> but there's nothing late news final
> as the dark night of the flesh.
>
> Come then Venus lay me back there
> hang your heavy breasts above
> I am growing nightly older
> give me one last taste of love.

XVI

I did fall asleep and it's evening again. Outside the window times and seasons march inexorably, in spite of the solipsist in all of us that would say they don't when we're not watching. I dial David and persuade him out for a drink.

'Oh I don't think so.'

'Come on. It will do you good. We'll go to the Nevern. You can't get into trouble there.'

'How can one be sure? Now that I've begun it may have already become a habit.'

'If necessary I'll take you home.'

After a bit more persuasion he agrees. His voice is lighter than when he answered my call at first and I feel a small flicker of achievement but I shan't risk telling him about Eamon O'Halloran yet. Should I ask anyone else to join us or is it best for us to be by ourselves, best for him to be distracted or to talk about it? Undecided still I go up into the hall and stand as if I'm waiting for the answer to come trundling down the stairs on round plastic disks, our equivalent of tablets of stone, jackpot from some great fruit machine above, but nothing comes. Clearly I'm not nudging that right button.

There's the sound of a key in the front door lock. It's Jemal, closely followed by his compatriot Chloe. She's very short with broad hips and inches herself up on the highest heels.

'Oh Al! You can help us. Come up to my room and give us your advice. I'll make some coffee.'

I follow her flame-coloured skirt and black jacket up the stairs. She lives in a cupboard. Jemal and I sit on the bed and our knees are half a foot from the wall. There is a narrow table with an electric ring and grill, end on to a small wash basin. At the other end of the bed is a wardrobe. Somehow a chair squeezes in, and on every available sill and horizontal surface are the tall barren glossy leaved Mediterranean plants Chloe grows from pips and stones, single flat palms branching from the slim green stems, avocado and citrus.

Chloe housewifes about, putting on the kettle, getting out mugs, instant coffee, a carton of longlife milk, the basic stock every room carries. Her hat-box fridge hums at the foot of the bed. She squeezes past our knees to the wardrobe, angling the chair dangerously above our heads. Jemal doesn't offer to help and so neither can I.

She hangs up her jacket and kicks off her shoes so that she is barely chin high and climbs onto the chair. Jemal leans back on his elbows on the bed, reclining Emir. Chloe reaches up to the cupboard above the hanging rail and hauls at a suitcase.

'Can I help?'

'No thank you Al. I can manage.'

I lean back like Jemal, not wanting to emphasize her shortness in case she minds it. Her waist is wasp pinched between jutting breasts and buttocks. Her hair falls in a black mantilla to her shoulders and her face is soft and sweet without cloying. She manoeuvres the suitcase above her head and steps precariously off the chair, breathing heavily, to dump it beside us as the weight drags at her arms. She smiles happily at her achievement.

'First I'll make the coffee. Then we'll see what there is.'

Deftly she spoons and pours and stirs, nips the corner of the milk carton, produces sugar, at ease in her doll's house. 'Now we will see and Al will advise us.'

'What do I have to do?'

'Jemal's cousin is in Nuneaton on a visit to his uncle. He is coming through London on his way home and Jemal must send his mother a present for her birthday home with his cousin. But he hasn't got anything and Harroun is coming tomorrow and Jemal is at work all day. So I say I will give him something to send her.'

'Chloe my darling, it isn't necessary. It doesn't matter.'

But Chloe knows it does. She knows the passion of mothers, whose marriages were arranged, for their slim sons. Jemal takes money from her, I know, as he does from all his women, as he is sent presents from mother, elder sisters and aunts. He

127

princes it among his harem; not that he sleeps with Chloe. 'She doesn't attract me. She is like a sister,' he once said when I asked him.

'Good. Because if you did you would break her heart.'

'She is a grown woman, Al; she can take care of herself. She chose to live here, away from her family and be independent.'

Yet I sense in her wide hips and full breasts and in the face which softens like clouds passing their shadows over downlands that she wants love and is vulnerable to every thrust. Sometimes in the mornings, if I'm out early I see her and Clara, the Italian cook, and Léonie on their way to the bus stop in a small brightly coloured flock, their heels clattering on the pavements, their cries falling sharp in their common language, Marsellaise, Roman, Afro-Asian fetched up on the high tide of a London rush hour and flung at the pillars of the city's bridges.

Chloe opens the blue leather suitcase and shows her treasures. 'I collect all the time for when I go home. Otherwise it is so expensive if you must buy everything at once in a rush. Now when I see something I buy it when the price is good.'

'Chloe my darling you should be a business woman. I will ask Ibrahim for a place for you on his market stall.'

I see her flush a little with pain. She opens her mouth to say she hadn't bought them to traffic in but knows he will only laugh at her where he leans aloof, making her jump to his will with the detachment of those accustomed to being waited on. His mahogany mouth is a scimitar or new sickle moon smiling up at her.

Each object is wrapped in sibilant tissue paper. There are cut glass vases, butter knives in silver plate, and silver frames for photographs, bottles of perfume, twisted glass like seaside rock, snap-legged animals. Each one says: 'This is from my daughter in London,' in the pursed tones of Bourne and Hollingsworth.

'This you can have. I have bought three of these.' She holds up a shining fluted shell, opens its lips and shows the gleaming glass membrane. 'Isn't it pretty. It's for butter balls. This would be good to give your mother, Jemal, and I can easily spare it.'

'Anything, darling, anything. I tell you it doesn't matter. Really I can't concern myself about such things.'

I stand up. 'I think that's the perfect answer. Thank you for the coffee Chloe. I'm going to the Nevern. Perhaps I'll see you later, Jemal?'

He lifts a hand. 'I don't know Al; I'll see.' I ease myself out of Chloe's cupboard door. She still holds the silver cockle shell in her hand and suddenly I am reminded of 'Mary, Mary, quite contrary'. There's something young nun-like about Chloe. I wonder idly if there are Muslim nuns but suspect not since it's a creed even more patriarchal than Judeo-Christianity, unlike our native Indo-European pantheons with their bevy of goddesses. I am out in the hall again, laughing at myself for such thoughts. I've always assumed that everyone has them but sometimes I wonder if I'm wrong and they're not common as measles as I've supposed but more a rare disease of the blood.

It's time to go and meet David. 'How are you?'

'Not too bad really. I've slept a lot. The case comes up in a fortnight.'

'That's very quick. They've definitely decided to prosecute?' I am keeping the words clinical.

'Yes. I've seen my solicitor. He thinks it's all nonsense but he says I must have a barrister and that I mustn't see the boy or speak to him. I wanted him to represent us both but he says he might have to try for special treatment for me and that I must look after myself. I rang him all the same.'

'Who?' I'm confused among the pronouns.

'The boy. Funny thing is we'd probably have gone home, had a night of it and never seen each other again. By bringing this case they've forced us into a relationship. He says he'll lose his job if it's in the papers. So shall I of course.'

'Not necessarily. And anyway they probably won't report it.'

'Today I don't care. Yesterday I was very frightened. That's how it goes. It's something I suppose to follow so closely in the steps of one's heroes. Maybe I shall die with a pain in my ear. I was given to earache as a child. I know so much better now even through this little experience how Oscar must have suffered.'

'How that went on reverberating. It must have been at least partly responsible for all those right-wing closet queens between the wars, Maugham and Forster for example, and who can blame them. I had lunch with Hector Spurling today. He's a brave old thing when you think about it: dignified, not ostentatious, yet making his point.'

'It's easier for a distinguished man of letters than, say, a plumber.'

'True. But you still have to steer a course between professional and private; either way you can end up in a ghetto.'

I look about at tonight's inmates. We make ghettos all the time of clubs, pubs, work places; invent sub languages, dialects and jokes for comfort and identity. In the Nevern the couples form, break, reform in kaleidoscope patterns, a midsummer night's dream of shifting desires. Sandy waves at me, his long lantern Christ's face sallow with drink. Tonight he has his arm across Clare's shoulders. His sister Billy leans her full flesh against Chris laughing and holding his young eyes. Those two are paired for the night, no lone bedding and drunken tears. We all cling for comfort.

'Dear bed-companion. Wasn't that the Anglo-Saxon for it?' I ask David.

'For what?'

'I think, technically, it was a wife, but what we're all looking for.'

'I shall go back to celibacy after this episode.'

There's a shout from the cluster around the dart board. A last throw has gone home. At the same moment the bell rings.

'. . . The lights go down.

Time calls across the bar into the dark

Bang the swing door. Don't cry who won or lost,' David is saying. My own words from so long ago are somehow shocking.

'Fancy you remembering that.'

'I use it still for literary criticism with the first years. It wears well I find. And what about you?'

'What do you mean?' But I know of course and it's the second time today someone has asked.

'I'll get us a last drink.' He turns and pushes through the crowd to the bar.

'It's your dialogue of heart and body again, master.

Qu'est ce que j'oy? – Ce suis je! Qui? Ton cuer.

My heart hangs by a thread too and I have no more strength, substance or sweetness . . . What comes next? Oh yes: 'when I see you so withdrawn into yourself like some poor dog cowering back.' No, better: 'cowering and flinching away.'

130

'They're out of IPA so I brought you Bass. Is that all right?'
'That's fine.'
'So to return to my question: what about you?' He sips himself into a froth moustache. 'When will you finish with Villon?'
I want to say 'never' in my panic. But I know we need friends to say these things to us, pose the questions that it's time to answer.
'Yes I have to let him go. You're right. I suppose I'm dragging my feet because I can't see what or where next. Nothing calls loudly enough.'
'I misquoted just now. It should be:
Time calls across the bar into the dark
The lights go down; goodnight knocks at the heart . . .'
'You mean "physician heal thyself."'
'Or "gather ye rosebuds" except that I'm not very good with my own medicine. But you're different. I'm always on the verge of hibernation.'
I think but don't say in your complaint, master:

> *Se celle que jadis servoie*
> *De si bon cuer et loyaument . . .*
> *If she from whom I had such pain and grief*
> *And suffered so much torment*
> *Had told me at the first*
> *Her will (she never did alas)*
> *I'd have made the effort then*
> *To escape from her toils.*

'He's become me or I've become him; I don't know which. Half my waking life I spend in that upper room with the bell of the Sorbonne ringing into the chill evening while my ink freezes. But I know that I have to get up, close the door and come downstairs into the streets outside. Only it's strange sometimes to see them full of buses and lorries and cars.' I laugh at myself to take the edge off what I'm saying even though I know that David understands. He's finishing his drink now. The bar's almost empty. Kevin comes out from behind with a cloth to wipe the mushroom tables.
Outside David goes off right into the dark while I take a left turn, each following our stage directions. As I unlock my own door there's a phone ringing. I reach it just in time.
'I'm sorry to ring you this late but I have tried several times

before. I expect you've seen about the row in Hornton.'

Caution, caution. 'No, I don't think I have.'

'I felt sure you'd have been following it with your involvement in all the different facets of literary politics, if I can use that term.' I am silent. 'Well if I just jog your memory: the writer in residence there, Eliza Teuson, has published a volume of poems and pieces by local people that's caused rather a stir: sex and drugs on the rates that sort of thing. I'm trying to get some comments for my column tomorrow. I'd like a few words from you if possible.'

I sigh. 'In the first place I haven't read it; in the second whatever the contents it isn't on the rates since Eliza Teuson is appointed and paid by the Arts Council, so it would be on the taxes as part of the arts budget. Thirdly, sex and drugs, if that is indeed what it's about, have been with us since the Garden of Eden and the aphrodisiac apple that Eve pulled, and I imagine Hornton, although as far as I've heard no paradise, has its share of them like everywhere else.'

'But should public money be spent on encouraging them?'

'I take it you know Coleridge's *Christabell*? It was written under the influence of opium. Then there's De Quincey of course and a long and distinguished line of literary alcoholics. As for sex...'

'But on public money?'

'When Queen Elizabeth I and the Duke of Leicester subsidized the two main London theatre companies was that public or private money? Jonson in his old age said Shakespeare was a drunk.'

'Then you think it's all right to spend public funds, taxes in this way?'

I sigh again, seeing tomorrow's headline in my mind's eye and trapped because there's no way out of this one. 'I think Shakespeare enjoyed state patronage. No doubt there were Mrs Grundys, probably given the times *Brother* Grundys, who objected when Hamlet said to Ophelia that something was "a fair thought to lie between a maid's legs." You may quote me. Goodnight.'

My hand is trembling as I put the receiver down and my mouth is dry. Get a bottle out of the cupboard. Pour a shot of Côtes de Ventoux. Grape after grain you must be insane. No, but I'm mad. I tell thee they have made me so.

XVII

The whites of my eyes are yellow, with red rivers running in them like the Nile delta in a Geography exam paper. This bowl of muesli is as hard to get down as a plate of sawdust. There's the telephone again shrilling between me and this week's composer countertenoring winningly.

Sure I must perish by your charms
Unless you sa-a-ave me in your arms

'I expect you've seen this morning's *Post*.'
'No.'
'Oh. Well it has a quote from you on the Eliza Teuson affair.'
'Oh yes.'
'Well we're doing something about it on *Morning After* at ten-thirty. We'd rather like you to come and take part in the programme.'

Think quickly: if you don't they won't ask you again and if they get someone else that person may say the wrong thing, be on the wrong side. The gates have to be held.

'Okay. I could probably manage that.'
'Great! That's marvellous.'
'I'll charge you for a taxi.'
'Oh. Yes. We're told not to encourage that by our paymasters but as it's such short notice . . .'
'Quite.'
'Can you be here by 10.15 so that we can have a chat?'

Then Sir Galahad had accoutred himself at all points and rode forth and when he came to the place he struck sword on shield and cried: 'I have come to do battle for the honour of

133

this damsel.'

End of fantasy, for Lizzie is no damsel in distress. She's a tough cookie and frightens me more than a bit. Her face is radically clean of paint and powder, her hair washed with a harsh shampoo that makes it always look faintly greasy. Why should I care? Why can't I just treat her as a person her feminist wing would say. Instead I try, and fail, to make a sex object of her so that my responses are all wrong and even my voice comes out at the wrong pitch. I like my feminists soft-centred, a touch of the violet or rose cream about them. Is there inside, a tender Liza not struggling to get out?

The worst of the rush is over as we trundle past Queen's and plunge behind Grub Street where the hacks sharpen their paper darts like quills. Half the illuminated sign over the doorway has fused and all that's left is '*adio*', like a Hispanic farewell, esperanto of despair.

'*Morning After* please.'

'If you'll just take a seat. What name is it?'

These girls are glossy. Eliza would disapprove of them perching on their padded swivel stools, perfect secretary birds, groomed with not a feather out of place, claws pointed redly to snatch at the little plastic terminals on their wires, plug and unplug. 'I have someone in reception for you.'

'Someone'll be right out.' She smiles at me: on, off; plug and unplug. 'Please take a seat.'

The seats are low and broad, bringing your knees under your chin and your eyes at mid-trouser leg. It's impossible to get out of them quickly. The human body hasn't that degree of levitation unless for acrobat or ballet dancer. When my Hermes comes I stare up, neck craning, while I try to open the hinges of my knees with thigh and calf muscles and feel myself put down, overawed till I'm upright.

'Very glad you could come. Tony Wallis is the presenter this morning for your slot. We've got a couple of other contributors: Alderman Mrs Jardine from the opposition and the chairman of the Ratepayers' Association.

It's a fix, a put-up. Why don't I just turn and run or say politely, 'No, thank you very much'? But I'm being ushered along between desks in the open-plan office strewn with stained plastic debris from the vending machine, and papers. We used to sing about a paper moon but it's become a paper world. How lucky that the volume of matter doesn't increase but is merely constantly transmuted, or the earth would sink out of the sun's orbit, out of the galaxy with its paper weight. A heraldic tree looks down from one cardboard wall with the badges of the London Boroughs and their mottos as progeny leaves at branch tips. A dart sits bullseye in Westminster.

Tony Wallis appears from behind a studio door patting down his hair as though we were on television. I see at once that's what he aspires to and we are his stepping stones, shoulders and heads to rest a foot on as he leaps upward.

'Now we're all such professionals we don't really need a run through. I'll just fire the questions straight at you. That way we'll get something really exciting, not stage-managed. Let me introduce you to the others.'

Never again, I vow. Next time Al, remember this moment and say no. 'I'd assumed Eliza Teuson would be here too to put her own view.'

'I thought you could speak for the writer's viewpoint. I'm sure you can deal with all the objections straight off the top of your head. No problem.'

Flattery eases me into the studio where the others already sit at 'the round earth's imagined corners', the green baize table with the pump-handle mikes and earphone muffs. Their mouths are set in thin lines I read as disapproval but it may just be nerves. I smile and try to look at ease.

'Now I've already had a chat with Alderman (is that right?) Mrs Jardine and Mr Timberley so we're ready to go on the green. I'll just sketch in the background for the benefit of the listeners and then I'll ask you Al, how you react as a writer to the charge of the public funding of pornography. I don't know whether you've seen a copy of the book?' He pushes a slim paperback across the table towards me.

Rose From the Dust is the title. A girl (is she Rose, a rose rising phoenix from Hornton's dusty streets?) leans long-haired, white-faced against a wall stippled with graffiti on the cover, her thighs slim in jeans, her jacket collar turned up like Michèle Morgan in a French Resistance film. What happened to yesterday's snow queens?

Quickly turn a page or two. The usual mixture of verses comes off the page, the people's poems as they try to grapple with inarticulate loneliness among the shopping precincts, car parks and underpasses of outer city perimeters, euphemistically called 'Greater'. The green glows. Tony

135

Wallis puts his penetrating question.

And I am sick of my own voice answering, querulous. I want to be a hedonist and lie on warm sand under a palm tree with the waves shushing behind my closed eyes and a silken girl bringing sherbet.

'First what do you mean by pornography? Secondly even if we agree on what it is and that *Rose From the Dust* contains some of it are you saying it's all right as private enterprise but that public funds must imply censorship? Thirdly today's pornography may be tomorrow's great art or tomorrow's yawn. Can you judge?'

'We know it goes on. It doesn't need encouragement at public expense.'

'Sex is one of the basic materials of art, especially painting and literature. Music less obviously so, which is why it's easier to subsidise.'

'We don't need this young woman to tell us what to do. That sort of thing comes naturally.'

'What about drugs? Surely that's a different matter?' Tony Wallis steps between.

'You must show me what's being complained of. I can't discuss it in the abstract.' I hear my own language becoming pompous, falling into the jargon of bureaucracy by imitation.

'Well this poem called "Snow" seems to have given the most offence.

> My nose drips, candles
> as it did when a child
> for another snowfall
> a white innocence
> that chilblained toes
> in socks wet from hours
> of balling, fisting the stinging
> handfuls, tasting . . .

'It mixes up drug abuse with childhood. That could be very dangerous.'

'I should think glue-sniffing is pretty widespread in Hornton.'

'Exactly. We've passed a by-law prohibiting its display and sale to minors.'

That's what happened to the wet afternoon with scissors and paste and a cut-out book. 'But as I read it this poem is about

136

someone trying to kick a habit. It can be seen as a warning.'

'It links throwing snowballs with taking dangerous drugs.'

'That's the way poetry works. It's a metaphor; a pun on snow.'

'Well we shouldn't be spending public money on it. It's not art, not as I understand it anyway: something uplifting that makes you see life as a bit better than it is, concentrates on something beautiful, Beethoven's Pastoral symphony for instance.'

Can a Spring symphony or even sonnet come out of Hornton? 'Look, take the title of the book itself: *Rose From the Dust*. That's another example of what I mean, of a pun; that use of Rose to mean a girl, a flower and to rise.'

'Why do they have to concentrate on the squalid? We've got some very nice estates in Hornton; some council, some private, with trees and lawns. They only see the other side when the housing committee is doing its best in very hard times . . .'

Tony Wallis intervenes. The hoped for punch-up isn't happening. We are ambling onto parallel paths that can't meet. 'One last word from each of you: Alderman Mrs Jardine.'

'It's typical of the party in power in Hornton at the moment that money should be wasted in this profligate way . . .'

'Mr Timberley . . .'

'The way to keep the rates down is to concentrate on essentials.'

I shall jump in before I'm called. 'Poetry, art is essential. If it does nothing else it keeps a few people out of the doctor's surgery . . .'

'Thank you all of you and listeners we want to hear from you about this week's issue: Pornography on the public purse. Please write, postcards please, to . . .'

I stop listening. The others have had the last word in Tony Wallis's invitation to the public. They sit back complacently knowing that those who bother to send their views will be on the right side.

'Can I have this?' I pick the rose from the dust.

'Sure.' The producer comes in.

'That was fine everybody. Just what we needed. Thank you all for coming along. Tony a word on the next piece . . .'

We get up, our moment of glory over. We have spoken to the nation. I don't know who I'm sorriest for. Perhaps Eliza

Teuson who will have to live with it until the wind changes and blows a fresh collection of half-digested scraps along the gutter.

I insist on my right to a taxi with producer and doorman and have the luxury of sitting back in the Holmsean-smelling interior for the ride home. Then I am out on the pavement again and still seething. Do the other two feel as disgruntled as me? What did you do in such a case? You cocked a snook as the saying was, and whatever indeed was a snook? Snoek I remember as a poor grey utility relation of coley we turned into fishcakes.

> Prince what did you do on that occasion
> But put your case to the high court of the nation,
> Lest you should feel your heels a-dangle
> When you prepared to leave this world?

I almost feel like singing or tap dancing along the pavement. No one would notice here or even turn their heads. It must be the effect of increased adrenalin in the blood that couldn't be drained off by taking a swing at someone.

Suddenly I want to pee with fright or rage. I can't get the key in the lock fast enough. Now there's the hall to cross and the steps up. Pray god there's no one in there. Ah the relief! Even so I can see someone has jettisoned a dog end that revolves lazily sending out a yellow distress signal. Why won't they be flushed away at once? They spin round in the vortex of the flush and bob up again, their paper skins a little more fragile, a little heavier until they sink to the bottom of the pan. Even then they won't be seen off straight away. I've known one lie submarine for two or three days sending out its squalid smoke signals.

There's nothing more to be squeezed out; bladder's all flat and empty. What a strange system it is of conversion and excretion, this machine for processing matter to fuel our individual self. Yet we are the machine although we can apprehend it; each of us is an informed sphere, Jack Donne's 'little world made cunningly'. Maybe that's why we had to have an indwelling god: energy, light, spirit in the matter of the universe. Maybe Aristotle or Lucretius had their sublimest thoughts in the kharsi too.

I let myself into my own room that seems somehow smaller even than usual as if I've suddenly put on different glasses and got a changed perspective. In here I become like Orton and Halliwell with a mind circling these *Huis Clos* walls. Out there for a moment I saw in Tony Wallis the curtains, the battlements, the outworks of radio city, the concentric circles of the media feeding off each other and broadening the ripples of their kingdom further and further from the original tossed gobbet of print in a local paper, through the radio waves and the telepictures bounced off satellite into dozens of countries and millions of homes until the trivial becomes universal, the world is Coronation Street taking in each other's dirty linen over the back fence. The air is thick with chatter and the trick Augustine taught of silent apprehension inside the head, the communion with the printed page may soon be gone forever.

XVIII

Time for a round of cheese and pickle and half a pint. Push open the swing door of the Knackers as it becomes I notice when I've been writing about death: love and death, knickers and knackers, the eternal themes. I'm late. I've got the last cellophane-wrapped round. The sweet brown goo of the pickle has begun to ooze up through the larger pores in the bread. There's a table at the back where I take it and today's book page.

Every newspaper has to be a compendium these days. I suppose because we don't listen to sermons any more we have to be fed our ethics some way; instead of features from the pulpit and news from a broadsheet we get the priesthood of the press. In your day master foreign news was just novelty by the time it reached the outside world, as mythical as history or the doings of the gods in your set texts. Now the daily rags encompass every circle of our lives – money, marriage, murder. You had that great picture text of the Celestines you described in your mother's ballade: 'Paradise painted where there are harps and lutes, and a hell where the damned are boiled' with its suggestion of cannibal cooking pots and demons poking the blaze with their prongs, set against a heavenly choir. I remember the day the old man looked at me quite suddenly and straight in the eye. 'I don't believe in a hell hereafter. Here and now is hell.'

There are the shadow projections of the city, our world, light and dark, heaven and hell. As sunlight falls on a wall through a window or as dark casts its shade we cast forward and back, into hope or guilt, our vision of the city. Here at the tail end of the paper is the tidings from Mammonsberg, Croesusville, Divestown. Here on the front are three children burned to death by a paraffin heater in a tenement, winter's last pyre of offerings from the bottom of our heap. In between come the cracked shell of a Beirut basement with a fledgling face looking out, the brave new worlds of fashion and technology trailing their fake feather boas in front of us, last night's first nights and this week's hot off the presses.

A little group swims into the shadowy bar from the bright street, a chequerboard of faces: two black, two white. One's that young pro who eyes me from time to time; eighteen if she's a day. The two white boys I haven't seen before. The other's that slim black girl Paul once mistook for a boy.

'So I said to this fat Arab I'm no fucking prossy. I work for my money. Not that I've got anything against it, Sally, but I just do and I don't like no one to think *I'm* one.' Her accent is South Thames, Lewisham to Peckham. The face is fine carved in ebony like an Ethiope but not so chiselled as Raphael, the true Nile serpent.

Sally leans a head on a *caffe latte* hand looking at me, hunting out my eyes across the room. Their voices fall clear into the still pool of the empty bar. The music box is silent.

'It's that Tony,' one of the white boys says explosively. 'She wants to give it up, don't you Sal, but he won't let her. Fucking queen.'

'I want to give it up. I do truly.'

Now you're whispering in my ear. What are you saying?

> Let me really know whether these young girls
> I chat to every day weren't once honest?
> Honest they really were without reproach or blame . . .

Until, you say, each of them took clerk, layman or monk to put out love's flame, a secret love until the girl got bored as they do with just one lover. You said it's woman's nature or rather feminine nature to need love so sharply, old heartaching chauvinist. 'Six workmen can do more than three.' Hogamus, higamus woman is polygamous, her genes wanting a different coupling each time, new fresh blood to make her children healthy. In every little human universe stasis and change are at war. She wants the love bond too: higamus, hogamus woman is monogamous. And she wants to dream of dead, lost loves like in Joyce's story, the tale Nora told him that shook his

141

complacency out in a blizzard of beautiful words, black snow
falling.

> Only for you lover she has no compassion.
> Small birds can have her palm to peck
> but her hands are busy elsewhere
> when you want her to pull down your zip.

> Yet she can walk with long gone lovers
> through the landskip of her heart
> where leaves fall, hands lock, toast is buttered
> and memory holds the toasting fork.

'But every time I say I won't he makes me.'

Was Sally destroyed by seduction, maybe by her brother or
father alone in the house one afternoon when they were off
work sick and she was skiving from school? Or is she just a
victim of a home never made enough to be broken, of poverty
and the whole wheeling circle of deprivation as it's called now?
And if I took her away, did a Sabine Baring-Gould with this
treadmill girl, how long would it last? How long would she
stand the boredom of stability and comfort?

I could do it. We could both manage in my room. I'd push
harder with someone to push for. You'd have to go my friend.
You're not cost effective. The care I lavish on you could knock
out a couple of block busters. We both have our fantasies, Sally
and me.

Anyway it wouldn't do. I'm too old for her. Crabbed age and
youth and all that. But you never feel it inside; that's why the
mirror on the stairs as you round the bend is always such a
smack in the face. Still Aristotle was at least fifty before he
married Herpillus. Then they laughed at him for being
uxorious and said she rode on his back while he went on all
fours like a donkey. I wonder if he cared about the gibes at her
extravagance or was happy to have her youngness to dote on.
She gave him a son, or he gave her one, and he gave us the
Nichomachean Ethics; tidy, even parsimonious, old
philosopher fathering a child and a book in one. And what a
line of descent that is with Socrates as progenitor, Plato as
pater familias, Aristotle the flower, Theophrastus the
consolidator, Menander the poet; a genealogy of the head only
humans can propagate.

Has she had an abortion or two already? Raffael says

sometimes the girls allow themselves to get pregnant to go on social security and get off the game for a bit. Then they find it isn't enough to keep two and they have to go back on again.

'Why don't you tell him. Just tell him to fuck off.'

Suddenly they are all silent. A figure has pushed open the doors and stands looking around: pale clown's face, black smears of hair, collar turned up on the long overcoat, the eyes sooted round, hands beringed. 'Come on Sal.'

'She don't want to go.'

He speaks to her low and urgently. I can't catch the words. Her head hangs. She isn't looking at him. Suddenly the white boy explodes up from the table and catches him by the lapels.

'She don't want to go. She wants to stay here with us.'

The pimp shakes him off and goes on with his low monologue. Sally still stares down. I know the blow is coming even before the fist moves and plants itself in his face. He staggers. Two bar men bundle out from behind. One's apprehensive but determined; the other eager, pushing forward to mix it.

'Out. You and you, out.' He grabs the pale one and hustles him towards the door. The other barman grabs the other. There's a struggle. The slim wilting clown is suddenly a coiled wire and as tough. He twists and tenses but the other's greater weight bears him on and out. 'Now you, all of you, out! There's nothing but trouble. And you're barred anyway.' He turns on the thin black girl.

'I wasn't doing nothing.' She is indignant.

'There's always trouble where you are. Out!'

Sally begins to plead. The tears come up in her eyes. Even from here I can see them. 'He was only trying to help me. Teresa didn't do nothing.'

All this time the other white boy has sat quietly, his face quite clean of expression as the volatile passions spend themselves around him like St Elmo's fire, 'the flame that cannot singe a sleeve'. His quiescence comes from whatever he's high on I realize, not a stoic calm.

The bar settles down again. I go back to my paper, the printed words punctuated from time to time with cyclical rumblings from the far table as they chew over the happening and Sally's future. For everyone knows the clown will be back to make her jump through his hoop, that she has no real will to escape and nowhere to escape to unless someone will take over

143

her life and bend it into a new shape; they all know that any job she might find would be a new prostitution of long hours and tired feet or a spirit gone soggy with repetition on assembly line or checkout. Her body and self are softly pliable now. Unless she can get out they will harden, become fibrous and brittle at once as if a carapace grew outwards, rooting through the flesh of body and brain, fungoid, consuming and changing as it grows from the sperm spores sown in her again and again.

What would the *Daily Puke* have to say about that? Inky fingers would be held up in horror while our readers were fed every greasy morsel. Remember the literary scandal of the decade when Veronica ran off with Fred and the rags couldn't track them down. How they sifted and poked and turned every stone to see what could be made to waddle into the daylight.

'You do know where she is.' My silence filling the line. 'But you're not going to say.'

'I think it's a private matter, that, particularly at such times, people should be left alone to sort things out.'

'Oh I agree with you personally of course. But our readers want to know. You're not going to help me . . .'

'I don't think I am.'

Yet I couldn't lie to get him off my back, couldn't pretend I didn't know when I'd been with them the night before. The little white lie wouldn't have been wrong or caused harm but I couldn't frame it. Lavinia's speech in *Androcles* about the hand refusing to stretch out and put a pinch of incense on the altar fire describes that sheerly physical inability better than anything. My tongue just wouldn't get round it. If Satan is the father of lies then all scribblers must be his offspring got on the OED.

Here's Quill with his week's fiction. Let's see who's in, who's out. There's a new book by Simon Carte but that isn't his lead review. He's given that to a first novel. Yum, yum, the best thing since sliced bread: perception, wit, breaks new ground, most promising for a long time. Ah, poor piglet who dared to dance, bummed up, it's just so they can eat you later but you don't know that yet of course. You'll think it's all true. Now what's he say about Carte? Listen piglet and I'll show you your fate in a glass.

You must understand that Carte was never as good as he was cracked up to be. It wasn't his fault he was overpraised in the beginning. When they took him up he had a living to earn and

144

the glitter of constant mention can dazzle and warp the vision. He had a long run, three books, and the lionizers all ran after him as if he was the boy with the golden goose tucked under his arm. He was dined and partied and snapped here and there, put on this panel and that programme like a pop star. But it doesn't last piglet, because it's not built on sane appraisal but on flattery and that jade fashion again, and the time comes when he must be pushed back into line while some new face is fondled, some new prodigy dandled. So:

> *Or y pensez, belle Gantiere...*
> *Prenez a destre et a senastre*

but be prepared that you too will become old coin, no longer current.

But as for Quill and Co. they, I suppose, also have a living to earn by their traffic in ephemera. I don't know whether to pity them or rail at such a world in classic old high Swiftian. The satirist is meant to believe in the extreme wickedness, degeneration of his own times but I can't. I know there's always been Sally whatever her name or dress. Indeed there are far fewer pros now than a hundred years ago or in the days of the Puritan Commonwealth or, come to that, Aristotle. Our only real advance on the downward scale is in the size of our weapons. That doom we foretold ourselves for so long we can really do. Our minds have played with it so often we had to invent it: megadeath by fire and the pestilence of radiation, our horsemen of the apocalypse, the rocket riders.

Someone, a tipster maybe, has left a copy of the *Puke* on the bar. Even the print is murky, stains and smears worse than the *Grauniad*. This one's thumb and finger printed too. The edges of the pages have become furred and the words are fading and smudged already along the fold although it's only today's. The page three nude kneels in grainy, grimy sand.

Our pornography is so graceless beside Titian's, our beauties hard celluloid, or rubber dolls with moulded faces and breasts painted flesh tint and glazed with a smile. And here's the gossip column: *Slopbucket* by Sewerman, so much flung shit some of it must stick to us all: writer and reader, and wretched victim of our prurience and self-righteousness. Sewerman paddles, dabbles, gobbles in filth. In his hands love turns to lust, fragile things are fractured, their parts encrusted with the crap with which he tries to stick them together in a new monstrous form for our amazement. He dips his trembling pen in pure piss and bile as he sits farting into the old tweed trousers he has never had cleaned and picking at his hairy left nostril with a deft little finger or bangs away two-fingered, black marking his ribbon of snot while a scurf snowdrifts up the keys.

XIX

I look at my diary and see I've forgotten I'm dining with Bumps Brunet. I agreed because he rang me up and I couldn't think of an excuse quickly enough on the phone. Now I wonder, indeed I've wondered ever since that call, whether I'm being disloyal to Guzzle in dining with another publisher, especially dining and on a Sunday. Guzzle lunches with other writers of course but that's different. There's no parity between us. Guzzle would sack me tomorrow by turning down something I offered him even though we're an old married couple of fifteen years. He would justify himself on grounds of expediency and his duty to the firm and his other authors to keep afloat and maintain a high standard.

There's the phone just as I'm trying to wash the mud off my best shoes with a damp cloth and the sink is full of dirty rivulets and my shoes are still too wet to wear. Put them on the top of the bloody radiator Al and answer the bloody phone.

'370 102 . . .' I hear the sound of weeping.

This has happened to me before. Then it was the old lady ringing to say the old man had died but unable to speak. Well it can't be that. I knew that time at once who it was. Now it could be anyone 'Who is it?'

The noises of distress go on, wordlessly as we become beasts in pain only able to howl and snuffle, brute speechless. 'Who is it?'

'Al?' A woman's voice.

'Yes it's me. Who is it? I can't hear you properly.'

'It's Mary.'

'Mary? What's the matter? What's happened.' I think I know

147

who it is but the voice is barely recognizable.

'I'm sorry. I know we've only met a couple of times but I don't know who else to talk to. And you're so strong; you understand it all.'

And because she says so I shall have to be though my legs buckle and my shoulder grows numb under the extra weight. I see her late at night in the hotel the festival organizers had booked us into, both of us pretty celebratory pissed now the strain of the reading and the questioning are over, trying to unwind. She's saying: 'I've come to it so late you see. I still can't believe it's happening, that I'm really being published. It makes me somebody at last. Can you understand that? Your experience has been so different. After my marriage failed I didn't seem to be a person. I wasn't a wife any more and that was what defined women of my generation. How can you possibly understand that? You're so much yourself.' I know I must get up and make my unsteady way to my own room while I'm still cool and tough and yet I have to leave her with something too, that I mustn't seem to be rejecting her because of the gap between us and Lea and Chérie parade through my head and out while I flinch away from a mind that sees a literary parallel even at such a moment.

'What's happened? Tell me.'

'I'm sorry; I can't seem to speak for crying. You must think me an awful fool, a silly old woman . . .'

'You're not old; that is silly. Don't worry about the crying; just tell me.' I'm trying to throw a lifeline through the air forged of air itself, words and the intangible expressions we lace them together with.

'Farrow have turned down my new novel.'

Why is life always imitating bad art. If I put this in a book, this coincidence of Mary ringing into my thoughts, some just-down-from-Girton reviewer (watch it Quill they are hungry for your column inches) would say it was too contrived. Yet it would be purest realism. Life does it all the time, farcically sometimes or hideously like now as if thought had the power of generation over events or we were all locked into one circuit with chance crossing the lines in the great game of random.

'Then more fool them.'

'Oh, Al.'

'Listen, that's what you have to think: that it's their loss, and you must send it off to someone else straight away. You have to remember it's nothing to do with talent, more to do with accountancy, cash flow, the times we live· in.' I'm dredging hard, trying to find the right phrase that will encircle her head and keep her afloat.

'I don't make them any money, I know that.'

It's a talent too fine for these rough times. 'Think of Elizabeth Courtney: never went into paperback in her life. I doubt if she ever sold more than three thousand copies. She'd be down to two now if she were still alive. Yet everyone who knows anything of writing knows how good she was.'

'Oh, Al you're so strong. I knew you'd help.'

'Listen, send it to Goetzle. He may not take it because he's a funny old thing in his taste. But I can keep an eye on him if he does, make sure he gives you the best terms. But if he turns it down remember he isn't God although he'd like to think he is, and it's not talent he's looking for but sales. Let me know what he says. Have you got an agent?'

'No.'

'You should have. We'll think about that. I'll ring you next week and we'll have a drink.'

I'm exhausted yet curiously high now I've put the phone down. Mary, I hope, has been snatched off the cliff face and I have to go and meet Bumps in the fittest state of mind with all that adrenalin flowing. My best black velvet I think, and a symbolically red shirt to go with it. Bumps has picked the Gay Hussar where Victor will welcome him and he can be seen to be known. For Bumps I shall be a little late so that I can make the entrance and try to upstage him.

I see at once I've failed and remember it's silly to try. He's wearing an open-necked cream silk shirt with white ducks and midi-jacket in something unidentifiably expensive. His aftershave is a heavy musk cloud around his dark curls, touched here and there with an elegant frosting like a Christmas tree. He is a rare moth pale in the candlelight against the bruise-red plush of the interior, a Fabergé artefact in a lined jewel case. His style as always amuses and irritates me at the same time.

'Al, you're looking splendid.' The hand is sinewy, well manicured and banded in gold and silver as the fashion is this Spring. 'Victor, do you know . . .'

But Victor is there first shaking hands and saying 'Good to see you.'

'Now this is nice. What will you drink? Jay Waterman is over there but we won't look. I love that red . . .'

Bumps is lavish, attentive, amusing. I'm in the mood to like him a lot. That's dangerous. I must slow up. Perhaps he would take Mary if Guzzle won't. How would she respond to him? She's sufficiently *grande dame* for Bumps to cultivate at first but perhaps too shy, too unassuming. He might break her heart when he's sucked her dry. Not meaning to, of course. There's no real malice in Bumps.

'So how are you? How are things? What are you writing?'

I'm wondering if these are just the questions you're supposed to ask a writer or whether there's more to them.

'Oh this and that. I went to give evidence to the committee on censorship the other day. I think you'd have approved of what I said. Have you been?'

'Lord yes. I wore my most sober suit but I think I still shocked them. They take it all so seriously. I wanted to laugh. But I suppose they could do a lot of harm if they decided to put the clock back.'

'I don't think they'll do that intentionally, and anyway I can't see this government giving time to it unless they want a moral issue for the backwoodsmen to fill in with in the run up to the next election.'

'But if they get back again?'

'Ah then who can predict anything?'

Bumps chatters through our order and into the first course. He's very amusing, full of publishing anecdotes told with verve and much waving of the hands so that the gold and silver glint in the candlelight, and I laugh a lot.

'But to business,' he says as his steak tartare is put before him. Here it comes. I have a moment's satisfaction in having been right.

'I've had a marvellous idea for a book I think you could do.'

'Oh yes.'

'It came to my mind because someone was interviewing me about *Mayhew Revisited*. You remember all those years ago? It's become something of a rarity. The forerunner of all sorts of things, I'm told, a kind of classic.'

'So it was in its way.'

'You do remember it. Well I was looking through it for something for this rather dishy girl reporter and I saw your piece about prostitution. I didn't think much more of it while

150

she was there but when she was gone I read it all through twice. It was very good Al. You're actually a very good writer.'

'I'm too old to deny it.'

'I don't know whether you've kept in touch with that world at all. You'd probably have to do a lot of research; I realize that.'

'There've been dozens of studies of prostitution, probably hundreds. Surely there isn't room for another.'

'It's a perennially interesting subject. But anyway I wasn't thinking of a study of it. I was thinking of a novel about it.'

'The prostitute with a heart of gold. It's called *Never on Sunday*. It was a great movie. I saw it years ago.'

'So it's time for it to be done again.'

'Why not make it a historical, the hetaira with a heart of gold. You could revive the great days of Cecil B. de Mille and have a cast of thousands. Equity would love you: all gold paint and nylon cheesecloth.'

'You're not taking this seriously. I'm putting a serious proposition to you. I will pay you a hundred pounds a week for however long it takes you to write it.'

'I could last it out for years and never write a word.'

'But you wouldn't. I know you Al: you're irretrievably honest. If you took it on you'd do it.'

He's right and I hate it. To be honest is to be dull, boring, worthy almost. Much better to be a flash rogue like you, master. Or were you really? Maybe underneath the swagger you were honest at heart, a conman in this too, probably an incompetent crook at best; a Hemingway: the poet playing the man of action.

'Why not a science fiction: *Callgirl 2000* or *Galatea of the Galaxy*, all about how a little green extra-terrestrial brought comfort to millions. Thrill to the pleasures of weightless sex. Is it possible do you think? Did the Russians try when they put a woman up there?'

'Be serious now Al. I was thinking of a really big blockbuster. You could weave in some real-life material and catch the wave for faction. Maybe we should claim it's all true, was told to you, is a kind of novelization of the serial that plays daily in our streets.'

'You're writing the blurb before you've seen the book. Or do you want me to write the book of the blurb?'

'There are certain episodes we'd have to have.'

151

'Such as?'

'Well I haven't decided whether she's a poor girl doing it for the money or a rich bitch doing it for kicks. That rather dictates the necessary scenes.'

'It would, rather. How about this: there are identical twins found abandoned at birth. One's adopted by a rich family; one stays in the home. That way you'd get both situations. Then they could meet and change places. Maybe when they meet they fancy each other, like having it off in the mirror. How about that for a scene?' I'm laughing a lot now. 'Perhaps they're not girls but twin boys who both grow up to be transvestites. One goes to Eton. Did you have any TVs there Bumps? And the other goes to Rippledean Comprehensive.'

'No we didn't, not in my day. Where's Rippledean?'

'Nowhere. I've just made it up instead of using Neasden which has been gravely over-exposed. Where were we?'

'Your preposterous idea of twin boys.'

'Why preposterous? The girl bit's all been done by the Americans and their imitators. Let's go continental. If Pasolini were still alive he could make the film. Should they be black do you think?'

'What's the matter with you Al? I put a perfectly serious idea to you for discussion . . .'

'No, you haven't. You offered me a piece of pseudo-pornography, no I don't mean that, sub-pornography to write for a hundred a week, less than the average male industrial wage.'

'You'd get royalties. It could be a real best seller.' Bumps shows signs of being hurt. 'I'd thought of some marvellous scenes.'

'All you need is someone to rewrite *Fanny Hill* in a modern setting with word processor language and high technology backdrop.'

'Exactly. Just what I want. You've got it.'

'I prefer my twin boys.'

Bumps' eyes focus on my face. 'Do you know them?'

My joke has gone far enough and is in danger of catching Bumps on the rebound. 'I thought you were, as they say, into girls at the moment.'

'I've always had a weakness for youth and beauty, however it's packaged. You know that.'

'Well I'm sorry to disappoint you but they're as true, and as

152

false as Rippledean Comprehensive.'

He sighs ostentatiously. 'I'll have to take my brilliant idea to someone else. But you would have been just right for it Al. That piece really was good. I must confess I can't really see the difference. If you did it then, and for peanuts, why not now?'

'Then it had a purpose for me that wasn't just to make money. No one had done it for one thing. And it was true, as true as I could make it. No one knew any more than I did or could have done it any better. That's why you can read it now and still say it was good.'

We have reached the coffee. Bumps leans back and takes out a slim gold case of cigarlings, leans forward and offers it. I accept.

'Your trouble Al is that you're an old-fashioned puritan. It isn't becoming in middle age. One is supposed to mature, don't you know.'

'I know it's very boring of me but I can't seem to get the knack. Too early an exposure to Yeats I suspect. I was very susceptible to my early influences.'

'What do you mean? Why Yeats? What early influences?' Does Bumps scent a tale?

> 'I pray, for fashion's word is out
> And prayer comes round again –
> That I may seem though I die old
> A foolish, passionate man.'

'You worry about it all too much. I'm older than you are.'

'But you've got your Dorian Gray safely locked in the attic. Some of us have to carry it around on our faces.'

Bumps is pleased. 'Tell me now about your early influences...'

'An adolescent exposure to some great singer, I never discovered who, on a wind-up gramophone and a much-played seventy-eight. I can still hear the little toc as the needle hit a chip, and the surface noise of chips quietly frying or small surf. She was singing *Casta Diva*, from *Norma* you know; and at that moment where the aria takes off it took me with it. I didn't understand the plot or what she was saying in those days but I felt she was singing for love of me or I wanted her to.'

I hadn't meant to tell Bumps any of this. It's the drink talking and he won't understand it. But he doesn't laugh as I'm afraid he might. Instead he's saying: 'Perhaps you could work

that in somewhere.'
    'The twin who's been adopted by rich parents . . .'
    'Why do you have this thing about twins?'
    'It's a sign of a split personality, of my deep moral ambiguity or the world's. These are really very good little cigars.'

XX

My head aches and a drowsy numbness pains my sense after all
that good Lethe I poured down with Bumps last night. I must
ring my guardian agent and tell him I've turned away fame and
fortune, and I must go and do my duty as a citizen. There's my
pollcard, behind the candlestick I keep in memory of the
winter of discontent and power cuts. Who was it, Herbert
Morrison, who wanted his ashes scattered on the Thames
during a sitting of the LCC? It had such glamour that old set of
initials to conjure up the ghost of Keir Hardie, and *Fifty Years
a Borough*, the story of the growth of radical London with its
monuments in schools and paving stones, chest clinics and
grants to sixth formers to make its children stay on, swimming
baths and libraries like some mediaeval Italian republic, our
own city state caring for its people, one of the intertwined
strands in our Lighttown, so that it isn't just Mammonsberg.
How I do run on.

'Ah Al. We were going to call you. Tell me your news first.'

I describe the glowing future I have turned my back on. He
is non-committal, not chiding me for being irresponsible.
'Why were you going to call me?'

'The film treatment on Villon we've been pushing around at
producers has got a bite. Ben Nicholas is very interested. He
wants Larry Lofts to direct it. He wants you to meet as soon as
possible.'

'Larry Lofts!'

'Yes, that's right.'

'But that would mean something very lavish.'

'We'd expect to build some element of budget percentage

155

into your fee. When can you meet them?'

I'm almost trembling as I put down the receiver. My mouth is quite dry. I've never actually seen a Larry Lofts but they're famous or notorious, big films in every sense. I must look through the cinema guide and find out if there's one on I can get to at once. Best to be boned up on him before we meet. In a couple of breaths I'm off on a dream trip. I can even see the credits. Scenes begin to shape themselves in my mind. I begin inventing dialogue for you, master. Who would play you well? It needs someone like a young Scofield, remembering you were only in your thirties when you died. A well-preserved forty-five could do it. What was his name: a whey face, thin body, beautiful passionate actor; brilliant as the deserter who's shot? Perfect. But I might not get any say in the casting, I must remember that.

I'm walking through the square behind the Knickers in a delighted daze. The sun shines obligingly and my track shoes kick up puffs of pink cloud and occasional stardust. Come down Al, get a hold of yourself. You have been here before, well almost, and it came to nothing. But shouldn't I, in that case, enjoy the dream? Then at least I've had this.

> *Appaise toy, et mets fin en tes dis*
> *Por mon conseil prens tout en gré ...*

How should that go? 'Calm down and stop what you're saying. By my advice take everything as it comes.' You didn't follow your own counsel though. 'And look where it got me.' Perhaps I should write a dialogue between us in ballade form.

> Prince, I'll listen to what you say.
> 'Amend your life or go the same way.'

There's a froth of green breaking out on the branches in the private garden in the middle of the square and the grass beyond the padlocked iron gate is a quick viridian almost as if you could see it grow. The playground's quiet and empty today with the school turned into a polling booth. Usually it seethes and screams with every colour and sound of child. I puzzle about where they come from in bedsitterland.

It's a bleak enough building, late-nineteenth-century ecclesiastical with two stretches of tarmac playground; no single-storey picture-window primary where children were meant to grow up bright and beautiful but an old-style junior mixed and infants with the classes cut in stone lettering over the gates: BOYS and others. The usual three dedicated women are sitting on infants' chairs inside the gates, wearing their rosettes like the prize jumpers they are.

I approach the one sporting the Labour colour. They all have knitting protruding from plastic bags and are exercising British tolerance towards each other. Each will go for the tea in turn, scrupulously.

'Hallo. I haven't had any literature through the door about the Labour candidate. I don't even know his or her name.'

'It's Stigwood. Jeffrey Stigwood.'

'No relation, I take it.'

'Oh yes, the son.'

'And do his views follow in father's footsteps too?'

'I think so. We've got some pamphlets here if anyone's interested.' She dives in the plastic bag among the tangled spaghetti of her knitting and fishes out a bundle. 'We had a few printed but there aren't enough people in this area for a proper street-by-street canvas.'

I'm faintly shocked that she admits this so freely in carrying middle-class tones while her rivals are sitting as close as the Norns passing their one eye between them. I take a copy and turn back towards the gate. I want to be able to go on into the school, to take part in the always slightly nervous-making ritual of identifying name and address and being ticked on the register and being given a ballot form. I want to be able to go into my little booth by myself, to read through twice to make sure I've got it right and put my cross large and clear in the correct slot, but I can't.

The sunlight seems harsh, sharp without warmth as I walk back reading the pamphlet young Stigwood's sect have put out. The trouble with the Leadites is that they're so dull and heavy. I like my nickname for them because it smacks of 'Luddite' and is from the village of Lead where they drew up the latest manifesto. I can just imagine them in shorts, sandals and open-necked shirts in that Edwardian fake manor become adult education and conference centre, arguing over the stew on earthenware platters as if the Beatles had never been born, and without even the humour to see that the village of Lead could only provide ammunition, sprayed gunshot of satire for the opposition.

All the time they're looking over their shoulders to a world

157

that never was except in the country-house politics of the Webbs. The new wed young technocrats in their first Shergold home, carpets and furniture provided for you to move straight in, and saving for their first video recorder, don't want a cloth cap except for the golf course when they've got on a bit. And these are the voters, not the down and outs, Asian outworkers, mobile bedsitterites. Only their opposites, the Shiremen could drive Mr and Mrs New Average into the Leadites' arms for long enough to win an election, and then divorce when they began to do all those token things dear to their hearts. They are the New Sandal Army and they have to exist to balance the extreme of neo-imperialism although I'm not sure that either is chicken; more two terrible twins hatched from the same cuckoo egg.

Gadget technology that will really change the surface texture of our lives, which is what most of us apprehend, doesn't exist for the Leadites. The New Imps of course are busy harnessing it to their counting houses and executive jets while their wives and daughters drive out on Sundays in a horse and buggy. The Leads are like oozlum birds looking up their own arses and trying to see the future there. They have their magic signs and abracadabras to counter the jingoisms of the Imps but Mr and Mrs New Average really want the simple language of *Crossroads*, the Fortran of the private housing estate, consumerese whose only poetry is the visuals of the tellyads. Someone should do a research job on the new basic vocabulary. I reckon it's less than the number of classic Chinese characters by now, less than an Anglo-Saxon bard would draw on in an evening.

The fifties children don't know what it was like before watershed 1960 and I'm glad. For once the start of a decade was actually a discernible starting point. And I don't want them to know except as a matter of history. Both political extremes walk around arse about face, peering into the past for a future while the rest of us struggle to live with our present, to seize it as it flows under us like a moving walkway.

My dream and my pleasure are all gone in a flurry of anger. That's what Stigwood Senior and Co. want of course; no, perhaps not him. He's too astute a politician. He's carried on the shoulders of his camp followers as their talisman. I open the front door into the quiet house and stand for a moment in the hall watching a water dazzle of sunshine that filters through

158

the fanlight onto the floor. If time and space are infinite then they must be circular and the past will come back to us, is indeed still accessible like a distant star if we could reach it. But if everything began with the big bang then time and space should be finite and what's lost is gone for ever. And what, you might ask, master, have such ideas to do with the price of cheese?

I step down the few stairs to my basement burrow. The door to the other room is open I notice. I don't know the occupier of that room. Chance has dictated that their hours of coming and going are different from mine, and they don't drink in either the Knickers or the Nevern. Just occasionally we smile at each other at weekends. Sometimes it's a boy; sometimes a girl I pass on the stairs.

I stop at my own door, key poised. Some animal perception beyond reason is alert. My psychic ruff is standing on end. My throat burrs with suspicion. Now I can see them, the jemmy marks on the frame and door but my lock has held. I go across to the other door. It has burst. The wood is gashed with a yellow wound. I can see into someone else's life. I resist the temptation to step inside and peer at their few possessions, to see if the bed is unmade single or double. I might be caught or suspected.

Back upstairs again and into the hall where there are no rooms but on the first half-landing the door is ajar. I go on up through the house noting who's been visited, who's escaped as though some angel of death had passed over. Jemal in his pride has been taken; Léonie with her Gallic caution has escaped.

At the top I find the Major's door intact. My newly awakened animal sense tells me he's in there. I knock hard.

'Major, Major, are you there? It's Al from the basement.'

There's a rustling inside, a shuffling as of down-at-heel slippers, a half-click of a lock. 'Al?'

'It's me. Open the door.'

The clicks are completed. A crack appears, chained across, with his withered brown pippin face slung between like a counting bead on its wire. 'It is you.' He unhooks the chain and opens the door.

'I think the house has been burgled. You'd better call the police.'

'I heard them, going from door to door, smashing . . . They tried mine but I think by then they'd had enough. What have they taken?'

'I don't know.' I see him huddled in the darkness of his room, in the bed where he sometimes brings the Asian boy he's managed to pick up in his trawl of the streets in the small hours, restlessly up and down, the night air plucking through his trouser legs at the spindle shanks, two scrawny chicken necks of skin and bone. He doesn't like trade. He prefers the plum-eyed Philipinos from the kitchens of the big hotels, their smooth olive-oiled skin and black olive hair on the oval heads laid against his spare ribs and white sparse down. He told me all that one night when I came home late and caught him in the hall weeping, Horace's thin tears riveting the flat cheeks when he'd failed to catch the unyielding boy in the Martian fields behind Gloucester Road tube. 'Captain or colonel or knight at arms . . .'

'I'll telephone them now. Stay there.'

He retreats into his sett and I can hear him dialling and speaking. 'They say they'll send somebody but there's not much they can do. It's so common in this area. I'll dress. Where will you be?'

'Downstairs in my room. Fortunately the mortice lock kept them out.' The door slowly closes down his brown and fawn woollen dressing-gown and pyjama bottoms above the veined ankles. He doesn't want to be alone but he has no choice. Modesty conquers fear. I go down through the ravished house noting the broken doors more carefully. They hang forlorn. I hope the thief didn't find Chloe's treasure chest.

I have hardly time to fill my kettle before that's him knocking on my door. 'Al! Al, are you there?'

'Come in and have some coffee. When did the police say they'd be here?'

'As soon as they could. I knew today would be a bad day. The *Standard*'s prediction last night was very inauspicious.' He jigs a little on the chair I've pointed him to, hands clasped over the knees so that his tendons stand out.

'You don't believe in that.'

'"There are more things in heaven and earth Horatio . . ."' He smiles. 'I learnt that when I was out East. I was brought up a Catholic, you see, and although I don't do anything about it I still have a residual belief. I suppose it never leaves you.'

Suddenly I see him as a character from mid-Greeneland. I could almost write the book, pastiche it together. Instead I'm

160

saying: 'We have a murderer in our midst. Did you know?'

'A murderer?' His hand rattles the cup in its saucer.

'Yes. He seems to like or dislike older middle-class, possibly upper-middle-class men. They take him home and he cuts them up.'

He winces. Then he lifts the cup to the thin bluish lips. 'But I am quite safe. My boys are so gentle. That's why I like them. And they respect ... age. No, I think I'm safe, as safe as anyone can be in life.'

'I thought you should know in case you hadn't heard.' I know that as a non-frequenter of the Knickers he may not have.

'No I hadn't heard. But in any case I have a certain fatalism and then again what is one to do?'

'Take care.'

'That's a Protestant ethic you see. My parents took care but my brother and I both caught a fever. He died: I lived. We were treated the same and loved as much. If my parents had been given the choice they couldn't have made it. But that isn't the way it works. The finger falls...'

'"The moving finger writes and having writ..."'

'A beautiful poem. I don't read much poetry now, much anything except the *Standard* and the *Telegraph* of course, but that poem says it all, I think.'

I wonder fleetingly if he was drummed out after being caught with his houseboy or merely retired, or if the rank is just a nickname he's erected over the years. 'My father was an assistant governor in Bangalore. I can still remember when they brought me home to England and school at seven, running down the drive as their car drew away, crying: "You will come back tomorrow won't you?" and waving.'

XXI

The policeman has been and gone. He will come back again this evening when everyone is in to list missing possessions they have no hope of tracing. 'This area's got the highest burglary rate in London, that is in England.'

But we're lucky. The break-ins seem clean. There's no sign that anyone's crapped in the beds or written rude words on the walls. As far as the Major and I can tell by the quick look round each door, only the expensive electronic shrines have been spirited away. I speculate again on whether the house is really his or whether he's allowed a free room under the eaves as caretaker.

The cups of coffee have consumed all my milk. I must go and buy some. Looking at my watch I see it's nearly lunchtime and I've done nothing, written not a word, and not resolved the question of whether, for the first time in twenty years, today I shan't vote in an election. I go up into the street. The pavements are stippled dark with a shower. I haven't seen Ramon since I signed the form for his nephew. I'll buy the milk there and pay my respects.

'Al, just the person.'

'How are you, Rick? How's the scourge of the mighty?'

He laughs hugely like a bull might, the big barrel of his chest and belly tub echoing with it under the flecked brown and white wool links of his guernsey, and tugs at his beard. His beached sea-dog eye twinkles with deliberate merriment. Almost he slaps a booted thigh.

'We've got them on the run. Come and have a pint, then we'll go along together to this afternoon's meeting and you can

162

see the sport.'

'I can't. I've got to get back.'

'What for? Nonsense. This is important. You can be an impartial observer and write it up for the news-sheet. Yes, that's it. That's brilliant. It will give the whole thing more validity.

'Suppose I don't see it your way.'

'You will. You can't fail to. They've really overstepped the mark this time: knocking down the Cartwright Hall at six o'clock in the morning before the preservation order could be delivered at nine. I'm sorry Cartwright's statue didn't fall on them and brain the buggers. Not that they've a handful of brains between them, just low cunning. Come along now. We'll pay you a fiver, not much but all the *Watchdog* can afford and better than a bob in the eye with a sharp stick. There's a little pub just round the corner from the borough offices where you can get a decent roll and some real ale. We can walk there and I'll fill you in on the background as we go.'

I'm carried along because the only other course is to be loudly rude and then Rick will be hurt. His black donkey jacket is powdered with dust and his brown cords bag at the knees as if he were slightly stooping. His nails are black-rimmed and broken by the assorted junk he stuffs his secondhand shop with, ancient grease-veneered cookers and fires, doorless cupboards, foxed mirrors, chairs with split pod seats and cracked rungs. Sometimes when I'm in the dim necropolis of his shop I marvel at the lives that could need such battered furnishing below the hire-purchase line of melamine and teak coated chipboard, our equivalents of the marquetry inlays of yesteryear.

Rick is impervious to the noise of traffic. He booms above it a Captain Ahab in a school of combusting whales. I lengthen my steps to keep up with him. Now we're beyond the tube station where the stream grows quieter and waiting to cross the dusty veldt of the Cromwell Road, whose plane trees pattern the air with their still leafless tracery. Once over we're in an older trellis of handsome streets, relic of the Kensington of cabs and housemaids. We pass the miniature crystal palace of the gardening shop, plucked out of Kew by a giant hand and set down here, and turn right along the High Street. We have walked for ten minutes into a different world of leisurely shoppers swanning from window to window, dipping their beaks to sample and catching their own faces in the glass before drifting on. Sometimes a whole gaggle of brightly coloured girls breaks through the stream, arms linked, chucking and gabbling with high-pitched squawks on their way to or from offices and other shops by sandwich and coffee bars. The rain has stopped and a touch of sun has wiped the pavements.

Rick's decent little pub is all coach lamps and horse brasses but the roll is fresh. Should I order fizzy keg beer out of perversity, a stand for independence? I settle for IPA, the old man's favourite. Rick takes an obscure aggressively country brew, smacks his lips and blows loudly over his first sup.

'You know all about this. The meeting starts at two.'

'It's open to the public?'

'Had to be. The *Watchdog* saw to that.'

'Power to the people.' I raise my glass.

'Grass roots involvement. Maybe they're learning that they can't ignore us.'

'Still, the Cartwright Hall is gone.'

'Yes, but if we pass a motion of censure, make enough fuss they'll be more careful next time.' He savages his roll with sharp white teeth. The drops of beer darken the fringe of moustache like sweat until he cuffs them away. I wonder if the office boys raising their elbows in the bar care about the Cartwright Hall or only about their own pecking order and when they might make it to a company car.

'Time to go. Drink up. We'll pass it on the way there. You can spill some of your best purple prose on a touching description.'

I want to shout: 'The expense of spirit is a waste of shame,' but even here the traffic is too loud.

Someone has tried to cover up the ravage with a board skirting but it doesn't reach high enough, as if an elderly stripteaser had dropped her veils to thigh level letting us see the demolition of time above. No one, I notice, has put a name to it. Above the boarding there's a Victorian rococo shell dome that might have backed a Venus birthing from the waves, broken columns and moulded frieze. The mechanical jaws have munched and torn away the whole façade so that the interior is exposed like the pitiful slashed houses of wartime I remember.

'Come on.' Rick urges me up the hill to council city, the huge redbrick and glass complex that's our new monument to civic pride with its courtyards and fountains. Rick fought this too. For him it's bureaucracy made concrete; small is beautiful. That's what he'll want me to say. But I think of the palace of Knossos, Mycenae gate, forum and temple, palazzo and parliament. Ever since we learned to put mud brick on brick or daub between split tree trunks and knap stone we have been making new castings of the universe and filling them with clerks and priestlings.

The council chamber is modelled on a Greek theatre with the mayor presiding from the stage, the actors in the audience and the few spectators barred high up in a harem gallery, impotently mute.

'Everyone rise; Her Worship the Mayor.'

'Complacent cow.' Rick shuffles to his feet. Scratch his radical skin and you let out the closet chauvinist. Her Worship has crinkly permed hair and a jut of bosom broad enough to display the second best mayoral chain. She is the pantomime dame, drag mother, despised by Rick and the Lysistrahood alike, yet I know she will stand in front of the mirror in the mayor's parlour patting nervously at the crimped blue waves, saying, 'Is me hair tidy?' and longing for a piece of bread and honey.

'That's our man. He'll go after them.' Rick is pointing out his clone in full hairy set, bellying sweater, feet ostentatiously on the next but one seatback.

'Councillor Edwards to move the motion number one on the order paper.' He untangles his legs and gets on to them. The mayor leans to talk to the Town Clerk. Three councillors get up and walk about the chamber in search of someone to have a word with. No one seems to be listening.

'Hear, hear!' Rick punctuates Edwards' words. The mayor looks up briefly and goes on with her conversation. I suspect that at least two of us in the public gallery have just come in from the cold. Already the old man by the next pillar has leant his head comfortably against it and closed his eyes. Down below is the aquarium where the fish are slumbering off their lunch, apart from stickleback Edwards of the raised spines. No natural light or air penetrate our enclosed world.

'And so I should like to be reassured by the Chairman of the Housing Committee that he has no interest to declare in the company of Wollfit and Bludgeon who have acquired the property and the permission to bulldoze away part of our historical and cultural heritage.'

165

'Good boy, good boy!'

'Alderman Wirral.'

'Madam Chair, really the opposition will seize on the slightest thing to score a sparring point. I can say here and now, indeed categorically affirm that I have no interest to declare in the firm of Wollfit and Bludgeon . . .'

'On a point of information, Madam Chair . . .'

'Councillor Edwards?'

'On a point of information: is it not the case that Alderman Wirral's brother-in-law is a consultant retained by Wollfit and Bludgeon. . . ?'

'Well done Teddy, keep after him!' Rick is on his feet.

'If I have any more such demonstrations I shall have the public gallery cleared. Alderman Wirral?'

He shifts uneasily from foot to foot. If the light were sharper we might catch him blushing. 'Really I don't think I can be expected to know every contract my brother-in-law has on a consultancy basis. We don't meet that often.' He smirks a little. 'It's hardly the sort of thing you discuss over Sunday lunch.'

'Will the Chairman of the Housing Committee tell me whether or not his brother-in-law is retained by Wollfit and Bludgeon. Yes or no.' Edwards bulldozes away at him.

Wirral hesitates. 'It is possible. It could be so. I can't say any more at this present time.'

Rick is on his feet shouting and hefting his fist in triumph. The old man by the pillar jerks awake in fright.

'I warned you. Clear the public gallery.'

'Don't worry me old dear, we're going. That's all we need. The *Watchdog* bites again! We never sleep!'

A uniformed man starts stoutly towards us puffing a little.

'Here you, out!'

I stagger after Rick, upsetting another sleeper as I crawl past her knees. She looks up at me blankly.

'I thought for a minute I was in the pictures. Must have nodded off. Is it over?'

'Only for us.' She closes her eyes again. I cast a quick look back down at the Chairman of the Housing Committee. He is sitting with his head in his hands. Several fierce consultations have broken out. A girl is getting to her feet.

'Councillor Mrs Naismith!'

'In view of what we've just heard, Madam Chairperson, I move that the censure motion be put forthwith.'

'I second that!' Several voices cry out. Wirral's companions show signs of discomfort, rout.

'Come on,' Rick is shouting at me from the top of the gallery. I dot and carry up the steps.

'Order, order.' The gavel is banging. A bell begins to ring. 'The motion is that the censure motion be put forthwith. Those in favour say "aye". Those against? Clear the chamber.'

The bell is still shrilling as we go.

'What will happen?'

'The opposition will win the censure motion because some of the wets will abstain and a lot of them aren't even there yet; Edwards sprang it too fast for them.'

'Was the Naismith girl in cahoots with him?'

'Of course.' Rick looks at me contemptuously. 'All parties stink.'

'You're really an old-fashioned anarchist at heart.'

'That's right. Well you can't pretend that if we were somewhere else, Tony Cwmri or Blenkinsop East, where the others are the ruling party that there wouldn't be any fiddling there.'

'No, I don't pretend. I know power corrupts.'

'That's why you need an opposition.' He is a goad, a gadfly. He almost dances along the street as we walk back. Huge billowing grey sheets and white aprons of cloud that have been slung out in our absence begin to fling their heavy drops down again, huddling the shoppers under awnings and into doorways. Rick is impervious to this too.

'When can you let me have the piece; tomorrow morning?'

'I didn't say I would. I'll have to see what comes.'

'You'll do it. I'll be in the shop till one.'

Suddenly I'm too tired to argue. Leave me alone, world. Let me lie down and the snows of yesteryear cover me while I sleep. I'm almost stumbling. Dimly I wonder how the censure motion has gone. Is it as Rick has predicted? I shall have to telephone somebody to find out before I write the piece. But not now, not now. 'Let us sleep now.'

XXII

But I'm not allowed to because all of a sudden everything is happening at once. Life is like that too. When I get in exhausted from my overdose of Rick there's a long brown envelope with an invitation to attend for interview for a writer-in-residency I'd forgotten I'd applied for. Then my guardian angel is on the line telling me the meeting with Larry Lofts is fixed for tomorrow and I must make it, and as I go to write it into my diary my head reels because there's David's trial in the same little slot but mercifully in the morning so I'll be able to scurry from one to the other, quick changing as I go. What a busy life you lead, Al, to be sure.

Now what do I know about Ledwitch? Not much. Cathedral city: that's about all. Go along to the library and look it up. And while you're there you can see if there's anything on Lofts. 'On loft' rings a very different bell. Must be the Old English for 'high up' or 'in the sky' or something. What it is to have a button jar for a mind.

But in the hall there's Hannalore. 'Oh Al, I have knocked and knocked on your door but you have been out. And now the examination is only in a day or two.'

'Let's have a session now. I'm sorry Hannalore. Life has been . . .' I spread my hands to indicate. We are so chameleon I find I'm foreignizing my personal dialect of English in response.

'We will have a drink in the Nevern yes?'

'Yes. First you have to go and see if you've been burgled.'

'Burgled?'

'Somebody broke in early this afternoon when only the

168

Major was in. Until everyone comes home we don't know what's missing. The police are coming back to make a list.'

'The Major was in and did nothing to stop them?' She is contemptuous as a Valkyrie.

'He's an old man. What could he have done?'

'He should have telephoned for the police.'

'They came to his door. He thought discretion was the better part of valour.'

'What is that: discretion is what?'

'Discretion is the better part of valour. It's a proverb or an aphorism. I'm not sure which.'

'I must write it down. I will go and look if I am burgled and then I will see you in the Nevern at seven o'clock.'

Brunhilde has spoken and I bow my head obediently. 'Should I come up with you to see if they've been into your room?'

'They are not there now?'

'No, I'm sure not. They were in and out very quickly.'

'Then there is nothing to fear. I will see you soon.' Coolly she goes out of sight round the bend in the stairs. There's just time for me to get to the library and back to the Nevern. It's not quite dark yet. The evenings are lengthening. How poignant that always seems. We're still animal enough to begin to lift our snouts to the Spring, to want to build and breed new hope. There's a notice about Easter closing sellotaped to the cold glass door.

Ledwitch, Ledwitch. Geography, English by county. The guide to Loamshire. Ledwitch is the capital of Loamshire. One of the oldest bishoprics and seat of Kings of the Jutes after the collapse of the Hegemony. Much besieged in the Civil War, much militiaed against Napoleon. I could have guessed all this. It's the pattern of non-industrial, non-metropolitan England. Yet somehow it helps to read it. Now for Lofts. Look for cinema among the arts.

Books, books, walls of books. They still seem precious, forbidden fruit we didn't see much of at home and those few were all bought or culled for me. I can still feel the paper and smell that damp cardboardy effluence of my first library books. *The Cinema of Larry Lofts*; that will do. That grey-coloured girl is on, the one like a stern mouse. She's got a wedding ring on the right finger. I wonder what sort of husband she goes home to, what sort of nest. No time to take

169

the book back indoors. It must come with me to the pub. There's no time either to read it all but then I don't need to, just dip and fish about for titles and subjects.

'Hallo Al! Where've you been? You're almost a stranger.' Kevin is pulling me a pint. Even your pub expects loyalty from you as a regular and gives you in return this recognition, this sense of belonging, of somewhere to go.

I perch up on a bar stool and turn the pages of *The Cinema of Larry Lofts*. It's written in an obsequious jargon that can't be in any way its subject's fault but does nothing to incline me towards him. Best to stick to dates and films if I can dredge them out of this slurry of fawning pretension. Nothing is more opaque than the outer reaches of movie criticism.

At the end of the bar the last of the early drinkers are planning where or what to eat. Shall it be chopsuey takeaway or hamburger sitdown? Alistair waves me over.

'Al, come here and decide for us!' He sways a little and his kind face is ruddy as Bardolph's nose.

'No fear. Too great a responsibility.' I am saved by the entrance of Hannalore.

'What will you have? Is anything missing from your room?'

'A pint of bitter, thank you. No. They have tried the door. You can see the marks but it has held. Now the Major will have to have, how do you call them, strong locks on all the doors.'

'Chubb or mortice.'

'Chub or mortiss. I will write that down in case I have a piece on burglary in the examination. Jemal's stereo has been taken. He is very angry and says he will sue the Major. How is it spelt the mortiss?'

'M-o-r-t-i-c-e. It's always explained to everyone that the responsibility is the tenant's.'

'Of course. But he is angry because he is robbed and Léonie is not, and he is not insured because he says insurance is a capitalist invention.'

'I agree with him.'

'But we live in such a world. One must be practical. I have both insurance and the strong lock.' She sips carefully at her drink which matches her long hair when the light falls through the liquid. 'Henry, I think he is called, on the top floor is robbed of his radio and Chloe of hers. And also beside you in the basement of, I think, a whole music centre.'

'They must have an outlet for hi-fi equipment.'

'I think so, yes.'

All the little tin gods have gone from their shrines. 'Now what did you want to ask me for your proficiency exam?'

'There is too much and I am tired. It is better if we talk, yes, and that way I practise.'

'Why are you so tired then?'

'It's my boss. He pursues me all the time and it is tiring to try to escape always or to avoid to give him the opportunity. Is correct, yes?'

'To avoid giving: the infinitive is followed by the participle as a gerund in English. You can't have two infinitives together.'

'Ah, that is so? I will write it down.'

'Go on with what you were saying about your boss.'

'He does it with all the girls.'

'It's called sexual harassment. You could complain.'

'I think so, yes. But then I lose my job.'

'He can't sack you. That's the whole idea.'

'Yes but it is not nice to work there any more.'

'But it's not nice now, is it?'

'No, but it is better, I think. And sometimes he is so foolish I am laughing. Today he leant over so far to pat me he lose his . . .'

'Balance?'

'*Ja*, balance, and fall over. He is rather fat you see. So if I expect that the hand is coming I lean also very far and then he falls.'

'The bigger they are the harder they fall.'

'This is another proverb?'

'Yes. I think it comes from boxing. Perhaps it isn't a true proverb but just an idiomatic expression.' My own tongue is faltering under Hannalore's questions. And now to confound it more Léonie is coming towards us. She offers me the smooth cool planes of her cheeks to kiss.

'I need a drink.'

'What will you have?'

'A glass of white wine.'

'Is Jemal coming?'

'I hope not. I have just left him. He is angry because his stereo radio has been stolen and mine hasn't. I offered him mine to borrow but he won't have it. He wants to be angry, I think.'

171

I don't want the evening to become a vicarious extension of their lovers' quarrel. 'Hannalore and I are discussing sexual harassment for her Cambridge Proficiency exam.'

Léonie laughs. 'Oh we all have to suffer them: the gropers and the grabbers.'

'What is that?' Hannalore's biro is poised.

'Nouns made out of verbs by adding "er" as in "to run; a runner".'

'This we have done. But the verbs? What are they?'

'To grope and to grab.'

'Spell them for me please.' I do so. 'What do they mean?'

'To grope is to feel for; usually in the sense of a person who can't see, groping for a way. To grab means to seize in your hand.' I make a snatching motion. 'Like this. Grope especially has a rather unpleasant sexual meaning.' Solemnly she writes it all down.

'If they are too persistent,' Léonie says, 'you have to slap them or say, "What do you think I am, hey?" Then they will stop because they are frightened if you speak about it openly. When you say nothing it is a kind of conspiracy between you and they think you like it. I always say: "Look here I don't want to mix my business with your pleasure so lay off."'

'"Lay off", that is an Americanism yes?'

'Definitely not for Cambridge Proficiency unless it's Cambridge Massachusetts you're doing.'

Hannalore frowns a little and then smiles. Léonie laughs and swings on her heel, her eyes drifting towards the door where Jemal might appear even though she doesn't quite expect him. And I long for a girl's eyes to go seeking for me like that.

'Al, I will buy you a drink.'

'Only a half. I have to go home and write a report.'

A half later I'm leaving. Jemal hasn't come and Léonie has nearly given up watching for him.

How shall I cast this report. The *Watchdog* is eponymous. Putting the simple facts in its clarion style doesn't interest me. It must be a *Romance of the Devil's Fart*, your lost work, master, you bequeathed to your godfather and re-invented by Rabelais. What devil's dance shall I make of it, what infernal saltarello for Tusker Edwards, Cur, Dogstooth, to ballet with Cupidity Wirral, Swindler, Rogue? Lay on Demons. Have at them. I pick up my pen.

XXIII

Carried away last night I scrawled on, sipping at the Côtes de Ventoux until the last paragraphs are the bemused wanderings of a drunken fly fallen into the inkpot, an insect *Iliad* of dragged feet, Codex Bacchus. Now up early reading it, I find the words just about decipherable. I beat them into type shape two-fingered. The need to hurry gives me no time to be apprehensive. Dressed in my best denim suit I go out into a raw morning with the weather echoing the heart and setting the blossom ashiver. The grey light drains all resonance from the pink and yellow petals and dims the grass in the cemetery opposite Rick's shop as I pop the envelope into the hazed chrome letterbox lips and back away. Grave monuments jut like broken teeth among the stretching arms of branches hung with thin cloaks of mist. Making love in there must always be a kind of necrophilia, death presenting himself to couple with in denial of love.

I catch two quick stops on the tube, fall out into the throng scurrying to work, and then have to double back overground. Obscene faces leer at me out of the novelty shop window. A dragon coils its green length. Demon and Hecate beckon among the carnival trappings of ticklers, streamers, vizards, bat wings and unfunny hats.

The houses are tall in dark burnt brick. I turn off down a side street that seems entirely residential and begin to panic that I'm mistaken and not in the right place at all. Suddenly the houses fall back and there's the magistrates' court, unappetizingly grimy and David standing outside with two young men, one neatly suited with briefcase who must be his

173

lawyer and the other thin in windcheater, jeans and a pale Bob Cratchit face.

'Thank you for coming. This is Mr Dove, my solicitor and this is Harry, Henry Peters.'

I shake hands all round. 'How do you see it?' I am asking young Mr Dove.

'I've been trying to persuade Mr Wilson and Mr Peters to plead not guilty. I don't think the police have a case. Nothing happened. No crime has been committed. They allege behaviour likely to cause a breach of the peace. I dispute that. They can't prove any such thing. I think the whole thing is nonsense and they should plead not guilty.'

I look at David. His hands are bloody with his bitten nails and his face is blank with prolonged shock. Henry Peters shoves his hands into the pocket slits of his thin jacket and shivers. His face is pinched and waifish, the sparse moustache droops as if he's damped it with licking his lips.

'If we plead not guilty they'll make much more of it.'

'I know you're right in principle,' I say to the lawyer, 'and I wish they could fight but if they attract the interest of the press it doesn't matter whether they win or lose. David will lose his job.'

'And so will I,' Henry Peters' starveling lips put in. They gleam a little as he moistens them again. There are deep bruises of exhaustion under his eyes and his boy's skin is grey and muddied.

'You look tired.'

'I haven't slept properly since this. If my boss hears I've been in court I'll be sacked.'

'I'll do whatever you want of course.' Dove looks at David.

'I don't think we have any choice.'

We all walk silently up the steps, through doors curtained with dust into an entrance hall like a station waiting room. There are doors marked 'Police' and 'Public' and one sinisterly labelled 'Gaoler'. There's a couple of wooden benches scarred with the black fingerprints of burns where cigarettes have been rested and forgotten. The walls have a Dickensian dinginess. Expressionless policemen pass to and fro, sometimes calling out a name. A figure detaches itself from a group or unsticks from the wall and goes into the room marked *Gaoler*. The lawyer is explaining that when their names are called David and Harry will go in there too.

'I'll go into the public gallery and see you outside after your case. Then we'll go and have a drink. Don't worry: it'll be over in a few minutes.' I try to put reassurance into my voice. They are called. They're to be charged together. They disappear into the dark hole behind the gaoler's door. I wander over to a list hanging on the wall.

Most of those shuffling their feet nervously in the hall are some shade of brown. I look down the rota of people appearing today and their charges: maintenance arrears, driving offences, drunk, disorderly, debts, soliciting. The faces around are depressed; their clothes seem to fit them badly perhaps because they've hunched into themselves. The stuff of them seems thin and cheap but that may be an effect of the poor drained light.

David and Harry Peters are spat out of the gaoler's mouth. We stand a moment or two waiting and then the number of their court is called and they fall in with the slow queue of defendants. 'I have to go into court now. They'll tell you when the public can go in.' Dove smiles at me and takes his neat suit and unscuffed briefcase away down a corridor.

We, the supporting cast of friends and relatives, are left backstage to eye each other surreptitiously. From time to time someone bold or exasperated enough asks the guardian policeman if we can go in yet. I don't hear the word but suddenly everyone is pressing forward into the square box of the small courtroom. The benches for us are like box pews, narrow and hard so that we're banging each other's knees and ankles trying to get in. I sit here alone feeling criminal. At any moment the judge will come in and sentence us all to deportation, hanging or life for surely we must be some rebellious crew, some rioting rout or rabble penned up together.

The magistrate comes in. He looks a neat fatherly man in a dark brown suit. A trail of dismal cases begins. I can feel my anger growing at the pettiness of them. You might have found yourself here, master, for rolling home to your room one night from the Pomme de Pin unable to keep a straight line, falling in the gutter. Who's this now? *Maistre Jean Cotert, pour boire tost et tard.*

'Don't ask me to give it up, sir, because I can't. I'd rather be dead. I've tried.'

'Did you go to the rehabilitation centre last time?'

'Yes sir. I went there for a fortnight; it didn't do me any good.'

'I shall bind you over to keep the peace.'

'But it's no good. I can't promise not to take a drink.'

'What are you saying? Do you want me to send you to prison?'

'It's no good me promising.' He is passionate. He spreads his hands in appeal.

'Either you agree to be bound over or I send you to prison. Which is it to be?'

'Bound over. But it won't do no good.' We all laugh.

The magistrate has nothing else he can offer. The drunk is pleading for honesty, for a recognition of his reality but the law can only offer the rote in tattered ermine and wig disguise and he must lie and appear again as soon as he's picked up until he is sent down for the first time and then, once begun, again and again. Does the fatherly magistrate never drive home pissed from his Sunday drinks party and be helped to bed by his wife?

The trail continues. Blue uniforms give their evidence in the official garble. Bald tyres and no insurance, the small dealer pleads for a fine rather than to lose his licence and livelihood. A girl who could be Sally appears for soliciting and is formally slapped down for a tenner.

And now it's David and Harry Peters. They stand shoulder to shoulder in the dock with their backs to me. They plead guilty. I can hear the buzzing in their ears, feel the taut skin over their cheekbones, the chokepear in the throat, the trembling legs that threaten to let them down. The policeman opens his notebook and clears his throat. In response to a complaint from a member of the public car number X12 investigated and found the prisoners embracing in the street. The gallery laughs out of relief and disbelief. The magistrate looks up sharply. The evidence of arrest drones on.

'Is that all? Do the defendants wish to alter their plea to not guilty? I am rather surprised that the court's time is being taken up by this. Have you anything to say?'

Harry Peters says, 'No sir,' in a very little voice.

Young Dove bounces up and pleads David's good character and respectable position and suggests without actually saying so that there is no case to answer.

The fatherly figure listens impassively and then says: 'I am not convinced that you have been well advised in your plea, however in the circumstances I must order you to pay a fine of five pounds each and be bound over for six months.' They turn and hurry out. I get up and begin to push past knees and ankles again, hoping that the magistrate's words haven't aroused interest in the breast of some cub reporter eager for glory.

I wait for them in the empty hall. Dove bustles back. He is cheerful, triumphant. 'I said the police hadn't really got a case. The magistrate knew it too. They would probably have got off, had it dismissed completely.' What we neither of us say is that now they both have records it will take five years to expunge, perhaps never from the police computer.

We have been playing the subtle game of hypocrisy where all the pieces are yellow and everyone loses. David and Harry Peters come into the hall, both a little flushed and breathless.

'We were paying our fines.'

'Let's get out of here.'

We go out into the late morning where the mist has lifted and the sun is trying to come through.

'Well that's over. I don't think you'll have any more trouble unless you get rearrested in the next six months.' We all smile weakly.

'What about a drink?'

'I've got to get back to work. I told the boss I was going to the dentist,' Harry Peters declines. 'I'll ring you.' He shakes David's hand and then mine and Dove's.

'We'd better not kiss each other goodbye,' David jokes.

'Not for six months anyway.'

He goes off down the gritty street still looking small and pinched.

'I've got to go too I'm afraid.' Young Dove smiles.

'Thank you for all your support.'

'I still wish you could have pleaded differently.'

'Ah well, next time.' They shake hands and he swings away with his briefcase.

'Nice lad.'

'Yes.'

We turn and walk the other way. I know he feels eyes are on him from every window and passer by. 'You need a whisky. Let's go in here.' I lead the way into an unknown pub where elderly women are just raising the first Guinness to their lips and the first dart game is flighting quivering into the board.

'I'll get them.'

'My legs seem to have gone.' He sinks down on the split padded bench beside the window.

'There, put that inside you. I don't think the press were there and if they were I'm pretty sure they won't bother to report it; it isn't exciting enough for them.'

'I'm going away for a few days, down to Elizabeth's cottage. I've told them at work I've got the 'flu.'

'I'll monitor this week's papers and let you know if there's anything. Give me her number again in case I've lost it.' His sister will cosset and restore him. 'When are you going?'

'This evening. I'll have a little sleep and get myself in a fit state to drive.'

'I've got to go and see the great Larry Lofts,' I say to change the subject for him, knowing how the mind wheels and circles a sharp point to pitch down again and again and start away.

'Thank you for coming. I couldn't see you but I knew you were there. It helped.'

XXIV

I feel too sick to eat. David and I have parted at the station and now I'm on my way, still in my best denim, to St John's Wood. You knew prison and torture, master, but then so did many people in your day. It didn't carry the stigma it does now. You could call your jailers: 'treacherous curs

> *Who made me cry for hard crusts*
> *To munch many a morning and night'*

and expect to be pitied, even paid. You could rail against Bishop Thibault and his flushings of iced water funnelled into your lungs till you thought you would drown or the frail tissue burst, tell it to the world without shame or disguise.

My breath seems shallow as if I'd been climbing. It's the altitude of fear I suppose, vicarious guilt like children know in class when someone's accused and you feel your own cheeks begin to burn, your tongue to stutter in sympathy. I've got a piece of hard potato in my chest that won't go down. We use shame as a social control for all those little failings flesh falls into, with all the panoply of the law, the formal charge, arrest, evidence, a court that's the Old Bailey in little.

It's no good worrying about it. Turn your mind to this meeting. It's hard to know in advance what to say. Lofts must like the idea or I wouldn't be seeing him. I'm glad Simon is going to be there to hold my hand. This is my trial too. Twice in a day is too much. Here's where you get out. Hang on to the rail as the train slides in. Mind the gap that reaches up to swallow foot and leg and gulp you down into the pit below to be fried and mangled.

There now, you can poke your head out into the air. That's better. Rooks are tossed about a windy sky like charred letters. Is it because I know that I'm further north that the canopy of clouds in air seems higher? You can't even tell with humans. We make the world to fit us and our mood. There's more space on the ground too: just a few people walking and some going north in cars. Up there's the Heath and below it Belsize Park where I used to visit Karl and his mother when we were in our first year. I'd never been that far north before. It seemed a different city. I had such a sense of their flight from Berlin, of great dragon steam trains trailing plumes of smoke and bearing them across frontiers, a continent, to fetch up with weak tears of relief in this redbrick backwater. Freud died in Hampstead too.

This must be the turning and there's Simon at the end, unruffled as ever.

'Have you been waiting long?'

'No. I've just arrived.'

'What do we do?'

'Ring the bell and play it by ear.'

The houses are tall, double fronted in stone cladding with classical porch and broad tall windows looking out onto a hedged garden. Lofts' has a dry stone fountain basin heaped with the bright blue berries of grape hyacinth. Daffodils hold up their poached egg heads along the path. I realize I'm looking down very carefully to place my feet. There was a boy in a children's story I remember called Johnny-scan-the-dust who found a ruby and got the girl after they'd all laughed at him for always looking where he was going.

A woman answers the bell, secretary, wife, mistress and takes our coats. Then we're shown in to an elegantly proportioned room that was probably the library when the house was built and is again now. One of the two men gets up to shake hands. He's the producer but I can't hear his name properly because of the singing in my ears, the siren's song of fright that blots out all other sounds and memory. Simon has told me, I know, but it still hasn't stuck or struck any root in my mind.

Larry Lofts lounges green lizard in a deep armchair. He holds up a hand. I go over to shake it.

'The trouble with these things is that you can't get out of them. Have one.' He waves at the rest of the furniture. We all sit. His belly fills out an emerald sweater with holes for elbow patches.

'Larry,' the nameless producer is breathlessly deferential. 'You've read Al's synopsis.'

I tell myself that this is the movies and that I must expect him to use just my nickname even though we haven't said more than 'Hallo' to each other. If I understand these things aright he's the one who will have to find the money and organize the whole affair. He looks like a kindly old-fashioned grocer, the sort who wore a brown overall and called the customers by name as he parcelled up sugar and soda into stiff blue bags.

'He's a fascinating character, old Villon. I did some reading up on him. I see him as a prince of thieves; the movie as in the tradition of Brecht's *Threepenny Opera* with Villon as a Macheath figure. We'll have to update it a bit. Can't have him running around in a long nightie. Set it against the French Revolution; that way you get a comment on both periods at once and by extension our own; makes it more universal. Actors can't handle those night shirts. It makes them look as if they're in fancy dress.'

'*The Lion in Winter* worked quite well,' I hear myself suggest tentatively.

'If you like that kind of thing. How do you see this character? We'll have to call him Frank by the way. François's unpronounceable in English.'

'Yes, I'd decided that too.' I'm glad to be agreeing with him. 'I see him as a rather incompetent crook, trying to be one of the lads but running off at the crucial moment.'

'Essentially a weak character?'

'Yes. His strength is a writer's strength rather than that of a man of action. He's flexible and imaginative, a survivor.'

'The mastermind. He devised the robberies and was laughing in the pub with the birds while the rest were falling off roofs and getting picked up by the fuzz. Now what about the gay angle. One of the things I read said all the Coquillards were bent. What about the relationship with Charles of Orleans?'

'He turned up there cold and hungry during his first exile and Charles took him in. He liked to surround himself with poets. He ran little poetry contests where he gave them the first line and they all had to write a ballade, himself included.'

'Did our Frank win?'

'History doesn't relate and neither does he which rather suggests he didn't.'

'Suppose he did. Charles was a rich old aristocrat. Up comes this poor boy, a poet and a thief. Charles offers him the prize in return for a favour or two. I can see the scene. Light from the sconces falling on his very pale thin young body and the old man's hand shaking a little as he reaches out.'

'Villon wrote a poem for the birth of Charles d'Orleans' daughter while he was there, saying she had saved his life.'

'How old was he when he came to Charles' court?'

'About, about twenty-five or six.'

'That's it then. He offends the Duke, holds out a bit against him maybe and is thrown in jail. Then the baby's born. Frank writes a poem in celebration, is let out and this time he gives in. We could make a whole movie round that. Forget the French Revolution. Plenty of dungeons and torture and corruption. The feasting and drunken riot in the city to celebrate the birth while Charles is thinking of Villon chained up and he's begging the gaoler for pen and ink to write the poem that will get him off. Or maybe he writes it in his own blood. The gaoler laughs at him and won't give him ink. Or maybe he gets the gaoler's wife or daughter to bring them. That's the classic. I'm thinking aloud. I like that image of the firelight falling on the blue-veined hand and the white city boy's skin. What else have you got?'

'There isn't any evidence that Villon was homosexual.'

'He doesn't have to be. He's poor and seducible. Maybe he ends up liking it. How do you see the end?'

'Well, there's no evidence there either. He could do a sort of *Scholar Gypsy*, twitch his mantle blue and go off into the sunset.'

'It's been done too often. I think he should die; makes a better ending.'

'But we don't know how.'

'That doesn't matter. We can try out two or even three endings and see what works best in terms of cinema. We can have one where he dies tragically with some faithful bint sponging his body and then lying beside him to warm him up like they did with King David in the Bible, only she does it for love. Or we can have him hanged, with crowd scene and Frank making a big speech before he's turned off. That famous poem of his about the bones being picked would make a theme song.

182

Or we could have him turning religious, going into a monastery but the sins of the flesh still being too strong. He falls for a young lay brother and they wall him up, both of them, together.'

'I think if anything like that had happened we'd have known about it. The story would have come down. The first one is probably the nearest to what actually happened. He says in *The Testament* that he's ill, his hair and eyebrows falling out, and gobbing up phlegm as I think I say in the synopsis.'

It's lying there on a side table. My carefully clean pages are out of their folder, crumpled and somehow grubby as though they've been around a long time. I can see the perfect round imprint of some sort of cup or glass as if Lofts has fixed his seal on them.

'So what do you see as the love interest if you don't buy the gay angle? Where does the sex come in?'

'There was a woman he was in love with called Katherine de Vausselles who treated him badly, had him beaten up and sent him away.'

'First she gives him everything. De Vausselles sounds rich. Rich bitch with poor boy. Then she takes this Noël you mention as a lover and Villon is beaten up. Then what?'

'He writes *The Testament*, gets into trouble, is sentenced to be hanged, appeals and is sent into exile.' I can feel myself becoming blockish, recalcitrant. I'm a mule crying. 'He, haw', and digging in its hoofs.

'There's no shape to that and not much sex. You've got to have shape and sex. Maybe she visits him in prison and they have it off in the straw. Then she takes out his letter of appeal. We could do something with that I suppose. Then when he's banished she goes with him. She's the girl sponging his body. But even her care can't save him and he dies. Then she's alone in this one-horse village with no money so she has to take a lover, the landlord of the inn they've been staying at and we end with him coming up to her room, his gross belly against her body: beauty and the beast. It's all been for nothing but somehow it's worth it because we've got the poems.'

I can't disagree with that. Aloud I make myself say: 'Yes, that could work. We don't know what happened and that could be a version of the truth.'

'I'd like to get Tessa Hargreave to play Katherine; someone bony-chested and classy. Very sexy. Villon's more difficult but he isn't so important.'

'I thought Leo Compton would be good.'

'He's a dog.' He yawns. 'Late night last night. This morning.'

'Oh yes,' the grocer is on his feet. 'We'll leave you. I'll call you, Larry, this evening. I think we can make a really good movie here.'

We all shuffle to our feet. I wonder whether to go and shake hands but Lofts is waving a hairy paw. The woman, secretary, wife, mistress appears, as if summoned. Perhaps there's a bell-push hidden in the armchair. She gets our coats, murmuring something about the weather.

'How's Chris?' the producer asks.

She makes a slight face. 'So-so. Better I think.' The door shuts behind us. We Indian file up the garden path and pause for a moment outside the gate.

'I'll call you when I've spoken to Larry,' the producer says to Simon. 'Very glad to have met you.' He shakes my hand and goes off down the road. Simon and I walk to his BMW parked at the kerb. I am filled with a brown miasma of gloom and feel sick again.

'I'll ring you as soon as he rings me.'

'I don't know what to think, what to hope.'

'Don't worry about it.'

'He'll make such a sensationalist stewpot of it all.'

He shrugs. 'That's the price... Do you want a lift somewhere?'

'No thanks. It's not far enough to the tube.'

'I'll speak to you soon.' He gives his usual reassuring formula that means: 'You're not abandoned. Keep going.'

I wave and watch the car purr off. The sky is very very pale blue behind a thin gauze of cloud.

XXV

But by the time I come out of the tube at the other end, a worm of meat extruded by the mincer, the cloud has thickened and towers over the rush hour street a chill wind funnels down, blowing wrappers, hurriers-home with turned-up collars, dogends, plastic cups along the traffic stream. The wind at my back, I'm bowled along too. On the corner flower stall freesias freeze in their cellophane jackets, daffodils tremble in their buckets. The seller stands massive in a lit doorway waiting for anyone brave enough to stop and be whipped cold. Often I wish I was a painter. Hopper, for instance, could have caught her there as she stands, forever. I need a great figurative to hold this city now. Perhaps I should advertise in *Creative & Media Appointments*: destitute writer wants mad painter for hopeless project. Money no object. Or is it one for the personal column: with a view to creative relationship?

Let me just get in out of the wind, make a cup of tea and collapse. I'll sort out the evening later. The teabag is doing its drowned mouse act. I draw the warmth of the room comfortingly about me like an old dressing-gown. The foxes have holes and the birds of the air have nests and city humankind have invented the bedsitter to lay their heads in. 'And I alone lie in my bed' or 'And I lie in my bed alone' as the lady said, one way or the other.

The telephone breaks into my sleep. Was I dreaming? Yes, but it's going as I pick up the phone, an image of a dead love falling back, fading like Eurydice. I'm still too asleep to say the number, just: 'Hallo.'

'Al?'

185

'Simon?'

'I've just heard from the producer. I'm afraid it's no go.'

'Well, I half expected that. What did he say?'

'Apparently Lofts said he couldn't work with you. It's a kind of tribute in a way.'

'I suppose he's used to yesmen.'

'I expect so.'

'So what do we do now? Will he try another director? Or give up the whole idea and we try another producer?'

There's a slight pause. 'It's not quite like that I'm afraid. Lofts is insisting on another writer.'

'But it's my synopsis, my idea. He wouldn't even have thought of Villon without it. Can he do this?'

'Well as you know there's no copyright in ideas so technically he can. I tried saying a few things to the producer but he's determined to go ahead.'

'What about compensation and a credit: from an idea by . . .'

'He doesn't acknowledge any obligation. He says anyone could have thought of it. Ideas are around all the time . . . Villon isn't exactly unknown.'

'But anyone bloody didn't. Isn't there anything we can do?'

'I'll talk to him again but there's not much we can threaten him with. Even if we had the money I don't think we could fight.'

'I know, I know. There's no copyright in ideas.' I don't mean to be rough with Simon but there's no one else.

'I'll have another go and talk to you soon. Meanwhile get on with the radio programme. I'm sending you the contract for that. Let's get it in before anyone hears that Lofts is going to make a film.'

I see at once the danger he's gently pointing out. I can lose you by this, book, programme, years of work. You're not mine any more. I've pandared you off to Larry Lofts and the grocer. I've been weighed, done up in a blue bag and put aside on a shelf, short measure.

'Okay. I'll do that at once. I've got an interview for a writer's fellowship out in the sticks at the end of the week.'

'That might be a good thing for a while. Give you some money and a chance to look around a bit.'

'You think I should take it if I get offered?'

'Oh I think so, in these hard times . . .'

Now I'm alone without his voice to hang onto. Who was it had the punchline 'We wuz robbed'? It sounds like Runyon. I can't even show the place where my treasure stood, the dust template where the thief lifted it away. Take off the top of my skull and you couldn't point to the bit of grey matter that contained it. It's as if a scalpel had lobotomized the small section that held you. It can't be. You're still there. My knowledge of you hasn't gone. It's changed, though. I feel its difference like looking on a face you're no longer in love with.

There must be words for this pain. 'No worst there is none'; that's it. Hopkins is the boy for a really jagged despair. Still Hamleting, Al? Where's the table so you can get down to your meat? There's an alternative reading no one's suggested yet. God it hurts.

> Larry was a welsher
> Larry was a thief
> Larry came to my house
> And stole away my breath.

Let me not be mad, sweet heaven. Ring Paul and see if he wants a drink; not David, he's had enough for one day and anyway he's probably on his way to Elizabeth by now. That snake in the grass, he'll make his fawning film about you and your poor poet's life and rob the living to do it. Ring telephone, ring. Oh my head's not the button jar today, it's the broken toy box that every battered scrap of childish comfort can be brought out of and wept over.

'I've had a rough day. Do you fancy a drink?'

'There's a show at the Hole; why don't we go up there for a change?'

'Good idea. Where shall I meet you?'

'I'll be in the last carriage of the first train from here in about twenty minutes. If you don't jump in I'll jump out and wait on the platform.'

'Okay; see you.'

That's best: movement, purpose. Jacket on; out of the house. I see his face peering out of the lit door as I run up and jump in.

As I look round at the faces going east into megapolisheart for their night out I feel suddenly old. The middle-aged natives don't travel in tubes. They're outside in cars and cabs or safely parked in front of the telly. Night trains are for the young and the lost. A tramp is asleep opposite in the warm, to wake at Arnos Grove, change tracks and slumber back to Heathrow. A tribe of young punks put their multicoloured coxcombs together in a corner by the door, supporting each other with their closed world jargon, argot of in-words like your rhymes in thieves' cant.

We bend our heads, rounding the corner into the wind's cut. The Wookey Hole Tavern looks a flat nothing on the outside; only the leaded panes let enough light through to show that there's life inside that engulfs us as we push open the door, with its warmth, press, falling fountain of light and sound. We go through the ritual of ordering:

'What'll you have?'

'You having a pint?'

'No, I'll get them,'

as we push through into the bar behind that's the black cavern of the witch's hole, the cave of light with high overhead an electric star or two pinpricking the ceiling. The lit corner bar and disco rostrum are pools of colour in the darkness letting enough spill over to make out faces and forms.

'So what's happened?' Paul hands me a pint.

I explain in short angry bursts that bring relief. 'But can he do that, Al? Hey, the bastard.'

I explain why he can and will. Telling him I've lanced out the poison, I can shrug and say: 'That's life. How's your job going?'

'Not brilliant. We've a whole block to wire out. Concrete floors and no heating. But they're a good bunch of lads. We have a lot of laughs. They think I'm a great one for the girls. I never say nothing but they make it all up because they think I'm crafty. There's a dishy boy over there. Can you see him? Don't turn round. In the stripey sweater.'

'How's Frank?'

'Very poorly since he's got his ticket. We had a really heavy scene last night. He said I was hard but it's just that he's going and I find meself drawing back all the time. It's an awful thing to say but I'll be real glad now when it's all over and he's gone. It hurts too much, you know.'

I hear my own words from earlier. 'Only the dead feel no pain,' but not much pleasure either, eh Mr Marvell? *Tous sommes sous mortel coutel:* we're all under the knife of mortality.

'Ladies and gents we have a special treat for you tonight: the fabulous Cockettes. This is their first appearance at the Hole and I hope you'll give them a big welcome. The Cockettes will be starting their show at ten o'clock so make sure you get your drinks in in time. Thank you.' The barman gives the microphone to the disc jockey.

'And now we've just got time for a couple more before showtime.' He presses his magician's buttons and the sound wells up taking over, making feet tap and lips mouth the words.

> 'Momma said you can't hurry love
> You'll just have to wait,
> Love don't come easy,
> It's a game of give and take ...'

I move towards the bar, doing as bid and getting us a fresh round. By the time I'm served the second record is nearing its end.

'Ladies and gentlemen give a big welcome to the sensational Cockettes.' They scuttle through the crowd up into the glare that highlights the wigs, one blond, one dark, the panstick, the yellow taffeta wedding cake tiers of stitched petals with matching bows in their false hair, the white ankle socks and dancing pumps, the lollipops as they mime to a childish female duo:

> 'I want to be somebody's baby ...'

flickering out long wet tongues to dab at the round headed sweets on their sticks with cheerfully obscene innuendo. The song lisps on as they shake their Shirley Temple curls and prink and pout. Then the tempo changes, the lights sink while the dark one scurries off stage, the blond whirls away the lollipop and seizes the microphone to mime the Streident classic.

> 'I'm just a girl who can't say no.'

The hands are white and small and there's only a suggestion of five o'clock shadow to deepen the jawline under the make-up. The effect is principal girl who will age to ugly sister. The song reaches climax, the head and arms are flung back so that the pink mouth and straining tongue glisten. Pearls of sweat are strung along the upper lip. The music fanfares, the lights bow again and the blond baby is replaced by the dark boy.

Now he's in leather pants and waistcoat with peaked cap and whip. His face is decadent clown's with streaks of gore and heavy eye shadow. His leathered groin bulges, his feet are bare as he slashes and prances in the Transylvanian transvestite routine, boy vamp, Dracula's young David with stony seed in his catapult. It's nearer to Isherwood's Berliner ensemble than we usually come.

He stomps his way to the end of the number, flings off and there's a pause while we wonder whether there's time to talk. But the music is rolling again and the two are pushing past, nice girls growing up, secretary birds who sing 'Sisters' with their arms round each other and then open oversize lunch boxes to produce a series of improbable knick-knacks: chains, whips, manacles, and other fetishist gear they toss aside to knowing laughter until they reach the giant rubber pricks at the bottom.

It's the old god phallus in dwarf hat, satyr rampant of ritual and vase painting, Priapus of the comedian grin, puckish ramrod dying of the doldrums that they kiss and nibble, puppeteering with its mobile head as they sing 'Give me a man'. The music changes; their backs are to us. When they turn again it bursts into 'Look what you've done to me . . .' as they show their ballooning bellies, aping dismay above them. The audience howls with delight at this new shape change that ends with a bang not a whimper as they burst them against each other and take flight in the half dark.

The music swells stately for the finale. Now they are queens promenading, managing their trains and teetering heels with counterfeit regality. In the voice of Vera Lynn they proclaim that there'll always be an England. From the back wall where we haven't noticed them leaning until now, they fetch and unfurl union jacks against their dark blue gowns. Then they march and countermarch with them, pomp and circumstance. I look round and see a few lips framing the words.

'Land of hope and glory, mother of the free . . .'

They face front and stalk stiff-legged towards us, managing to salute and hold the flags crossed at the same time. Many of the drinkers are joining in now.

'Wider still and wider may thy bound'ries stretch . . .'

Does nobody else see any ambivalence in this double parody of Mother England that drags at the emotions and lifts her skirts to show the hairy thighs in the jutting cami-knickers. Yet I feel my lips moving too as the old heart-jerker pulls irresistibly, bearing us all along with the pantomime dames:

Make thee my tear yet . . .
Make thee my tear yet!

XXVI

'Ladies and gentlemen the Cockettes will be back to give their second show at ten-thirty. Meanwhile let's give them a big hand before I play you a few requests.' The clapping is spasmodic. Already minds have turned back to the quest, the pursuit of the moment.

'Not bad,' Paul says. 'I thought the dark one was quite dishy when he was doing the David Bowie bit though I'm not into whips and all that sort of gear myself.'

There's a face, no not quite, more a back of the head and profile, I think I recognize down near the rostrum. She turns, she's coming this way and now I'm sure it's Lisa though I haven't seen her for a few years and her hair is almost white but in the same putto curls.

'Hello,' I step into her path smiling. 'I thought it was you.'

'Hello, Al,' she says back. 'You know Diana?'

'Yes of course.' I smile at the heavy set woman behind her, remembering that Diana teaches PE in a girls' day school or did. 'It's a long time. How are you?'

'We survive.' Lisa looks at me and then away at the crowded faces and I'm chilled as ever by her lack of pleasure at this chance meeting. She wouldn't want it to be known that she ever comes to such places.

'This is Paul.'

She brightens a little and prepares to be friendly until she realizes that he isn't an academic or even an office worker.

'What are you doing these days? I heard the Hathaway had closed down?'

'Yes. I got a good redundancy settlement so I'm doing

nothing.'

'That should give you some time to write.'

She makes a little face and I remember the time I kissed her and see her again smiling enigmatically across the English Library table at some piece of student wit when we were all young together.

> *Ou sont les gracieux gallans*
> *Que je suivoye ou temps jadis,*
> *Si bien chantans, si bien parlans,*
> *Si plaisans en faiz et en ais?*

Oh master how can I give you up to the Larry Lofts of this world? How does it go?

> *Where are those gracious gallants*
> *I ran with in the old days*
> *Singing and talking so brilliantly*
> *With such charming words and ways?*

'The old days' for *jadis*: how about that then? Where are the snows of the old days or where's the snow we used to have in the old days? Too many syllables.

'Have you seen David lately?' Lisa asks me almost coldly and I remember there was always something strange there, almost a touch of jealousy, although there needn't have been. She was the one who went to bed with him not me.

'I saw him yesterday. I think he's gone down to Elizabeth's.' I didn't mean to lie but it's said now and truly this morning feels like yesterday. Will he have told her about his Wildean episode? I'm not sure so I'd best keep quiet.

'And what are you doing now, I suppose one should ask?'

'Feel no obligation.' I'm annoyed as I imagine she wants me to be. 'However I'm writing a radio programme.'

'What about?'

'Villon.'

'Ah. Prose?'

'Some prose for the life; some verse translation.'

'Other men's coat tails. I thought you wanted to be the literary Lautrec of the underworld.'

'I do. But epics are unfashionable.' I laugh to plaster over the wound she gives me.

'You should try for an academic post. Then you could put your feet under the high table and sip sherry like Tolkien.'

'I don't feel old enough yet. Maybe I never shall.'

'Al, the eternal student, or adolescent. What are you waiting for? Nothing's going to happen now. Admit it.'

'Just because you've given up writing.' I don't want to say this to her. It cries out against me as too harsh but I'm lashed into self-protection. This animal bites if tormented. She's still pretty. Her skin is smooth, less bagged than mine though she's older. The white hair seems almost an affectation.

'I wasn't satisfied with the second rate. There are too many minor talents about.'

I won't give her the satisfaction of pushing her words to their logical conclusion. Better to bleed quietly inside and show a whole skin. The fires of the camp crematoria play round her still, as they do round Guzzle, I suppose, but with Lisa they have always danced and flickered like an impulse from that magnetic shield we all carry about with us, the aura of the parapsychologists. Her mouth is full of the boneash of those long dead and it chokes her with bitterness. What right has she to be alive, she asks herself, or to try to achieve anything when so many perhaps better people died. I must remember and not let her hurt me. She looks towards the door.

'Are you going?'

'I think we're on our way. They're all much the same: once you've seen one drag act you've seen them all.'

'Not Issyvoo enough for you?'

'There aren't any people of that sort of stature any more.'

'No doubt that's what they said in his time in lamentation for Hardy and Kipling.'

'You haven't changed Al. Why don't you grow old gracefully, give in like the rest of us? Accept reality.'

'There's no such thing. Or rather there are so many versions you can usually find one to suit your size. When people talk about accepting reality they usually mean the map without Utopia. As a good Wildean you know one shouldn't.' I'm laughing as I say it.

'Oh Oscar; he's no saint.'

'I always thought he was.'

'I was very young at the time.' She turns to Diana. They are about to go but the electronic drums are rolling and the lights going down.

'*Mesdames et Messieurs, faites vos jeux.*'

'Ladies and gentlemen for the second time this evening give

194

a big welcome to the Cockettes.'

The bar is completely dark. Flame leaps up in it and lights a second. The twin plumes begin a dance, not towards each other but over the body of each torchbearer stripped down to black leather leotard. As each torch flares across its owner's face in passing the set serious features have the look of priesthood. The flames demand complete dedication if they're not to sear and run riot. This is the Cockettes' real act. The other was dressing, dressing up in the Empress's clothes.

They run the flames over their arms until we think we can smell the singeing hair. They pass them between their thighs until we groan with the giant fiery pricks that can't be doused. They carry them to their lips to lick, tongue against red and yellow tongue, or firehead; they thrust them down their throats and gulp at them, shutting the fires momentarily from our sight so that we feel the red seed burning like lava down to our bellies and then letting them burst out of their mouths in fresh yellow flowers.

There's silence in the bar as we watch like children in the dark of bonfire night, the rockets go up and burst. Now each has a short fiery solo while he plays with his flame, feeding two or three spikelets into his mouth in quick fire, juggling glowing balls, pouring hot coals on his hair until we expect to see it break into a blazing halo like Blake's Satan. Sometimes we can see in their own light the hand that holds the torch; others, the fire seems to float and move of itself, Jack-o'-Lantern.

The boys' faces painted, demonic hover in the glow as they near their climax. This isn't the purging fire but the heat of passion they wield and suck at and we applaud like imps as they grow more daring, thrusting, cocky in their mastery. Yet each is alone with his flame. Our eyes go first to one, then the other. It's a kind of seeing who can shoot farthest. There's a new crescendo of drums. Their single flames split into three and they begin to gobble them, quenching and relighting the globules of fire, hissing out in the wet pink mouths and snapping on again in a mounting climax that doesn't come but ends as the lights are washed over the two slim black figures bowing, smiling and running off with the trip of trapeze artists. The air is full of smoke and the rancid smell of burnt grease. Their flame was real. When I look round, Lisa and Diana have gone.

'Who was that then, Al?'

'An old friend I haven't seen for years.' Should I have said to him: 'That was temptation, the demon despair that sucks a small wound in the throat to let the lifeblood ooze away.' An image out of Spenser and Hammer horror, overblown, yet Lisa has always had the ability, power to demoralize me, perhaps because she, the refugee, was always more at home in English society than I was, or seemed coolly so.

Lisa had no accent she need fear losing. What accent did you rhyme in, master, the *bon bec* of Paris, Les Halles Billingsgate for the *jargon et jobelin*, Coquille cant? It was a game, a mask. You weren't really one of the boys, just a young pretender, dancing in the straw for their amusement while keeping half of yourself apart and your tonsure in trim. There I go, still making you in my own image or me in yours. I can't tell any more.

You thought you were old, dying even when in our time span you were a youngster still, not old enough for middle management. Even I'm too young to be Prime Minister and yet Lisa makes me feel, tries to make me feel decrepit, *passé*, as if it all has to be given up, the juice and flush of hope. Why?

Because hers was doused in those bonefires. If I'd tried, all those years ago, a quarter of a century, could I have poured my blood through her veins and made her live or would it have been another face of my phantom that Nightmare-Life-in Death, *La Belle Dame*, old beldam that rings the changes through my heart?

Paul's handing me another pint but I'm alliteratively pissed already. Look back at the footprints in yesterday's snow and see them walking up their own path to where you stand. And tomorrow's white drift; does your shadow already lie over it? Yet there's nothing to do but go on, unless, like Oates, you turn aside and let the blizzard brush out your steps.

Lisa's chill fire gnaws at the mind's bone, turning my will to ash that crumbles and sifts down to a little nothing, not enough to boil an egg by. I've lost my way on your gibbet hill, master. The wind blows too cold and my flesh blackens. The streets press against me as if the houses had your lowering top storeys that keep the rain off but block out the sun.

The last bell is ringing. Drinking-up time's over. The music is killed.

'Are you all right Al? You look a bit pale.'

'I'm a bit pissed.'

No I'm not all right, as the old man used to say. I'm half left; the leftovers. The air smacks my face but it's numb and hardly feels. A wino veers past, mumbling on his way to some vacant lot. We have to go through the railway arch to get to the foot of the pedestrian bridge. The dark grey bundles have beached here. Three of them huddle round a heap of glowing oddments on the pavement. Each has his own bottle that goes from torn overcoat pocket to mouth in a hand gloved in grime. Their eyes are screwed up in red-lipped purses of skin. They look up as we pass, wondering whether to try a touch but by now too sluggish to move fast enough. Their three shadows cartoon the curved roof. A train fills the brick tube with its thunder, and walls and pavement tremble.

Out the other end I find I'm trembling too. Roofs, gantries, hoardings are cut out in black on the red sky. The whole city seems to be burning, falling into the dark Thames soundlessly and yet still the sky glows with a cold heat while its reflection drowns.

'Are you all right?' Paul is asking again.

'No, I'm half left,' I say, this time aloud.

XXVII

Waking I feel that shame of half remembrance. There was Lisa. I can see her quite clearly but what did I say to her? Maybe I made a pass at her. No, Diana was there and I certainly wasn't that far gone. What then? 'Words, words, words.' I don't remember getting home yet I'm here and I seem to have done everything as usual. Habit is a wonderful thing, Al, and now it will get you up, wash and dress you and make you eat a sensible breakfast.

The muesli is going down like the chaff it really is. How do horses enjoy it without the dried fruit and milk? I turn on the wireless but it seems aggressively loud. In all yesterday's excitement I missed the election results and media-life is so instant, just add boiling water and stir, that it's history already and unmentionable today as yesterday's cold greens.

This morning I must sit myself down to the radio programme with Simon's quiet warning ringing in my ears. Larry Lofts shan't leech you quite away, master.

NARRATOR: It is nine o'clock on a cold winter evening. *Sound of an old bell heard distantly.* That's the little bell of the Sorbonne. Its Angelus notes mark the beginning of curfew. Sometimes they find our hero lurking in an alley or still banging his cup on the wooden table of the Pomme des Pins but tonight he's safely home. He's home because he's broke, and because he wants to finish the poem he's writing before he goes away tomorrow, leaves Paris for an exile he doesn't know the length of yet. It's December 1456.

That's it. I'm off. Narrator: that's me. Voice over or under;

inner voice. Will they let me do it I wonder, or will they want to use an actor? Continue.

His candle has burnt down to an end, a drunken wick in a pool of tallow with the flame grown long, yellow and smoky before it finally cants over. He's been scribbling for hours with the ink threatening to freeze in the pot and wearing mittens to keep his fingers supple enough to write. But he's nearly finished. He's written his will, a last list of mock bequests before he goes out, perhaps never to return. They'll enjoy this when he's gone, his roistering rogue companions. It'll remind them of him. Frank Villon won't be quite forgotten, not while this joke's still going the rounds.

Is that really my voice? It's one of my public voices, the one I like people to hear; tough, amused, throwaway, yet capable of getting a catch in it. We speak so many dialects to ourself and others, especially those of us who grew up bilingual, home- and school-tongued. Get on with it. O'Casey had GET ON WITH THE BLOODY PLAY pinned up over his mantelpiece. Or was it pasted to the mirror in the overmantel? It doesn't matter. It's the message not the medium that counts. Time for your voice to come in, master.

Now there's a problem. Should it be in French or English? French followed by a translation breaking in and taking up as the French is faded out. Will they wear that? Come on, it is Radio Three. It's standard practice for the glorious foreign dead. Just do it that way and wait for anyone to object. Get on.

> *Fait au temps de ladite date*
> *Pour le bien renommé Villon . . .*

Fade out. Fade up.

> *Done on the aforesaid date*
> *By the well-named Villain,*
> *Who eats neither fig nor date,*
> *Dry and black as an old mop,*
> *With no tent or pavilion*
> *He hasn't bequeathed to a mate,*
> *He's nothing left now but a little bullion*
> *And that'll soon be his last drop.*

He jabs the quill at the paper for the final full stop. That's it; he's done it. If only he had a drink. Or a girl. But he hasn't. Now there's nothing to do but creep under the covers thrown over the straw mattress and try to sleep the night away.

What would they do if I had him tossing off there before he falls asleep? Not for Auntie Beeb I think, though it's probably the truth. He was young and alone, a little afraid and elated with finishing his verse bequests. He'd have wanted a girl to snuggle up to. Don't we all. Aye there's the rub, rub-a-dub-dub.

Most of the time in the Middle Ages it must have been too cold and not private enough to take your clothes off. But then they didn't have much in the way of underwear so you could turn a girl's skirts right up and she would lie there like a flower, with spread petals, and belly and thighs for its heart of stamens and nectarous pollen-brushed seedbox.

> Lightly into bed you leap then
> wrap your arms around the prize
> suddenly she turns her back
> and begins to close her eyes
>
> What's to do then hero conqueror
> force your way into her charms
> or be tender, smile and hold her
> sleeping in your conquered arms?
>
> I am not the one to tell you
> night by night I weep and pray
> that the dawning near tomorrow
> sends me a victorious day.

Oh god that softness, that curve of breast and the quickening of a soft fruit nipple to firm life. How can I write in this state? Better to get it over quickly, take the head off lust and try again. You and your girl, master, are my soft porn and I'm you sinking down on her mouth, her arms going round me and then the lush burst of entry. Oh god make me chased!

The phone, the bloody phone at the crucial seconds. Hang on whoever you are, I'm coming.

'Hallo,' I'm too out of breath to say the number. Will they hear my hot quick pants?

200

'Al?'

'Yes.'

'It's Greg, Al, Gregory North.'

'Oh.' A voice from the dead.

'Were you working? I'm sorry to disturb you.'

'No, no. That's fine.' Pull yourself together. 'How are you?' Why am I asking him? I don't really want to know. I don't want to talk to him at all. I'm asking because he's caught me with my pants down.

'Never better. I'm starting a new series of programmes for Channel 4. That's what I'm ringing you about.'

'Oh yes.'

'An alternative voice to the trendies who've rather taken it over.'

I almost gasped with amazement then. Lust is in full flight, open-mouthed as you might say. Can he be putting this forward as a serious proposition and expect me to swallow it?

'It's thought it needs a broader spectrum so I've been asked to do something about it. We've put together a small consortium to make a series on social and ethical questions.'

'But you're still the Member for Arlington? I haven't missed a bye-election?'

'No, no.' Greg laughs solidly. 'No you haven't. I'm still the Member.'

'But not PPS for Clegthorpe?'

'Not since I joined the Greens. That wouldn't be acceptable to either of us.' He laughs again.

'I never quite knew how that happened.' I am probing disingenuously.

'I was approached. People knew I wasn't happy.'

When you saw you weren't going to be made a junior minister straight away without an apprenticeship, that people wanted to watch you for a bit and see how you would turn out having jumped into a safe seat on a telly ticket because your face was familiar. You saw the years passing while you sat on the back benches being loyal with that as its own reward and you began to feel qualms of conscience about the way things were going.

'And are you happy now?'

'I do believe it was the right thing to do. I don't think the party can be saved. They've got too much of a grip. A little bird told me you weren't too happy either.'

'Who is.'

'That's why I'm ringing. You see in this series I want to really explore the question of conscience.'

'"Doth make cowards of us all . . ."'

'What? Oh yes. But that's consciousness isn't it, over-nicety of conscience. It's something we might explore in the course of our discussion though.'

'What discussion?'

'Well what I had in mind was a sort of Putney debate on the air or rather the sceen.'

'Isn't that rather the stance of the other lot, the Leads, digger-levellers all, and ranters too.'

'One mustn't let the devil have all the best tunes or arguments. The other side has to be heard.'

'How do you intend to *structure* this great debate, to use the cant phrase?'

'Well I think a fairly simple series of interviews, no gimmicks but really lengthy, in-depth discussion so that you can really get down to the roots of unease. That's what I'm calling it: *The Roots of Unease*.'

'And you'll do the interviewing?'

'That's what they seem to want.'

'The North Debates.'

'Something like that.'

'Who else do you have in mind?'

'Well, it's early days. I'm really just taking soundings.'

'Oh come on Greg. I'd have to know what company I was keeping.'

'Well Tania Sizeman has agreed to do one. Do you like her work? I think she was quite brilliant as Millamant.'

'I didn't see it. The theatre's too dear for me to go often.'

'That's something we must change, of course.'

Tania Sizeman signed the original Ladywell declaration in *The Times*. I don't blame her but I can just see what Greg will do with her. I can see him leaning forward with great concern on his face, hear her impassioned reply: 'My voices were right.' Not a dry eye in the audience and another clutch of votes for the Greens.

'I thought we'd do the discussions live. I've booked the old Shepherd's Bush studios and we can get in a live audience. I want that degree of reality, of involvement so that you can really open up, let people see the inner workings: a conscience at work.'

I can't believe it, can't believe what I'm hearing, that anyone can deceive themselves, himself so much. Does he or is he just an emotional sharper, deliberately trying to pull the wool over my eyes? Wool, what wool? What does that mean? The hangman's blindfold. Or just a mat of hair falling forward and blinding you like an old English sheepdog, sheepishly.

'Suppose I say the wrong thing, don't fit in with your thesis?'

'I'm not worried about that Al. Truth is truth, don't you think. I know you're totally honest . . .'

'Indifferent honest. Suppose the wind is southerly . . .'

'I'm not with you . . .?'

'Hawks and handsaws. There that's your *Times* crossword clue.'

'Crossword?'

'Yes. My cross word Greg. I don't think so.' Not today thank you. Take your wares somewhere else, huckster.

'I'll ring you again. You think about it. It'll take some time to set up. It's a chance to say what you really feel without pressure.'

Only the pressure of your scalpel, the blade of your ambition dissecting, slicing me through for the watching students until I cry out, bleed, pull my viscera through the slit stomach wall with my own hands and in the process tear down people, beliefs I have trusted, or no that's too simple, not trusted, loved.

There's a strange smell in the room. What is it? 'I have to go Greg. There's something burning.' I put the receiver down and turn. The room's full of smoke. Now I remember. I put a slice of bread under the grill. I snatch the pan away, almost dropping it it's so hot. The toast flames. It's charred black as your gibbet flesh, master. The terror of fire, that half-tamed thing Prometheus brought us as flowers from the fields of the gods, strikes at me. I blow on it to put it out. The flames sink, die. Soon it will be cool enough to throw into the waste bin. I lie down on the bed again but this time feeling only a little sick. I take a deep breath or so. My fire's out too.

XXVIII

I have to find out what's happened with the election, the one I didn't vote in. I don't suppose elections went on much in your day, master, or if they did that you bothered yourself much with them. Will you forgive me if I leave you for a bit? I'll come back and get on with the radio programme. Now I need a newspaper.

It's colder this morning. A few flakes, Cocytus feathers, drift down to leave damp fingerprints on the pavement. I feel one that lights on my cheek, a chill touch that dissolves to a tear. The passers by are pinched and hunched down in their jackets. The bones in their faces show under the reddened skin and their wrists are raw between sleeve and pocket. I'm glad the seventy-year-old newsboy on the corner knows me. He puckers his currant-bunface in a grin and pulls out the *Groan* from the neat fan on the pulpit of his wooden hut that seems as if it's been there since Victoria commissioned the Albert Memorial. How much longer, though, I wonder? I should like to be the chronicler of such ephemera, put them into loving words to keep for ever.

'Parky this morning. You all right?'

I grin back, warmed at this small contact. 'Fine,' I lie. 'You? Keep warm in there.'

He nods and winks with the old Londoner's gesture of cocked, cocky head that means the world's still going round as it should. I tuck the paper under my arm and cross in an oasis of calm in the traffic to the big delicatessen whose pavement front is set out every morning with boxes of bright fruits and vegetables, a miniature Covent Garden. I remember someone telling me that was a London custom too, spreading out over the pavement in a perfect display of the coster's art. I need coffee to help with the writing.

The girl at the checkout is a young Indian wife with belly full of child. This morning she looks grey with fatigue, and sickness I suppose. I want to send her away to lie down instead of perching on her hard stool in the purple sari, a tired bird of paradise pecking at the keys of the automatic till with soft thin fingers. I wonder about her life, whether she was born here or imported for marriage and if her husband loves her and her young brown body. Perhaps I should get myself an Indian girl to soothe my old age. Could you buy one if you sent to that continent and where's the difference in buying one-night stands? Ah, I would care for you, brown girl, and when I was dead you could take my money home and buy yourself a beautiful young lover.

I am not that old. This city has worn me down in its service till I feel as you did, master, on the eve of departure. She rings up my coffee and packet of buns and tries to smile. I go out into the cold loud street and hurry towards home like a hibernator fooled by a patch of sun into waking up too soon.

Good coffee I allow myself as an extravagance, and my trusty Italian coffee pot. I love the spiced pepper smell when the metal seal is broken or the airtight sack snipped. The taste is never quite as good as that. Perhaps I could become a gourmet, an epicurean substituting flavour for passion. The coffee pot chugs fatly. It's time to open the paper and find the post-mortem if there is one.

Yes. The middle-page spread is given over to pictures and my pain, analysis, figures, conclusions. The leader's face, haloed with patriarchal hair, looks out at me. The camera has caught a flash in the lens of his glasses so that he seems blind, the sockets filled with opaque milk instead of a sharp stare taking in the world, facing it down.

That's what we want of a leader, a bully boy or martinet, ambition with a goad. Instead he offers us reason and we stick our thumbs to our noses, and our tongues out like rude children, call him silly names and blame him for not beating us into the shape we want. We put him there to hold us together and then tore him in two between us. 'Things fall apart, the centre cannot hold.' We're the dogs with the coursed hare, a live end each in our mouths. Only he doesn't scream. He goes on trying to string his warring sinews in one body, patiently, cheerfully even.

Someday it'll all be seen clearly, as everything is in the end. That's one of the things Revelation gets right, the eventual coming to light, the sea heaving up its wrecks and the earth its bones. Posterity will look at us in amazement, shaking its head when the skeletons come tumbling out of the cupboards and the long-yellowed love letters give up their tales.

And the schismatics who've torn great holes in our body while searching for our soul are like all those fanatical soul-surgeons who never cared if the patient died as long as they held his repentance in their hands in the end. Look how Burnet harried the dying Rochester who only wanted to live, how roundhead and cavalier ripped at our bellies in pursuit of truth and the Jacobins offed with their heads until the blood baths were full and our ideals drowned in them.

We've been massacred. That's clear from the figures. No wonder Greg was so cock-a-hoop: the Greens have done very well. Stigwood's neoists have gone down worst. Where there was an old retainer the votes held up. What do we glean from this? That the British like what they know; that they're anti-intellectual, conformist. What do you do? Give them what they want while hoping to lead them gently on. But I wanted them to understand, to stand up for each other like men, not grab for themselves and their offspring because a greedy gene dictates.

And the sunderers don't care as long as their point is made, their purity kept. I go round and round it like the ox with the water wheel only I don't come up with anything half as useful. I don't even irrigate my own desert. I wonder if the Old Testament prophets felt like this. At least they could go up into a mountain and let off a Jeremiad. That must have made them feel better.

Leave it; look at the home news and then get on with the bloody programme. Here's a snippet: 'Man in Death Plunge. *The coroner returned a verdict of accidental death on Eamon O'Halloran... Drugs and alcohol.*' So that's that. His family will be glad it wasn't brought in as suicide but sorry not to be able to lay it at anyone else's door. That leaves them their bewilderment. Why? What else could we have done? He shouted from the rooftops too but it was a cry for help. I wonder if his mother wishes she'd never borne him to die in a

206

strange country so pointlessly.

Still he might have been an IRA bomber and been killed in Northern Ireland, shot by a soldier or blown up in his own blast. We hardly notice any more. The papers are filled with a steady drip of blood that no longer stains our consciousness. Here's a little sectarian tit for tat: a father shot in his living room in front of his children in return for a policeman gunned down on school patrol while the kids fled screaming from the bloody crossing.

Maybe the O'Hallorans came here to escape all that. It gives life or death a terrible inevitability. Your number's on the bullet. 'This one shall I save,' said God, 'and I do not care. And this one shall die, and I do not care.' It's the child's boot on the scurrying beetle. We have to live with randomness and violence. That's the message from the medium today.

We clamour to be allowed to destroy ourselves in the name of some mythical freedom. For years we wouldn't submit to seat belts. Now at last they're here and accident wards all over the country are closing for lack of custom. Sometimes freedom is another mask of Freud's old death wish. Not Eamon O'Halloran though. He didn't want to die. He wanted to live. He called out, 'Help me!'

Such pleas may lie. Most of us pretend to ourselves and others that we want life, more abundantly and then we can't grasp it. We let love die, nibbled away by habit, abraded by everyday. And yet love is the only thing on life's side, that can hold up time and keep out death. Love's a dear poultice over the mortal wounds we give ourselves or that are doled out to us. The barriers break down that lock us into our bodies. Loving, making love lovingly we no longer know ourselves from each other, transcend time and the self-absorption of the biological unit, the shell round every breathing mollusc. It's anti that sect of one we all subscribe to.

It's the carnivorous cycle of the world we imitate with our human violence, the dog eat dog, the old bitter chestnut of *Ilkley Moor Baht 'at*: 'Then we shall all have eaten thee.' Such feeding off each other can be a kind of loving cannibalism but we don't see it like that. We each make our stone pyramid and embalm our heart for our own immortality.

The strained face of Stigwood looks out too from the page. They have caught him, of course, with his mouth demagogically open, slightly askew when his more usual interviewing face is composed into a smile. Yes, I will come back to you, master. Now where was I or rather where were you? Leaving Paris, huddled under the quilt. I must go back to your beginning.

NARRATOR: He was born in Paris in the year Joan of Arc was burned.

XXIX

That went much better. You can rest now. I've kept you on the go for long enough and now you're starting to complain and sit down at the roadside crying that you're not well and I'm as bad a torment as Bishop Thib, that fat cat of Orleans.

> *Let his fifteen ribs be bruised*
> *with big mallets, stout sledgehammers*
> *with lead and suchlike balls...*

I'm so deep in it the entryphone buzzer makes me start.
'It's Paul.' Behind his voice I can hear a lorry thunder.
'Come in, come in.'
We both reach my door at the same time from our different sides. 'Why aren't you at work? Do you want a cup of coffee?'
'That'd be brilliant Al, thanks. It's cold out there. I had the morning off to go to the hospital. I've only got a dose again.' His face is strained and raw with the cold rain the snow flowers have become, that's somehow chiller than the flakes' light touch. It falls through the pores of exposed skin and seeps down to leak through the joints and into the bones displacing warm marrow with a freezing trickle. I put on the coffee pot and reach for mugs and milk.
'I must have got it off Frank because I haven't been with anyone else. When he went to Amsterdam that weekend he must have picked someone up even though he said he didn't.'
'Are you sure?' I pour a thick molasses-brown stream into each mug. One says *I Love New York* and I inherited it years ago when I took the room on. When I go I should leave it, like burying a coin in the footings. When I go?

The other has an old advertisement for Pears soap on it. On a bad morning I can't drink out of it or the one that says *Brasso* so suggestive are those old names and symbols. I shall give Paul the Pears soap one.

'Ta. Yes, I'm sure. I found a little spot last week and a bit of a discharge. I kept hoping it would go away like but it never. So I rang up work this morning and said I had to go to the doctor and took meself down the clinic. They're so nice in there. Eh Al, this is brilliant coffee. I must get into the real stuff.' He sips, the strain dying a little from his face but the eyes are still hurt and wary.

I imagine his misery looking every day at the little weeping eye in the puckered scarf of foreskin hoping to find it dry, feeling the hot piss sting its way out and dreading.

'It's always busiest on a Monday. Everyone gets up there then. Today wasn't so bad but I hate sitting and waiting so everybody can see you.'

'Well presumably they're all there for the same thing so no one can feel superior.'

'No, but they know why you're there and what you are 'cos it's mostly gay guys.'

'So are they, then.'

'I suppose so. Then this nurse calls us and puts us in a cubicle and tells us to take me pants off and lie down on the bed. Then in comes this really dishy young doctor and asks us some questions. And I asked him why I keep getting these things and he says, "You'll have to stick to one partner or be celibate." He's very relaxed about it all. Do you think he could be gay?'

'He might. Doctors are only human though you mightn't always think so.'

'This was a really dishy geezer.'

'You'll be going there more often then.'

'I've got to go back on Friday for the results of the blood test. I've got a whole file there now, inches thick.'

'It can happen to anyone. Think of the long-distance lorry driver who left his mark all the way up the M1. Nobody ever found out every girl he went with, so the chain will have gone on and on until somebody breaks it by going to the clinic.'

'Some blokes don't seem to care. They say they don't bother, don't even notice but I'm on the watch all the time and I couldn't not go and get something done about it. But I don't know why I seem to catch everything that's going while others get away with it.'

'Maybe it's your clean country blood that hasn't built up any immunity to nasties,' I joke.

'Now I'll have to have it out with Frank because he'll have to go too. That'll mean another heavy scene because he'll try to deny it.'

'At least you'll send him back a nice clean boy.'

'In some ways the worst of all was the crabs. I couldn't believe it. I'd never seen them before. I nearly went mad. I cut all the hair off with me nail scissors. To look at yourself and see something move. There must be some terrible dirty people about.'

'Unless they're like animal fleas and prefer nice middle-class homes with central heating and wall to wall carpeting.'

Paul sips again at his coffee, his hands clasped around the mug for warmth and comfort.

'It made me feel really sick. They ought to be able to find a cure for these things, stamp them out.'

'Perhaps they don't try hard enough. Anyway if it means giving a lot of monkeys syph I'd rather they didn't bother.'

'Fuck, there's enough human monkeys going about with it for them to find something out. It must be a funny life for that dishy young doctor handling people's dicks all the time. It must right put him off.'

'Maybe he's taken a vow of celibacy. That's why he wished it on you. Perhaps he's a reformed rake.'

'I think about it, you know, but I couldn't. I wish I could find someone really nice to settle down with. I wish they weren't always going off one way or the other.' He looks down into his empty mug. 'Thanks for the coffee. I'd best get back. I'll say I've got a sore throat. Shall I see you later?'

'I'll be in the Nevern about half eight or nine.'

I see him out and come back to you. Did you have the clap? Is that why your hair fell out? Even young Keats got it. I remember how shocked that young Japanese professor of Eng. Lit. was when I told him. 'You are quite certain?'

'I'm afraid so.'

'You have broken my dreams. I have thought he was romantic.'

'He was but he was human too, young and passionate and there was no going to bed with a nice girl like Fanny.'

211

'You are absolutely certain?'
'It's in the letters. Have you read the letters?'
'No. Now I don't want to perhaps.'
'They're very good. Strong and vigorous.'

It's a sad thing to break someone's dreams. Yet if they're based on a lie there's nothing else to do, and poetry and pox have often lain down in the same bed.

> Heine's racked there in his attic
> like the princess with the pea
> half a dozen mattresses
> can't disguise the pulse of pain
>
> Great venereal bitch you screwed him
> up and cracked his balls and spine
> still he wails above the walls of Paris
> stanzas of the one he never had
>
> Cockney Keats a-dying youngly
> he too felt your loss and pain.
> 'I should have lived and had her,'
> that's the harsh beat of his last line.
>
> Come then poets late or early
> Venus holds you at your death
> her last will is what you utter
> with your dying breath.

'Poetry and pox are curse enough for one,' as the satirist said with mercurial wit when they closed the door of the sweating tub on him. I could weep for that pursuit of lust looking for the alchemy of love to gild loneliness, clapped out nightly in the Knickers and all the others, the Nevern too. It's the price we pay for failing to find love, that or loneliness. In love we can float free, play, grow, a baby in the warm amniotic fluid hearing another heartbeat close, fed, warmed and not alone. How I wish you a happy ending, master, even Larry Lofts' version mark one with the girl stretched beside you holding you in her arms as you cough your lungs up. As long as you didn't give her the plague in payment.

XXX

Looking at my diary I see it's tomorrow I've got to take myself down into lushest Loamshire for that interview. I must be brisk. Ring the talking clock at Paddington for trains to Lugmouth or is it Haftesbury? What happened at Haftesbury? Something must have. It has a Civil War ring. Ring: that's it. The country of rings and tumuli, old rituals, gods and goddesses. That was the name of a dance we did at school, in the playground, grimy paw to paw when dry, in the hall with slap of Woolies sixpenny rubber daps when wet, smelling of old mackintoshes and children's skin that has still an almost sour-sweet milk savour lingering of breast or bottle. We weren't even princes let alone gods. Now I think about it I remember the title was just 'Goddesses'; simply that. I wonder who or what we thought they were or come to that what the title meant, whether they were great ladies come in their coaches to dance on the green or Clare's country maids out for green gowns.

All this because you're off to the wilds in the morning after a job you probably won't get and don't even know you really want. They want you there at 10.30 the letter says. You'll need to set the alarm. Clean your shoes now, look out a decent shirt, brush the scurf off your jacket collar. All you'll have to do in the morning is get up and put the lot on. Organization, that's the key to a productive life. Keats liked the Devon maids. Milkmaids were thought clean because their skins were clear of pock marks and because they dabbled their hands in milk. There must have been a confusion in people's minds between the poxes. Somehow I feel he picked it up on his walking tours with Brown rather than in London but that may just be because I want to think that, don't like to see him in bed with the rouged trulls of the stews but rather in the straw under a summer sky with a rosy peasant.

I don't want him squashed under a Fat Margot like you, master. You could handle it and come out more or less unscathed if there's any truth in that ballade and you weren't just posturing for the price of a drink, *En ce bordeau ou tenons notre estat*, 'In this brothel where we two keep state'. Now I'm being as bad as the Japanese professor and not wanting my golden boy sullied. I suppose it's because in spite of what I said to Nagasaki, or whatever he was called, for Keats it was a falsification of love when that wasn't what or who he wanted at all, whereas your Katherine of the twisted nose seems almost a conventional figure from a tapestry of courtly amour and your cries of pain troubadour triflings picked out on a lute. Your purse was more pierced than your heart.

There that's everything ready I think and the envelope behind the clock with the bumf I can read on the train going down. I mustn't get too pissed tonight; perhaps one in the Knickers first and then a quiet saunter to the Nevern for a couple and so to bed. I don't want to be muddy-eyed and thick-tongued in the morning. I'm talking as though I want this job. A bit of me must, I suppose, to have applied. Who else has been short-listed? Maybe we'll all be on the same train like some hideous eighties version of *The Orient Express*. Thank god it's stopped raining and my shoes will stay clean.

The bar's full for so early in the evening. As the door flaps to behind me I see into the smoky pool of light beyond the short funnel of the entrance, the silhouettes of a couple of dozen shapes and the music is loud, making the voices rise in volume to be heard above it. I push through to the bar and inch out a space in the red mahogany to get an elbow on with my pound flagging for attention.

With the glass held up I turn away to find somewhere to prop myself. There's my best corner. An angle between the glass and wood partition and the wall, with a ledge to rest the pint on where I can watch the world. The outstretched glass carves me a way through. Now I'm here I take a mouthful and look round. The music is frenetic disco. The sweet smell of pot drifts through the bar.

On the far side I can see the slim figure of Ismail deftly

214

picking up glasses. He comes towards me with both hands full, smiling his shy, sweet smile.

'You're back then.'

'They have kept my job for me.'

'How was home?'

'It was good to see my family.'

'You look very well, rested.'

His hair is like black wet boot polish and his skin is ivory. Sometimes when he's been working too hard at his classes all day and every night here, it becomes almost green. Heterosexual, teetotal he's like a figure from a Mughal book suddenly stepped off the page into here.

'I have found a girl, Al.'

'Oh good. Is she English?'

'No, she is from my own country.'

'Better still. Did you meet her at the school?'

'No she is living in my house all the time. I hope you will meet her.'

'I hope so, too. But I don't suppose she will come in here. Does she like science fiction movies?' I laugh.

'She begins to understand now that I explain them to her. I have taken her to see Kubrick's *Space Odyssey* and we have discussed it together.'

'What does she do?'

'She is a nurse. I hope that eventually we will be married but I will have to go home again and ask her father.'

Absurdly I feel happy at this unlikely flower blooming in Earl's Court so far from the banks of their native Nile, this fragile white waterlily cup they hold between them.

'You'd better get on.' I nod towards the bar where I can see the manager looking across to us. 'This isn't the time to lose your job.' We smile at each other with the secret of his girl held between us and he moves away, his fingers holding the bunches of empties in an everyday juggling act. I look at my watch. Another half hour before I'm due to meet Paul. I mustn't drink too quickly. I must think of tomorrow.

But the bar is very tense tonight and the feeling of expectancy washes over me, making me sip nervously and look around to find where it's coming from. There's a little group of queens down by the bar: four of the regulars and, a bit apart, two I haven't seen before, a boy in an apple-green boiler suit with a flop of blonded hair falling over his eyes and another

215

brown-skinned in pink trousers and a white tee-shirt. They let their eyes flicker over the other group and back and then across the other faces in the bar, testing.

The regulars chatter among themselves and push each other in the easy rough and tumble of young animals. From behind I catch a scrap of talk. 'Don't be bitter because life is so short and so trivial.'

There is a pause, almost the jukebox hiccoughs. Just for a second all looks waver towards the door and then the dropped syllable is picked up and the other lives go on. Raffaela is coming towards me across the room, the talkers parting to let her through, for tonight she is a movie queen. Her skirt is a full falling circle of red silk, her black heels raise her slim height even higher, the leopardskin top swells gently over the mounds of padding. On her head a hat with a bunch of poppies has perched. The make-up is perfect. She is well-kept Latin American mistress or business wife. I bow as she reaches me. The long eyelashes flutter. She puts out a hand.

'Do you like it?'

'It's quite splendid.'

'I do it for a friend, for a dare. He likes it, likes me like this. He dared me I wouldn't walk down the street and in here.'

'I'll get you a drink.'

As I push back towards her with it I can see the full effect. In any gathering she would be beautiful and undetectable. It's a perfect performance with none of the usual giveaway touches.

'You almost deceive me. Be careful I might fall for you.'

'Oh Al, have I done it well?'

'You should be in cabaret. You're much better than all the drag acts in the pubs and clubs.'

'I want to please my friend. He is new, not like the others. He is very quiet. His life has been sad with an ill wife. He flies to different places all the time and he always brings me a present. You see this?' She fingers an opal pendant against the *café au lait* skin. 'He gives me this. He has very good taste, don't you think so?'

I look at Raffaela and say, 'Very good taste.'

She's so beautiful my own world shimmers as if about to dissolve.

'What's happening over there?' I turn our attention to the divided group of queens.

She tosses her head above the little storm. 'Those are two

216

new ones trying to get in. Did I tell you I have a new place to live too? It's very modern and clean. You must come and see it.'

Suddenly the two groups coalesce like pools of quicksilver running together. A tall regular with pigtail, knee britches, silk jacket tattered as a battle flag and fedora lifts a finger to the newcomers and wags it under the green boiler suit's thatch.

'There will be trouble. I shall go. I don't want my clothes spoiled or my face.' Raffaela pouts and empties her glass.

'What is he saying to them?'

'That there are too many here already trying to do business, that they should go back to their own pitch.'

'Why have they come here?'

'Perhaps they are banned as trouble-makers.'

I feel her tenseness. She's excited like the carnivore by the smell of danger. 'Perhaps there are too many where they are. But there are too many here.'

The green boy is answering back vehemently. His eyes flash and his head tosses. A very young brown queen starts forward and spits at him. I see the blob of spit hang on his cheek catching the light and beginning to ooze down in a glutinous tear. Their voices are harsh now above the music and the ground bass of others.

'You black bitch, you fucking queen!' The boy in green lifts a hand in the air. There's a shout, a pistol shot of cracking glass and the third boy snaps a pint against the rim of the table, steps in front of his group and touches the other's neck with a bright blade, drawing a tight lace of blood.

The green boy falls back, his hair flopping, a hand on his throat crying sharp and high with fright. The other new one puts an arm round him. His group pull off the boy with the glass who is screaming abuse, hysterical with self-justification, now that he sees blood.

'I've called the police,' the manager shouts as he bundles out from behind the bar with two of the staff. The screaming boy has dropped the glass and his friends are dragging him towards the door. The green boiler suit has collapsed into a chair and is whimpering as the blood trickles between his fingers.

My own breathing is quick and hard. Turning I see Raffaela has slipped away. I follow her out into the night and walk along towards the Nevern. The air is full of Spring scents suddenly. The grass in the private garden in the middle of the square has

217

had its first haircut of the year. I take deep breaths of its fresh scent as I pass and gradually my heart stops thudding.

It was that drunken brawl that nearly did for you, master. You'd gone to supper with two others at Robin Dogis' place at the sign of the chariot and you were all on the way back to your room in the cloister of St Benoït, to keep the party going.

'Come back to my place. I've got a couple of bottles there.' So you and Robin Dogis, Rogier Pichart and Hutin du Moustier set off through the narrow cobbled alleys, along the rue des Porcheminiers and into the rue St Jacques where you found the law clerks of François Ferrebourg still scribbling away like a battery of Bob Cratchits and spat at them through the lighted window, at least Pichart did.

They can't see your faces outside in the dark but they pick up the candles and run out: 'Do you want a fight?' Pichart says and belts one of them. Then it was all in together until they managed to capture Hutin and pull him into the house while he's shouting 'Murder!' This brings Ferrebourg himself out. He gives Robin Dogis such a shove he falls down but he's up in a couple of seconds. His dagger is out, glinting in the candles. He stabs at Ferrebourg and runs. Then all hell breaks loose. Ferrebourg calls the cops. They yank Pichart out of the sanctuary of the Cordeliers, Dogis out of his bed at the sign of the chariot, Hutin is handed over to the Watch and then they come for you where you're shivering under your blanket in St Benoït.

You were sentenced to be *pendu et estranglé*. It is Christmas 1462.

XXXI

The double horn blast of a police car going west tears at me out of the darkness, embodies itself in a white Rover with blue cyclops eye flaring on top, screams like a passing train and fades towards the Knackers. By now the boy in the green boiler suit will have been helped away and the bar half empty. I keep walking.

Spring is struggling out again in the gardens after that setback of snow. Daffodils stand up in the narrow beds, their trumpets frost-fringed a deeper tone. I feel their presence though they're hard to make out in the street lights. Yellow pools still lie across the pavements from the windows of Ramon's delicatessen. Inside a boy sits behind the till waiting for customers, dreaming, perhaps the nephew I signed the photographs for. I wonder how this cold Spring prickles his skin, whether he feels any stirring or it's only us who were reared on 'the soote saison' of renewal. I pass an uncurtained window where a head is bent with a telephone receiver held up to an ear I can't see under a fall of hair, a woman talking to lover or child.

There's not much traffic now. I cross the road obliquely, pass the bead-fringed windows of the Taj Mahal where two couples are dining in the red plush glow and the closed launderette whose big-bellied machines stand waiting for the morning's first command, and push against the door of the Nevern.

I almost back out again, the inside is so sea-changed, but Paul has caught my eye and is waving me into our corner.

'Al, what'll you have? A pint?'

'What's happened?'

Giant heads hang from the ceiling turning slowly in the updraught of hot air. The bottoms of their necks are hollow so that you can see up into the dark caves of the empty skulls.

'Is it Madame Tussaud's now?'

The heads are made of rubber or papier-mâché that sags a little making the features droop grotesquely as if carved from melting wax. I recognize a couple of politicians among them: Churchill bulldog and pekinese Prime Minister dangling together, John Bull and Monroe, the great tyrants Hitler and Stalin and a cowboy in a stetson who must be a forgotten American president. Cartooned they hang like monstrous carrion on a gibbet.

'Do you like them?' It's Kevin anxiously leaning across the bar.

'They're certainly unusual.'

'I got them cheap from a carnival shop. I thought it'd cheer the place up for Easter.'

'That one reminds me of General O'Duffy,' Connal says, pointing at a moustached ruddy head in the corner by the door to the ladies' lavatory. 'Though why he would be here I don't know. Though again he should be, strung up like the old villain he was. Did I ever tell you how I went to fight with his brigade in Spain, volunteered as a boy? I thought I was fighting for Catholicism. That's the way it was put to us. I was only sixteen but I've seen men tortured to death, on both sides. The first man I ever seen killed was a prisoner. They brought him in one night into the guard room where the guards, our lot, stood round the walls. They threw him from one to the other like passing a ball, you know, just shoved him around among themselves till he was all broken. He was only a kid too. I can see his face now. It marked me. I was only sixteen. There were terrible things done, on both sides.'

'Never mind Mr Connal,' Ellen says. 'That's all in the past. You've got to live for the present.'

'What present? No one ever made me a present of anything.'

'Is Frank coming in?' I ask Paul.

'He said he'd look in on his way back from the cinema.'

'There was a fight in the Knackers tonight. A boy got slashed with a glass.'

'Eh, all this violence. Why do people have to get violent with each other?'

'I'm going after a job tomorrow.'

'Where's that then?'

'Down in Dorset.'

'Everyone's going away.'

'I haven't got it yet. Even if I'm offered I might not take it.'

He shakes his head. 'Look there's Léonie.'

She sails across the bar, hands in the pockets of her long black coat, hands that when she takes them out are smooth, white and a little plump like those of Restoration portraits of beauties. I order her a white wine.

'Cheers Al, Paul.'

'Cheers.'

'I'm going to have to give this up.'

'Are you dieting again? There's not many calories in dry white wine.'

'No. This time it's another reason. Can't you guess? I am only telling a very few people, special friends.' She smiles over her glass.

'And cigarettes?' I ask, probing. 'Are you giving those up too?'

'Yes.' She laughs. 'You have guessed.'

'Are you sure?'

'Oh quite sure yes.'

'What are you going to do?'

'I am going to keep it.'

'What does Jemal say?' Paul asks.

'He says it's nothing to do with him, that he doesn't want to know anything about it and that I am trying to blackmail him.'

'But you haven't asked him to marry you or keep you have you?'

'Of course not. It is all his choice. He must do what he wants. He says he is going home soon.'

'Why did you decide to keep it?' I wonder what sort of a life it will have with this beginning.

'I think about it a lot. I want to have a child now while I am still young and it is better to love the father even if he doesn't love you.'

'Have you told your family?'

'Yes. They are all pleased for me to have someone of my own. My mother will come over when it is born to stay for a bit. Jemal even said that he didn't know if it is his but I say we shall soon see.' She laughs again. She seems happy. Does she

221

secretly believe he will relent and marry her or is it just that now she has a little of him for ever? I can't ask, only speculate.

I raise my glass. 'Well here's to her or him, whichever.'

Paul lifts his too and we toast while Léonie smiles, holding one hand over her belly as if to protect it. Suddenly she stiffens. I follow her eyes across to the other bar and see Jemal is standing there. He doesn't look at us.

'I will go home now and then he can come and talk to you. Anyway I mustn't drink any more. I don't want it to be born an alcoholic.' She laughs again, happiness oozing out of her. For a moment I wish it was my child she was carrying with such pleasure.

Paul and I watch her cross to the door under the grotesque heads. I almost cross my fingers that no malign influence rains down from them onto her dark head and through her blood. Let this baby be perfect.

Now she must be passing along the street under the lamps, taking in the Spring freshness. I look across at Jemal and beckon for him to join us. He's coming.

'I don't know if I want to speak to him. He's treated her rotten.'

'You must. There's a bit on both sides. She's not easy and she chased him.'

'He didn't have to be caught. But I suppose you're right.'

He comes a little uncertainly round the door with his glass nearly empty. 'What'll you have?'

'A half please, Al.'

'Have a pint,' Paul relents. 'I'll get it.'

'I suppose Léonie has told you. I will not feel guilty.'

'I don't think you should.'

'If she wants it that is her decision. It is nothing to do with me. I will not even discuss it.'

'Okay. That's fine.'

'How can I even be sure it is mine?'

'Well she seems pretty certain and when it's born... It would be silly for her to say it was yours if it wasn't.'

'I don't want to talk about it.' He shakes his head. Paul puts a freshly filled glass into his hand and then looks at his watch.

'Frank should be here soon.' The heads turn over us on the ends of their threads. I imagine touching a light to the edge of a neck and seeing the whole thing swathed in flame, the features blackening, crumbling. 'Hallo, may I join you? That is good? I

222

say right?'

'Of course.' I feel Jemal flinch and tighten. He will drink up and go because he doesn't like Suli the Libyan who is handsome and cheerful, and the girls all love him. They are like old melancholy continental Jew and thrusting Israeli, with only the same thin strand of shared religion uniting them.

'How's the football?'

Suli's eyes glisten with drink and smoke. 'I am too old to play. Now I have become businessman, learn English.'

'What will you two do for liquor when you go home? Will you give it up?'

'There are always ways,' Jemal says. 'Zimbabwe is pretty liberal.'

'When we are boys we make drink out of dates you know. Very good, very strong.' Suli shows his perfect teeth.

The noise is swelling now towards closing-time crescendo. I look round at the faces, the mouths opening and shutting, and let the sound pour into my ears like a giant bore. Cocacolonization has added a couple of tiers to the Tower of Babel and united our voices in Berlitz broken, a fractured pidgin that limps its message around the world. The gods have conflated our languages to confound us.

'There's Frank. I'll get him one in. Tell him, will you Al?'

And now we are five flung together on a pinprick of time with thousands of miles between our starting points.

'How are you? Cheers!' The ritual formulae are exchanged. Somewhere a thousand or so years ago Frank's ancestors were Phoenician traders, migrants from the island city of Tyre, Paul's were Scots from Celtic Ireland, Jemal's North West Indian, Suli's Sinbad's sailors and mine were mongrel, polymorph; a nexus, in me the lines meet. I know their pasts, their legends, I can hear the songs they sing.

Yet we are all here under Venus; hesper and vesper she rises on us and takes us by the hand towards morning so that we forget yesterday's snows and their blurred footprints, how the sun went down on them in blood and the long shadows that ate them all away.

XXXII

Why didn't I do as I promised myself and go to bed sober and early? The alarm was too loud and anyway I was half awake out of a confused dream I can't catch the tail of, or the train, as it's drawn away from me. My shoes are still quite clean. There's the shirt and pants I laid out. I must get up into the bathroom before anyone else bags it and shoots my whole schedule to pieces. I feel I need a bath to face the day on. I wouldn't want them to think I didn't bath enough, and fright will make me sweat.

Strange to think that as Léonie lies here now there are two of them lying together. It must be a very odd feeling to have your own body invaded, taken over, two of you living in one skin. There is no time for meditation. You must get on, Al. Pull out the plug and dry yourself. You must leave enough time for some breakfast so you don't rumble at some pregnant pause in mid-interview.

This morning's wind is a real gallows-jerker, master, stripping the flesh from the bones. I've brought nothing with me. I hope that's right. It's good to get down the tube out of the cold. I hope I've left enough time. Hope, hope: Pandora's last-born huddled in the corner of the mind. If we are really a multiplicity of systems with no boss, no ruler, a true fraternity of cognitive parts, the sense of I, me comes only from being bound in a definitive skin. This hope is the animal will to survive made conscious. I dream therefore I am. It's the power to hypothesize that makes us human, that makes procreative lust love. How you do go on.

It's time to change trains. I'm glad they haven't torn down

224

our cathedrals of travel and put up transit lounges. You can still hear the ghost of steam hissing in this vast nave. The commuters are all flooding in, office bound from clerical Surrey and executive Hants while I'm going the opposite way. I can have a whole compartment to myself. I wonder if the others are somewhere on this train too. Let's look through the brief. There's the map. Churchdown College. There's a bus from the station but it looks as if you'd really need a car if you lived there.

The city falls away. Tracks cross, spur off. Another train passes with faces looking out. We're all looking out. Even if 'I' is an illusion like free will, it's a necessary mode we inhabit. Those others are sucked away and I go on in this compartment I have to myself. A cold sleet specks the windows, melting into drops the rush of air streaks into slanting daggers. A wet green creeps up on the houses and pushes them away from the track. Men in archaic caps and knickerbockers are dragging golf clubs across the grass. The human web covers the whole world in its complexity. I wonder if I dare doze a bit.

Cows are standing about in the fields. They don't even look up as the train goes by. It's all country now like being evacuated again. I should have my name and destination pinned on my coat in case I get lost. There's no one to lead me here. No, that's not true. You learnt to speak with a country burr because two pretty girls taught you on your travels. There's the bus. Is there anyone on it who looks a suitable candidate or are they all locals? I mustn't peer about too much.

We wind through streets of yellow stone façades pierced by the ubiquitous household names of the national chains. Everywhere has a Litebite, a Jean Machine, a Tesco to give us all the fine tunings of infinite capitalist choice. In every minopolis in the land we can all buy the same spectrum of breakfast foods and shoes. All the crafts have vanished that made a small difference in our possessions if we were lucky enough to have any. The hand weavers are down in the factory, except that now they're not even there but in the dole queue.

> Where are the girls? I'll tell you plain,
> The girls have gone to weave by steam,
> And if you'd find them you must rise at dawn
> And trudge to the mill in the early morn.

Choice in our homes and goods is a delusion for ninety per

cent of us and yet I'm so much better off than that child that set out with a label on its coat. I wonder what the old man would think if he could see me now. That's another facet of the human ape: its infinite adaptability. Perhaps it's true that we've never grown up. Here's the gates of Churchdown College, white-painted, laid open with a drive between trees beyond and a stone front down in the distance. No one else seems to be getting off. Now for it. Walk along nice and slow like the old man used to coming out of the gates of a night so you don't arrive out of breath.

Head up, look around in a lively and would-be intelligent way. There's reception. Give the girl behind the desk a nice smile.

'You're all assembling in the library, where the Head of the English Department — — will join you.' As usual I don't hear the name; fright makes it into a public address garble. I follow her pointing finger obediently.

There are three other people in the room: a woman and two men. They all look up and nod. One says, 'Hallo, here's another victim,' and grins with wet lips making a red loop through a grizzled black beard.

I warm to this one. He's as frightened as the rest of us but he's playing it blitz style for laughs. I know I ought to recognize these faces. In particular, the one sitting apart whose nod was the slightest, believes I should know him.

'Not to know me argues yourself unknown,' his look says satanically. The middle-aged woman is tidily dressed in a smooth navy coat with a spotted silk scarf at her neck. I surmise a children's writer. I sit on a hard chair and am about to speak but the door is being flung open and Dr Garble comes in.

'I'm — — . . .' *Charley's aunt from Brazil where the nuts come from* my ragbag supplies and I miss the vital handle again. 'We thought you would like coffee and then a tour of the building. We shall start the interviews at eleven-thirty, break for lunch at one and resume again at two. We thought alphabetical order would be best. That means we begin with . . .' He works through the names which makes me third. I was right and she is a children's writer. The other two are poets: Pierce is the black beard; Hollingsworth, the other whose name appears blurrily and regularly in all the mags above slim verses that are unMartialled epigrams.

We begin our tour of the college. Hollingsworth is up in

226

front chatting up Garble. He enquires briskly, his vocabulary is latinate, his concern oozes over the tops of his shoes. Beverley, the children's author, tries to keep up, not realizing his game but wanting to be alert and polite. Pierce and I dawdle behind, sometimes exchanging a grin or a subversive murmur. Out of the window I can see ducks pushing against a congealing stream. I'd forgotten how London's walls bring the Spring, blossoms and all, on quicker. Here its finger has hardly touched the hyacinth bulb tips into tight flower still swaddled in their green jackets.

'We run a great many courses here for all kinds of people. We would want the person appointed to be available to the whole body of students not just the English Department although we would be directly responsible for you. This is the room we've set aside for the writer.' He pushes open the door of a space shaped like a sarcophagus on end. There's a tiny far window, painted over so that you can't touch the outside world with your eyes or it you. The central heating has turned it into a dry sauna. There's a desk and a hard chair. We are deep in the bowels of the earth with the building's weight lying heavily over us.

'Very nice,' Pierce says. Something in the tone alerts Garble.

'I'm afraid we're very short of accommodation here.' We all turn on our heels in the coffin of the corridor and about-face away up concrete steps.

'Now our pride: the Simpkins Theatre named after Elisha Simpkins, the actor-manager who was born in the town of course.' Silently I curse my folly in not looking him and his players up. 'It's the only theatre in the town. There used to be a Theatre Royal when this was a spa very briefly during the boom for those things but that's gone the way of all such via cinema, bingo and now as a furniture repository.'

'R.I.P.' I offer.

'What? Oh yes. A band of enthusiasts is trying to raise the money to turn it into an arts centre. Meanwhile we have the Simpkins.'

I long at once to get my hands on it. There's something about the silent playing place that excites me and makes me want to fill it with people and plays, poetry readings. Songs by Toad, speech by Toad. Clap, clap!

'Now I think the panel is probably ready.' Garble ushers us

back to the library. 'Mrs Acres if you'd like to come through.'

She goes. The rest of us sit nervously. Hollingsworth can't be still though. He gets up and goes to stand by the window. He wants this job very badly.

'Do you think that means what it says?' Pierce asks, jerking his head towards the *No Smoking* sign.

'I suppose it's because it's a library. You'd probably be all right in the corridor.'

'I might just do that.' He goes out, fumbling at cigarette packet and match box. I hope he doesn't set fire to his beard with trembling fingers. I look at Hollingsworth's back. I want to speak to him, to tell him it's all right and he can have it for all I care but his stance is not to be spoken to. It says we are all in competition here. It says I'm frightened but I'm also superior to you. I pick a book from the nearest shelf: *The Poems and Prose of George Gascoigne*, the sort of thing I'm always meaning, indeed wanting to read but never get round to. The words blur and dance. I read a couple of lines and no sense of or from them remains. Does increased adrenalin-flow inhibit the short-term memory? There's a question I'd set some researcher at as long as they agreed to use human guinea pigs. Footnote: an example of specialized usage from the world of vivisection; the animal's name has become a metaphor for an experimental subject.

Outside the ducks are still flaking icicles from the stiff stream with their webs. Pierce comes back. We begin to swap life stories. Time inches. Beverley Acres pushes open the door. She is flushed; her hair a little awry. Garble follows her.

'Mr Hollingsworth, we'll just take five minutes. Then I'll call you.' He glances at his watch. 'I should think after that it will be time for lunch. So the other two candidates will be seen this afternoon.' He smiles at us all and goes out.

'How was it?' Pierce asks.

'Very, I think the word is, searching.'

'Is it a large panel?'

'Quite big, yes.' She looks round at our two faces and Hollingsworth's back which he has turned on us again. 'I think I'm off. I shan't stay for them to announce the result. I've said they can ring me. That's the only advantage in having my name. You get things over quickly. Good luck to us all.'

'We wave and murmur and she goes out. Dr Garble comes back. 'Mr Hollingsworth.' The back turns about and stalks

228

after him.

Pierce goes out for another smoke. Gascoigne and I try to get together again but I fail him. It's not as bad as waiting in prison for royalty to pass and the gates to open I know, master, but bad enough. How would you have made out here? One biographer suggests your only attempt to go straight, get a writer-in-residency at the court of Charles d'Orléans ended in disaster, that you nicked the silver or something and only wrote your way out of trouble with that ballade to his newborn daughter: *Noble enfant, de bonne heure né*.

English society's never gone in much for the royal reprieve as Léonie said. Where's the princess that'll bring me pardon? I could compose some exam questions while I sit here: Trace the continuity in public patronage of the arts since the Norman Conquest. Time grinds. Hollingsworth has been in there a long time. It looks bad.

The door opens on Garble and Hollingsworth. 'Well now, half time. We start again at two. Has Mrs Acres gone?'

'I think she had to get back.'

'Ah. Well there's a, ah, pub just outside the gates on the right that does quite a good lunch. You should find something there.' Pierce and I get up obediently. 'And what will you do Mr Hollingsworth?'

'I'm staying locally.'

'Why not join us at the pub?'

'I don't think so.' He turns his back on us and speaks to Garble. 'I'll telephone later.'

'Yes do that. Though I can't say when the panel will make up its mind. You're such a good list we may be in here for hours.' He almost simpers at Hollingsworth and I'm getting a distinct fix on what his voting intentions are already. 'Two o'clock then.' He bows us away leaving him alone with Hollingsworth.

'What the hell, let's try his pub.'

'D'you reckon it's a fit-up?'

I shrug. 'Who knows?' We stroll out into the grounds where an east wind is shivering the pink and white lace of the prunus. 'It ought to be warmer down here but I'm chilled. There's the pub. What'll you have?'

'What are you having?'

'Well we'd better not get too pissed so I'll have a half of draught Guinness for strength.'

'Make mine a pint. I can't get me fingers through a little jug handle.' He grins.

I've warned him and the choice is his. I order the drinks and take him the menu. 'I'm not a great one for eating. A sandwich will do me.'

'Me too. What sort?'

'That beef looks all right.'

I order his and toasted cheese neat without onion for me, and take over the drinks.

'Jesus these things make me nervous.' Pierce gets his beard round the rim of the glass and tilts down a flow of oil-black stout. 'Cheers.'

'Me too. Cheers. Here's to us.'

'I came too early. Hollingsworth was already there though. I tried to talk to him but he wouldn't give you the time of day.'

'Maybe he's nervous too.'

'Bound to be. We all want the money. But you can be friendly. You needn't make it a competition, need you? She was a pleasant-enough little middle-class body that children's writer.'

I ask him what he's writing and what he's been living off, the usual stock-in-gossip of writers, to take his mind off Hollingsworth. Time scurries waiting for our sandwiches, taking a pee, walking back up the drive to the house, a little unreal now in the grey afternoon as if it's been conjured up there and might vanish into the trees behind and pressing against each wing.

'Must be beautiful in summer. You could lie out there under a tree and write or pretend to. Who'd know the difference? Well it's you now and then it'll be all over. Just me. Will you wait to hear?'

'No. I'll go home. It's hard though to get the balance between looking too eager and as if you don't want it.'

We laugh our way nervously back to the library. There's only a minute or two before I'm Garbled for.

Beverley Acres was right. There seems to be a sea of faces to coin a cliché. Count now. Six. Sit down carefully, smile round, say, 'Good afternoon,' nicely. There's Garble, the college principal Dr Something, someone from the Arts Council, the local literature director, and who's she?

'Member of the literature panel and a writer herself.' But I've missed the name in the principal's introductory round.

230

She looks across at me. She smiles. I smile back. She's so stunning I feel my stomach turn over. I sharpen up at once to impress her, sit straight yet with a touch of casualness, confidence on the hard chair, widen my eyes and field the first question.

On the table are piled our collective works. I can see Hollingsworth's couple of narrow spines under mine which are fatter and more.

How do I see the job? What interests me about Churchdown College? What would I say in answer to the comment that writing can't be taught? Who are the writers who have most influenced me? How would I fit in my own writing with the demands of the post? What other contemporary writers would I try to bring down to give readings?

I scent trouble. Is this a real question about my resources and tastes or what? It comes from the Arts Council representative but the local man leans in on it too. They snuff the air after some quarry I can't see. Not alone must I come but trailing clouds of tappable glory. Perhaps it's not me they want but access to all those unreachable great who didn't need to apply.

Almost I'm faltering but I catch sight of her face again and I pull myself together. I can die gloriously in her eyes if nothing else. I won't name the names that are current gilt tender but the ones I believe in for vision and craftsmanship and that I know I can approach. I do.

Now she's looking at me and her lips, such kissable lips, move in a question. She wants to know why I want this job. And I tell her and all of them, that I need it for the change, small change, all change.

'Have you any questions you would like to ask us?'

I scrabble around. 'What about somewhere to live in the area, or I could commute? Lots of people do it. Two days a week would be quite easy.'

'I think we would want you to live in the area, to be truly resident. We could perhaps help with finding somewhere or the council might. As the college is non-residential we can't of course offer you a bed here. Would this problem deter you?'

I look at her face again. Nothing would deter me. 'No,' I say with an open smile. 'It will be good not to be a Londoner for a while at least, to stand back and look at it, meet new people, find a different place.'

XXXIII

They were all smiling as I got up and bowed out. I smiled back especially at her, holding her eyes, trying to push myself through them and deep into her, a little subversive seed of love to take root. I wonder if she knew or felt it. Well it's all in the gift of the gods now and there's nothing more I can do. If the little winged one intends me to have her he must twang his bow. There's a pretty conceit.

I said goodbye to Pierce and we grinned and shook hands before he went in, and I out down the drive again and on the bus to the station. London begins to draw round me in my small cubicle, running up against the windows just as it did when I was a child coming home for a holiday from evacuation in a lull in the bombing. It will always be there, great nurse, grand mother. The tracks cross and run as though they were moving live things and we still.

I wonder if they've rung Hollingsworth yet. Instinctively I feel it was between him and me. What insufficiency in himself made him play it that way? There's no community of writers but there ought to be some fellowship. Each of us knows how hard it is and therefore how the others must struggle. Even for those who're always writing successfully there's a toll to be paid in that.

'I'm tired now. Reaction I suppose: the bloodstream running green with all that gush of adrenalin. I seem to have been waiting forever on this tunnelled platform. The stale wind is sucked down it, plucking at us as if signalling a coming train but nothing comes. We might be characters in a between-wars play outward bound, dead already, or strangely meeting.

232

I should have picked up a paper on the way back to divert my mind. I wish I'd heard her name. How old was she I wonder?

No good getting too comfortable; you've got to change at the next stop. We scamper about in our burrows like those hairless desert rodents that were on the telly the other night. Why should hairlessness have become predominant? There must have been a time when they were furry as other mammals. Then there came the great sickness and all the animals lost their hair. When they began to recover only on some of them did it grow again. The rest stayed naked. They were healthier than the pelted ones because they had no carrier parasites to bite disease into their bloodstream. So they increased and multiplied until the others died out. From time to time one is born and begins to grow fur. The others bite him to death.

That's the pessimist's ending. The optimist's is that he seems to be almost revered among them and is fed special titbits and allowed to lie with the queen. I seem to remember they had a queen like the hive insects, ants and bees, and workers too. Interesting that among some of them the worker class is female and in others male; there's equality for you.

Is that genetically possible as an explanation: that hairlessness caused by a disease might be transmitted or would it have to suppose a tendency for there to be hairless mutants already in the population? Thank god for a seat and keep far hence the aged and infirm, the *mutilés de guerre* and pregnant women. We are all *mutilés de guerre*. The headlines opposite announce a new bombing campaign for Easter. It's always the non-combatant who's hit by the stray bullet, whose blood flowers into red roses: O'Casey was right as ever. I must pick up some milk on the way in.

How I long to sleep. I'll dunk a teabag first. Are you there, master? You're very quiet. All that thought of hairless rodents put you off I suspect. Too much like sewer rats. I don't even know if there were any sewers in Paris then. Probably not. The road was lined with cars as I came in. There must be something on at the Exhibition. Did the rats run up Montfaucon gallows and help the crows to strip the bones? No answer. A little steam comes out of the nostril of the kettle and the red tongue at the back of the handle clicks off. There are no non-combatants and we are all *blessés* and blessed. My thanks to some Merry Queen for this sleep sliding into my soul.

Let me sleep. I don't want to answer. It'll be Paul asking me

233

if I want a drink. That's it.

'370 . . .'

'We've been ringing you for an hour. I thought I'd calculated your arrival time rather precisely.'

'I had to wait a long time for the tube train. Some sort of hold up.'

'I was almost going to offer the post to someone else.' Garble giggles.

I'm trembling. I'm glad he can't see me. I sit down on the bed. His voice is still going on: '. . . that's of course if you want it.'

It's the moment. I have to decide. I wanted to be offered it but do I want the job, exile, all change that may be only small change? But already I hear myself saying: 'Yes, please,' and giving a kind of nervous giggle too as if I'm taking the wickedness of a second helping of trifle.

'I'm very grateful to the panel for wanting me.'

'It is contingent on your being able to live in the area.'

'Oh yes. I'll get that sorted out although it may take a few weeks. I take it that will be all right?'

'Of course. We understand you couldn't have done anything about it in advance. May I say how personally delighted I am.'

Odd; I'd had him down as a Hollingsworth supporter. Perhaps he's lying. 'By the way,' make it casual Al, 'could you tell me who the other members of the panel were, apart from yourself and the Arts Council representative? I missed them in the opening panic.' Clever, rather clever.

He runs them off. Now I have your name little bird I can seek you out. Or maybe you'll come and find me. We garble on together, the Dr and I, planning another visit and confirmatory letters. Now he's gone I can dance and sing:

> *Que vous semble de mon appel*
> *Garnier? Feis je sens ou folie?*
>
> *What do you make of my appeal*
> *Garnier? Was it sense or daft?*

You had to beg three days' grace to pack and raise the wind before you got out of town. I've begged myself about three months if I'm careful. Shall I give up this room that's kept me, dry and wet? What colour were her eyes? It's time for a celebratory drink. I'll try Paul and David.

No answer. And again none. I'll ring them later but I need

something now: noise, music, not to be alone. I'll pop into the Knickers for a quick one and then come back and try again or on to the Nevern. It's nearly eight already.

The launderette's about on its last wash with hardly anyone inside it except an old tramp eating out of a paper bag. No it isn't; it's Ferdy Haslam. What's he doing in there? Will he recognize me? Should I go in and speak to him? He's seen me looking through the window. He recognizes me. Push open the door.

'Hallo.' He's eating a large sausage out of a bed of chips.

'Hallo. I came in here because it's warm.'

'Good idea.' His eyes are quite lucid but his face is grey with fatigue and stubble and his clothes scarecrow the gaunt body.

'I came for a poetry reading but I found when I got there it wasn't R. S. Thomas as I'd thought but Sean Henryson giving a lecture. So I came away.'

I don't know what to answer. I would invite him for a drink but it looks as if it's food he needs and he's getting that.

'I'm just going for a drink.'

'I shall go home again when I've finished this. It's really very good.' We nod goodbyes at each other.

His appearance like some figure in a morality has put a chill on me. I hurry into the bar, glad of light and sound and get my order in quickly. That's better. The first sup always goes down sweet. Pierce will be having a consolatory drink now. I feel sorry for him or rather for his disappointment and Beverley Acres too though I can't visualize her habitat or how she'll be drowning her sorrows. It's too easy to think she won't have them, to see her as cushioned wall to wall. I hope she's got husband or lover to lean her head on.

And should I feel sorry for Hollingsworth? I suppose so since we can none of us entirely help what we are and his let-down is probably harder from the height he'd been built up to. I fit myself between the spokes of the central wheel and feel the trembling die away at last and a calmness that's almost hope take over.

Across from me a small drama's being played out. Cast list: a man in suit and overcoat, neat almost smart; a boy in green army jacket and cap, black jeans, heavy boots and thick silvery rings through his ears, standing a little to his right, looking at him, trying to get his attention but he's deep in conversation with a flatly elegant Wildean young man I see in here from time

235

to time, in sweater, black jacket and unrolled umbrella he prods at the lino with and twirls. I can't get the plot.

Now there's another boy, neatly dressed, white-faced though and the eyes in deep shadow are trapped near frantic creatures. 'Ha, I smell poppers.'

The suited man smiles a thin smile, takes a flask from his pocket and offers it to him. He takes the cap off. There's a stench like I remember from the school's stinks cupboard, rotten eggs. He breathes in and hands it back. Now the man offers it to the other boy who shakes his head.

'I'm hungry. You promised me I'd eat.'

The man smiles. 'Come on Mark. Just do what I say and then I'll take you out to supper.'

The boy shakes his head. The man pockets the flask and turns back to his conversation.

'If you won't give us something for to eat I'm going.'

'Have a drink. Look I got you one.'

'I can't drink any more, I'm too weak with wanting food. It's going straight to my head.'

The man shrugs and turns away. The boy pushes at the full half pint of beer in front of him. He stands a bit, staring first at the man's back and then at the floor. His dark hair is cropped short back and sides. "You promised me three meals, breakfast, dinner, tea. I haven't eaten since the day before yesterday. Will you give me something?'

'I've bought you a drink.' He turns away.

The boy stands a minute trying to make him turn back again with his eyes. 'Well I'm going.'

There's no answer. The man keeps on talking low and earnestly. The umbrella twirls. The boy's face is sick with hunger. He looks for the last time then turns and pushes his way towards the door. I hesitate for a few moments. He's gone. It's none of your business Al, and anyway you haven't got much on you. You only came out for a quick one.

How much? Count up. Nearly a pound. I'm leaving my half-full glass on the wheel and pushing out into the street. I look up and down. Where's he gone? Isn't that him up ahead there walking westwards, the boots enormous weights on the thin young body. I hurry after. What will I say? He'll think I'm trying to pick him up. The coins are growing sweaty in my pocketed hand. I'm almost running.

'Hey!'

236

'What's that?'

'I heard what you were saying in there. I haven't got much on me but have it, no strings. Go and buy some fish and chips.' I hold out the coins. 'Go on. No strings.'

'No, I couldn't take it.' He flinches back.

'Why not? Go on. I've got more at home.'

'I'm not a scrounger. Not usually. It's just I've come down here and I've no one. He promised breakfast, dinner and tea if I'd go with him. So I did and he never give me anything except a cup of coffee and the offer of some hash. But I didn't want it. I've seen all that. Then he said we'd just go to the pub for a bit and then we'd go and eat. But when we got there he kept buying drink and saying I had to have the stuff. He was trying to get me hooked.'

'Can't you go home? This can be a very hard place with no job and nowhere to stay.'

'I'm from a boys' home. I've never done this sort of thing before. I didn't mind like if he'd given me a dinner.'

'Take it. Come on. I've had rough times. I don't like to see anyone hungry.' I push the coins at him. 'It's all I've got with me.' I get them into his hand.

He's looking down at them disbelievingly. Suddenly the tears begin to glisten on his cheeks, smooth still with childish pliancy. 'You sure? I'll pay you back.' He leans his head against a plane tree.

'Yeah. Some time. I'm often in there. But you'd do best to get out of here. You will buy something to eat with it won't you, not beer?'

'I've had too much already.' The tears have streaked and tickle his face. He rubs at them.

'The fish and chips is good over there.'

He looks across. He seems dazed. Then: 'I'll go back to the Stewpot where the food's good, better than fish and chips.'

We walk a few yards back together. 'Thanks. I won't forget. I'll pay you back. I can get a whole supper there for this.'

I watch him go off. He'll have to pass the Knackers again. Maybe it's all a con but what else could I do? I remember the old man who was clinging to the railings as I went past, then told me the story of his journey down to his daughter, the mugging that took his wallet, showed me his battered suitcase and asked how he could get to King's Cross. I saw him pulling the same act three weeks later at the Aldwych and laughed at

237

both of us, glad I'd allowed myself to be conned.

I let myself in and go down to my room. There's still no answer from David or Paul. I pick up some more money and go up into the street. I'll finish the drink I left if it's still there and then go on down to the Nevern. There's no sign of the boy. I could look in on the Stewpot to check. Instead I open the bar door and let the music pour over me again. My drink's still standing there but the little group has gone. I walk over and pick it up.

XXXIV

I'm still here another pint later. I didn't mean to be but when I went to the door to leave, big white marbles of hail were hitting the pavement like stone shot. The road was almost empty of people and traffic as if it had been swept clean, just a couple of steamed-up cars apparently driving themselves and one or two figures hurrying with faces bent featurelessly.

'What's on at the Exhibition tonight?' I asked the barman.

'Some sort of army commemoration,' he said.

The bar's filling up again now for the last gasp. Those who come in have numbed faces and hair plastered in slicks to their heads and sometimes an unmelted frozen bead sewn here and there in calcified tears. I can't decide whether it's worth trying to make a dash for the Nevern to get in a last one, hoping that I'll find Léonie there sipping an orange juice or Paul and Frank briefly together or . . . or . . .

The face of the murdered man still looks down from the wall. No one else has been arrested but people have begun to forget, and forget to be careful of their bedfellows. Raffael isn't in tonight and it's Ismail's night off the glasses. Maybe he's taken his new girlfriend to *Starsaga*. I hope Eamon O'Halloran is lying quietly in his box and his mother has stopped her crying. I'm getting sentimental. It must be because I haven't eaten. I'll go to the door again and see how the weather is. Maybe I should go over and buy some chips or up the road for a samosa and onion baghees. I empty my glass and unstick my tired body from the wheel.

The blast lifts me as I'm walking and slams me down. After the clap and roar there's the sound of wood and plaster splintering, cracking and crashing around. Showers of dazzling deadly glass icicles are hailing through the air that's fogged with dust and smoke. I smell again the unforgettable, unforgotten from childhood mixture of mortar and explosive that clings to the skin and coats the mouth and nasal passages for days.

There's silence and then the screaming and moaning begins. I try to get up but I can't at first. A glittering blade of glass from a pub mirror sticks in my right hand. I pull it out and put the left one over the open wound that begins to gush red, trying to pull the two edges together.

Even as I'm doing it I'm thinking: 'They've made a mistake. It's not this pub they want. It's the one down the road where the soldiers'll be drinking, not here.'

I'm trying to get up again. Time seems to be in the wrong gear. I get to my knees. Perhaps my back's broken. I daren't look down in case I see my own entrails poking softly through my torn trousers. I'm on one bent leg heaving myself up. The wheel has been sliced through with a cleaver of blast. Other shapes are stirring in the smoke but I can't help them. The blood's coming out between my fingers.

I stumble forward between broken chairs and lumps of fallen ceiling not daring to look too close at anything. I know where the door is. I'm making it. My back isn't broken. I pinch harder on the lips of the gash and stem the blood.

For a moment I can't see the door to push it open. I'm almost sobbing. It must be there. I know that's where it is. I hear myself moaning and try to stop. Then I see it's gone, blown outwards into the street and what's confused me is just the black gap where it should be. I stretch out my hands together towards it to make sure like a blind man.

I'm not blind am I? It's just the black arsehole of the doorway punched into the night and now I can make out lights and the street beyond as I go on towards them and out through the torn frame. The cold air strikes at me. I suck it in deep. Is this how it felt when the gaoler turned the key and let you out? I'm all right. I'm going to be all right. Blood drips warm down my fingers. I look up above the long black ridge of the housetops.

The sky's cleared and there are stars. They seem to be laughing. And I'm laughing too.

March 1983

THE HISTORY OF VINTAGE

The famous American publisher Alfred A. Knopf (1892–1984) founded Vintage Books in the United States in 1954 as a paperback home for the authors published by his company. Vintage was launched in the United Kingdom in 1990 and works independently from the American imprint although both are part of the international publishing group, Random House.

Vintage in the United Kingdom was initially created to publish paperback editions of books bought by the prestigious literary hardback imprints in the Random House Group such as Jonathan Cape, Chatto & Windus, Hutchinson and later William Heinemann, Secker & Warburg and The Harvill Press. There are many Booker and Nobel Prize-winning authors on the Vintage list and the imprint publishes a huge variety of fiction and non-fiction. Over the years Vintage has expanded and the list now includes great authors of the past – who are published under the Vintage Classics imprint – as well as many of the most influential authors of the present. In 2012 Vintage Children's Classics was launched to include the much-loved authors of our youth.

For a full list of the books Vintage publishes,
please visit our website
www.vintage-books.co.uk

For book details and other information about the classic
authors we publish, please visit the Vintage Classics website
www.vintage-classics.info

www.vintage-classics.info

Visit www.worldofstories.co.uk for all your
favourite children's classics